HOPE,
A HISTORY
OF THE
FUTURE

a novel

G. G. KELLNER

Published by SparkPress, a BookSparks imprint,
A division of SparkPoint Studio, LLC
Phoenix, Arizona, USA, 85007
www.gosparkpress.com

Published 2022
Printed in the United States of America
Print ISBN: 978-1-68463-123-0
E-ISBN: 978-1-68463-124-7
Library of Congress Control Number: 2021923166

Interior design by Tabitha Lahr
Block prints created by G.G. Kellner

Dedicated to Jordan

and

Matao, Madelyn, Lucy, Hannah, Nicole, Leila, Matia, Kian, Leon, Nina, Nicole, Aaron, Eli, Ryan, Caroline, Kellan, Hale, Carter, Brooklyn, Justin, Wilson, Blake, Madison, Chloe, Christian, Oliver, Lucille, Liliana, Aviva, Sam, Lila, Kieran, Zoe, Josephine, Marigold, Isaiah, Maddox, Hendrix, Evelyn, Colton, Emma, Ardea, Julia, Jillian, Jackie . . .

and all the world's children and their children's children—seven generations from now

The following story and characters are fictional, but the book uses scientific facts, historical documents, and legal precedence as the basis for a new society in the future that achieves world peace, justice, and verdant sustainability.

Documents referenced in the book include the Constitution of the United States (1787), the United States Bill of Rights (1791), amendments to the United States Constitution (1794–1992), the Treaty for the Renunciation of War (1928), the United Nations' Universal Declaration of Human Rights (1948), and the Parliament of the World's Religions' fifth directive (2018). These unabridged historical documents are included in the back of the book along with historical photographs and notes from the author.

There is also a timeline of fictional events and characters, an imagined Universal Bill of Rights and Responsibilities, a set of provocative discussion questions, an about-the-author page and interview, and acknowledgments pages.

CONTENTS

TIMELINE OF FICTIONAL EVENTS AND CHARACTERS

TTB = The Time Before
AGC = After The Great Change

1967 TTB	Birth of Ruth's brother, Gaylord Sr.
1969 TTB	Birth of Ruth
1984 TTB	Birth of Mia's parents
1985 TTB	Birth of Ruth's sister—Gabe's deceased mother
1985 TTB	Birth of Marq
1987 TTB	Birth of Joyce
2007 TTB	Birth of Sam, Marq's oldest son by his first marriage
2016 TTB	Birth of Kate, Zen, Gabe, and Mia
2022 TTB	Marriage of Marq and Joyce

2023 TTB	Birth of Grace
2033 TTB	Approximate birth of Little Bird
2040 TTB	Gabe and Mia's moon marriage
2042	The Great Change
2042	First child of Gabe and Mia is born at sea
2042	Universal Bill of Rights and Responsibilities is signed by world leaders
2045 AGC	Birth of Gabe and Mia's daughter
2093 AGC	Birth of Le, Gabe and Mia's great granddaughter
2109 AGC	Little Bird passes away
2142 AGC	The world celebrates One Hundred Years of Peace

PART I:

THE TIME BEFORE

"The arc of the moral universe is long, but it bends toward justice."

—Martin Luther King Jr.

Chapter 1:

THE HISTORY
OF THE FUTURE

The clatter of something falling in the library startled Joyce, who was in the kitchen making a cup of tea. She went to investigate. Through the old wavy glass panes of the French doors that separated the library from the rest of the timeworn house, she saw a large book lying facedown in the middle of the room.

It was a completely quiet afternoon—not a breath of wind outside, no music playing inside. No one else was in the house besides her daughter Grace, home from school sick, sleeping in her bedroom. Their cat, Plato, curled in his favorite library chair, seemed unconcerned by the noise or the large book on the floor.

Most of the books, antiques, odd collections, and curiosities in the library had come with the house when Joyce and her husband, Marq, bought it. A condition of the sale had been that Joyce and Marq be willing to take everything in the house along with the house itself. The previous owner, an old man, had left everything when he disappeared. Apparently "everything in the house" included the cat, for he'd insisted on staying too. Joyce had named him Plato because of his habit of holding his tail upright, in the shape of a question mark.

Joyce looked around the library. She suspected that had anyone attempted to remove the stacks of books inside, the entire room would have collapsed like a house of cards. It was filled, ceiling to floor. Books lined the walls and occupied every crack and cranny that wasn't stuffed with unusual collections and strange artifacts left behind by the old man—seashells from distant shores, maps of faraway places, fossils of leaves and insects, birds' nests of various species, and tiny colored glass bottles whose former contents she could only guess at.

The book in the center of the library floor was large and hardbound.

Joyce wasn't a believer in "signs"—but now, there was a book lying facedown in the *middle* of the room. *Maybe a sign.* But what does it mean? She walked in hesitantly. Peering down the hallway toward Grace's room, she could see her daughter's door was shut and that there was no one in the library—besides the sleeping cat.

Joyce looked up, half expecting to see a hole in the ceiling. She turned the book over.

"The History of the World" was scrolled in elaborate gold-leaf cursive across the front. The finely woven cloth was the color of a ripe plum. She ran her hand over the cover. It wore no jacket. She definitely didn't recognize this book.

Where did it come from? How did it get to the middle of the floor? Joyce pondered this for a moment.

She was an avid collector of used books, especially history books. She was sure she hadn't picked it up in any of her travels up and down the rows of half-empty bookshelves that now occupied the dark corners and back rooms of what were once thriving bookstores and libraries; she would remember it if she had.

It must have come with the house, she decided.

Joyce went quietly down the hallway and cracked open the door to her daughter's room. Grace was sleeping soundly, her tight curls spread around her head on the pillow like a bright halo. Joyce went back to the library.

Her hands shook a little as she felt behind a set of old leather-bound encyclopedias. She had two secrets; smoking was one of them.

"Ahh," Joyce sighed audibly. Behind volume VII— *giraffe* to *hieroglyphic*—she found a pack of cigarettes. One dry, lonely cigarette rattled around in the light cardboard box, like a slightly loony inmate in solitary confinement—for everyone's good.

She plucked it out.

I should take this outside to hide the smell, she thought as she lit it right there in the library.

She looked around the room at all the books. She was a reader. That was her job, to read—but it was also her passion. She took a nervous puff of the cigarette and cracked the window open. Then she knelt down on the threadbare carpet. The old-growth fir floor under the worn rug groaned slightly. Joyce's knees creaked back a reply. She opened the cover and turned to the first of the onionskin-thin pages, crisp in her fingers. Smoke and a bit of dust circled her head as she leaned close to read the delicate print.

THE HISTORY OF THE WORLD
To the Best of Our Knowledge
Researched and Compiled for the Hall of Records by
The World Council Committee for Remembrance
Published 2200

Published in 2200? That seems unbelievable! She shook her head.

But then again . . . the book had appeared out of nowhere. And Joyce was not above thinking there were things that she didn't know or understand, things about the workings of time and the universe no one could explain.

She turned to the table of contents.

Plato jumped off of the chair where he had been napping and came to investigate too. He curled his long tail around his feet as he sat upright, watching her. His long white whiskers twitched as he bent to sniff the pages. He was black with white paws and a white chest. One small white patch hovered above his left eye, giving him the appearance that he was always raising an eyebrow at the happenings around him. To Joyce, he looked like a butler wearing white gloves, ready to receive guests at a formal dinner party.

Or ready to go around the house checking for dust, she thought. *He'd definitely find plenty in here.*

As the smoke from her cigarette rose into her eyes, she scolded herself—*I really should quit*—and stubbed the cigarette out in what was a clumsy attempt at a clay "bowl," now turned ashtray, she had made in a pottery class one Saturday afternoon. Embarrassed by her creation that was more like a round brick or a paperweight than a bowl, she tucked the pottery back in its hiding place behind the encyclopedias. She never came close to mastering the potter's wheel. Of course, it was only a three-hour class. Her expectations might have been too high.

Joyce retrieved her lukewarm tea from the kitchen. But when she returned to the library the book was open to a new spot. She looked at Plato who was innocently licking one white paw with a pink tongue. The big book now revealed the section titled "Survivors' Stories." Joyce settled down on the cracked green leather chair with the book. The cat joined her, seemingly reading over her shoulder.

Under the starlit sky the children huddled close together, both for warmth and to be close to the presence of "Grandmother," as she was lovingly called by her community (and as all respected aging women were known). However, this Grandmother was special, for she moved throughout the daylight seasons surrounded by birds—small brown wrens, swallows, bright yellow finches, and, of course, her crow, Darkness, who was always near her. Some even called her Little Bird.

Tonight, Darkness rested on her left shoulder. His iridescent black feathers flickered in the firelight. He was her constant companion, as a crow had been since her arrival in the colony with her third family after The Great Change.

Darkness accepted the small gifts of food the children brought. This was a night of a Telling. The children came early to Tellings, for they knew they would not get to stay long. Only the adults and the oldest among them would get to hear the whole story.

"Tell us of The Time Before," the children's voices chanted musically.

Grandmother's features were strong, but her expression was gentle. Her hands, resting peacefully in her lap, were curled like old talons, but her eyes were sharp on either side of her beak-like nose.

"Yes, tonight I will tell of The Time Before, and then one last time of The Great Change and my arrival at the colony."

Le, a bright-eyed girl of sixteen known for her keen memory, sat closest to Grandmother. Grandmother touched Le's shoulder. "May you always live in the light of love," she said to Le, glancing up also at the other children in the circle, their faces lit by the fire's glow. Le's hands gracefully moved in the air, interpreting for the crowd that had gathered from far and wide to hear Grandmother's epic saga.

"This is not an easy story to tell, and it is even harder to hear. So go away now and think the happy thoughts of children," Grandmother said, and Le signed her words fluidly. Grandmother waited as several of the older children whispered to the younger ones to go on to bed, now that they had fed their treats to Darkness. It was not yet their time to hear this tale.

Le sent her brother off with the other youngsters. She promised to tell him the story one day, when he was old enough, for she knew she was now the Keeper of this story. Grandmother stroked the soft feathers along Darkness's back. Then, taking out a drum and closing her eyes, she began to tap it softly, singing under her breath:

Yene o'ti Maa koo
Hene Hene hono Yoko he Ashi kono kaa
Heya kana Wa'a ana Omi yori
Weyee kaw . . .

The sun, just below the horizon, cast a strange light upon the gathering. Before the Telling was over, it would nearly circle the sky.

The flames reached up like lively dancers into the night, lighting up the faces of the crowd. As Grandmother's drumming subsided, everyone leaned forward. No one wanted to miss this last chance to hear her tell the story.

Grandmother's song had been a combination of birdcalls and words no one understood, in a language no one any longer spoke. But her ancient song ended with lyrics and gestures everyone knew.

Her voice floated like an ageless river over smooth rocks as she chanted:

Water, water, cleanse my mind,
Make me peaceful, make me kind.

Water, water, cleanse my soul,
Make me peaceful, make me whole.

As she repeated the song a second time, everyone joined in, their voices filling the night air.

Joyce took a sip of her tea and looked at the grandfather clock, its back against the wall. She needed to get on with her day, but the story had already caught her imagination. She read on.

"With time," Grandmother said, "the memories have become easier to bear, but no one ever really forgets, for memories are stored deep in the body."

A tear traced its way down one of the many valleys of Grandmother's wrinkled face.

"In The Time Before The Great Change, the oceans were cool and waves lapped on the sandy shores of my faraway island. The sea around my home was full of giant turtles and bright-colored fish. Dolphins swam in great pods. Huge whales breached and splashed, frolicking with their babies in the turquoise waters."

No one but Grandmother remembered these creatures, but most had seen the pictures in the Hall of the Ancient Ones, next to the Hall of Records. They were framed alongside the condors, with their mighty wingspans, and the white bear, fabled to have lived on something hard and cold called *ice*. Pictures were all that remained of many animals and plants.

"Lots of fish swam in the ocean near our home. We caught them in nets and hauled them into our boats to eat and sell. The sky above was deep blue.

White clouds gathered in the afternoons and gentle rains fell, washing the green leaves so they sparkled when the sun came back out.

"My family farmed and hunted. We grew rice and taro. Papa and my older brothers tracked wild boars. We gathered ripe fruits from the trees. I would stand on the ground as my brothers climbed up and dropped mangoes and papayas down for me to catch. Sometimes I didn't catch them and they fell to the earth and broke open, revealing their juicy orange flesh and black seeds.

"Back then my island had many thousands of birds. At dawn's light they would begin to sing. I remember lying in bed as a child listening to them through the open window of the little room I shared with my sister. The birds would perch in the thick leaves of the green trees outside and call to one another that the day was beginning.

"In The Time Before, people on my island laughed. Food was plentiful and life was good. But there was also fighting and arguing—especially just before the end.

"Then The Great Change came. It happened slowly at first, like the coming of dusk.

"My small island became hotter, the waters warmer. My family began to stay inside during the day to escape the worst of the heat. We waited for the sun to go down so we could go outside again. My older brothers and my sister and I began to sleep outdoors under the tree in our yard. That is my first memory of the stars. I peeked up at them and they back at me between the dancing leaves and branches that swayed in the evening breeze. We would all lie together under the tree—our heads in a circle, our feet pointed in four directions like a compass. My siblings would tell stories until my eyes grew heavy. As sleep overcame me, I would nestle close to my sister, making us not quite a perfect compass any longer.

"Sometimes hard rains came unexpectedly, driving us indoors. My family huddled in the dark as a fury of wind roared in through the cracks around the windows. My grandfather sat in a corner and prayed.

"Floods began to wash away hillsides. Windstorms ripped roofs off of neighbors' houses and toppled trees. Long periods without rain would follow.

"After too many months with no rain, the trees and plants began to change. The silversword plants in our yard, with their soft green-gray leaves, shriveled and then simply were no more. Some of the trees put out great fruits, and the people thought this was a good omen. They did not understand that this was the trees' last effort at life.

"High tides crept into low fields. Shorelines started to erode. But it was only when the beautiful seaside houses began to wash away that the rich and powerful took notice. The water that came out of the faucet in our kitchen no longer tasted sweet and good."

Looking up from the pages in front of her, Joyce remembered the date on the first page of the book. Was it possible that the story she was reading was true—that it was really the story of someone from the future who was alive during something called "The Time Before" and who had lived through something else called "The Great Change"?

Disturbed, she shut the book. She hoped this wasn't the future. But the way the book had come to her—falling out of nowhere and onto her library floor—had her spooked. *What if it really is from the future?*

She shook the thought out of her head. *There are other things to do*, she reminded herself. *I'll go out for a short walk. Make up for that cigarette. Forget about this book.*

She wrote a note for Grace, opened the door to her room, and soundlessly left it next to her on the bedside table. Plato slipped into the bedroom behind her. He jumped up onto the bed and curled at Grace's feet.

Joyce shut the door tightly on her way out as she told herself, *I won't be gone too long.*

Chapter 2:

THE BOOK OF GRACE

Grace reached for her glasses on the bedside table and held up the note:

Back soon. Out for a walk.
—Mom.

Plato watched with one brow lifted above a green eye as she got up to go to the kitchen. Grace could almost but not quite reach the cupboard over the sink. She pushed a stool against the counter and stepped up to get a glass. She filled it with water and took a long drink. The house was quiet. Everyone was gone.

When she returned to her room, Plato was still on her bed, but he was curled on top of a large purple book. *That's weird*, she thought; she hadn't noticed it there on her way to the kitchen. She couldn't imagine where it had come from.

Maybe Mom left it for me to read. Well, I need something to do anyway, she figured. She wasn't allowed electronics if she was missing school. She nudged Plato off the book. "The History of the World" was written in large letters across the cover.

Grace liked school—well, mostly. She liked her fourth-grade teacher, and he liked history. And her mom had been a history major in college. As many times as they moved, they always packed the boxes of history books and brought them along.

Maybe this book came from one of those boxes.

When she was younger, before she could read herself, her father had often skipped to the end of the books he was reading to her. So, like him, she frequently started books at the back, too. She opened the big book on her bed toward the end.

Plato touched his cold black nose to Grace's arm, sending a small shiver down her spine. As she started to read, he settled down on the pillow next to her and began to purr.

In the spring of 2142, the world prepared to celebrate one hundred years of peace. Le stepped off the boat as it silently docked alongside the wharf. Its solar-powered engines shut down. The large white sails that collected energy were already furling automatically into place. The flag of the world, the round image of Earth from space, floated in the breeze. It was the enduring symbol of the oneness of humanity and the shared commitment to stewardship of the earth.

Le had taken a vow of austerity, the same vow all public representatives took. But the basket she was carrying was still heavy. It contained documents and a few personal items, but the most important things Le carried were in her heart and mind. The documents in her basket were light in comparison to her words. As a Speaker, she was practiced in the art of remembering details. Her early work as a Keeper of stories had helped train her already-keen mind. Sometimes she wished she could forget things—it would be easier.

As Le walked down the long wharf, her indigo robe fluttered open, revealing the talking stick tucked into her belt. Stepping to the ground, she knelt alongside the other travelers. She was greeted by volunteers, young and old, who were moving among the new arrivals like honeybees. They were passing out water for the little ceremonies taking place all around her. Copies of the Universal Bill of Rights and Responsibilities were being handed out too, for those not already carrying them. A young volunteer offered Le both. She smiled and gestured her gratitude, but she only accepted the water. She was already carrying a special copy of the Universal Bill of Rights and Responsibilities—the same copy she had carried with her for over thirty years.

Kneeling on the ground, Le placed her talking stick in front of her. She poured a little of the water out onto the earth where she knelt. "To which we all belong," she said simply.

Then she repeated the words she had said so many times, words that were being echoed around her by the other new arrivals:

Water, water, cleanse my mind,
Make me peaceful, make me kind.[1]
Water, water, cleanse my soul,
Make me peaceful, make me whole.

She drank a little of the water. It tasted fresh and clean and quenched her thirst. Replacing the stopper,

---

1. These lines have been attributed to the musician Hamza El Din, but after due diligence the author was unable to confirm their source.

she added the bottle to her basket and waited, still kneeling, as was the custom.

An old gentleman wearing a golden armband approached her. He supported himself on a long talking stick of finely decorated wood with elaborately carved symbols. The handle of the staff was shiny from age and use. His eyes were folded in deep pockets beneath his brow, but the centers blazed with light. His broad nose rose like a mountain from the placid plane of his kindly face. His large ears seemed to tune into everything around him. Le had a fleeting thought that she had met him before. There was something familiar about him.

"Welcome," he gestured.

Still kneeling, Le offered her talking stick to him with both hands. Offering a talking stick in this manner in a new community was a sign of peaceful intent and informed the hosts about the traveler.

The old man looked closely at the symbols as he ran his weathered hands over the talking stick's engraved surface. A large cat with a tail in the shape of a question mark wound itself around his feet.

As he returned the talking stick to Le, he introduced himself: "My name is Gaylord. May peace and love be with you." His fingers moved gracefully through the gestures, despite his age.

The cat now rubbed against Le, seemingly echoing the old gentleman's greeting.

"I am Le," she said, rising and offering her hand.

Gaylord took her hand gently and placed it on the outside of his robe just over his heart, averting his eyes. In turn, she took his hand and guided it to rest on her cloak, just above her own heart, beating faster at the touch of a stranger.

She noted Gaylord's pulse remained steady, quietly keeping rhythm inside the cage of his ribs. He wore a look of patient serenity. They stood together waiting for her pulse to slow, in this long important moment of nonaction. Gradually, her heart returned to a normal beat—the universally understood signal to raise their eyes and meet again, but this time no longer as the strangers they were moments earlier.

Gaylord's long gray hair and beard were neatly trimmed and bound. Had he been standing completely upright, Le would have had to look up to see his face. But age had brought him closer to the earth. He appeared to be in a perpetual motion of bowing with gratitude. Le speculated that he was very old. Perhaps even born sometime during The Great Change.

Grace's door opened. Her mother poked her head in.

"How are you feeling, sweetie? I brought you some crackers and . . . where did you get that book? Her mom asked, in a voice Grace noticed was a note higher than normal.

"It was on my bed. I thought you left it for me."

The color ran out of her mother's face as she hurried over and set the crackers and tea on the bedside table before taking the book and abruptly closing the cover.

"You need your rest, and this isn't going to help you get any."

She carried the heavy book to the dresser near the door, then went back to feel her daughter's forehead.

"You're still warm."

She got a wet washcloth and laid it across Grace's brow.

"This will help cool you off. I'll check in on you a little later."

"Thanks, Mom."

Grace gratefully slid down in bed. The wet ends of the washcloth dripping onto her pillow made a cool spot for her to rest her hot cheeks.

Joyce tackled the big book on the dresser and carried it out of the room with her. She shut the door behind her and leaned her head back against the outside of the door in the hallway.

How did this book get in there? she wondered.

She eyed Plato, who was gazing up at her.

"Did you have something to do with this?" she asked the cat.

Plato just stared at her and twitched his tail from side to side, *ticktock*, *ticktock*, in rhythm with the grandfather clock she could hear innocently marking time in the library.

Chapter 3:

ALONE

J oyce carried the strangely heavy book down the hall, back
to the library. Plato followed her. She put the book on the
table next to the old leather chair, near the grandfather
clock that continued to swing its tail, *ticktock, ticktock*, giving
time the illusion of a predictable beat.

A half dozen books sat patiently on the table next to
the big book. Joyce glanced at them—a light romantic novel
from a favorite author, an older best-selling murder mystery,
three books of nonfiction. She'd been plowing through them
like rich soil.

She needed to get to work reading online. But she had
a second secret in life: she really only loved reading real
books—books printed on paper. There was something about
the feel of paper. She liked the smell of books and the weight
of words. In an increasingly digitized world, they offered
her a kind of retreat. Real books weren't always convenient.
Yet walking into a room filled with them, she felt like she
was walking into a room occupied by interesting old friends.
Against her better judgment, she opened the big book again
and began to read where she had left off.

Grandmother looked out at the people arriving to hear her story.

"Papa said our well was being invaded by the sea. I remember carrying my tin cup in my hand while balancing a plastic jug on my head to carry water. Grandfather stayed home, but the rest of my family ventured up into the high hills to a secret spring. My mother carried my little brother, Ammah, at the front of the thin line. My older brothers and my sister and I all walked behind her. My father, at the very back, swept our footprints away so others wouldn't follow. I didn't know better then, but still, even now, I think of our neighbors that died from lack of fresh water, and I am sad for my part in that."

Grandmother began to beat the drum again, this time like a pulsing heart. *Boom boom, boom boom* . . .

"People began abandoning cars along the roads. I remember riding in one once. It went very fast. Everything went fast then. I have strange memories of giant shining machines that flew in the sky, leaving long tails of white clouds behind them. They were noisy, but not in the pleasant way of birds. They roared and I covered my ears.

"People waited at the docks. Long lines began to form whenever a boat or a barge arrived. Sometimes quarrels broke out among the people waiting. Then the supply barges stopped coming altogether.

"We were dependent upon the barges for many supplies: flour, sugar, paper, salt, cookies that came in packages wrapped in plastic that crinkled when I stole one from the bag in the kitchen. I was not always a good girl.

"Soon our fields were inundated with seawater. All the cars were abandoned, and in time they rusted over. They became home to the rats that my older brothers chased when food became so scarce.

"I remember Papa in one of our fields, only a few green shoots coming up around him, most of the crop turned to useless brown slime. He hung his head down and dropped to his knees in the putrid-smelling mud, covering his face with it as he wept."

The drumbeat stopped.

"That is when my first family began to die. My grandfather passed first. He refused to eat, saying he had already had more than his share. I remember gathering around his bed. We took turns sitting with him. One day when I was alone with him, playing quietly on the floor with a doll so as not to disturb him, he opened his eyes.

"Looking at me, he whispered, 'I am so sorry . . . please forgive me.' I have often thought of his words and what he might have been sorry for. He died later that same day."

Grandmother paused. Le's hands paused as well, waiting for her to continue.

"I heard talk that this was occurring not just on my small island but everywhere, the world over. Though at the time I didn't know about any world other than my own.

"The tree in our backyard no longer danced in the starlit sky. The leaves, like us, lay scattered at its feet.

"One day, Papa did not return from our fields. We never found out what happened to him. But now without him, there was even less help for me and my mother, my brothers, and my sister. My sister had brown doe-like eyes and long dark hair that she wore braided down her back like a thick rope. The neighbors told us she waded out into the water and simply sank below the surface. She must have had no will to live after Papa was gone and my two older brothers were killed in an argument with a villager over food gone missing."

The drum lay silent in Grandmother's hands while a faraway look lingered on her face, but soon she began to beat the drum again.

"The people that remained dug holes for the dead. But the rising seas soon covered the graves. As more and more people died, we simply took them to the water's edge and let them float away on the outgoing tides. My last brother, Ammah, just a toddler, was my only sibling left. I used to dress him and play with him, pretending he was my baby. In the final days of my first family, he grew very quiet, no longer a smiling, chubby boy-child. The life went out of his eyes first.

"Ammah's face was hollow, though his stomach was bloated. No more giggles, no more games. He lay still in my mother's arms like a limp doll. His gaze was vacant, as if he were already no longer of this world. There was nowhere for us to take him for help. The health clinic had closed months before—there were no supplies to stock it, no people left to run it. He stopped eating the small spoonfuls of food my mother and I offered him. We dipped our fingertips in water and rubbed them against his cracking lips.

"My mother rocked him for three days, wetting his hot brow with her tears. He was so small, his arms as thin as the bare branches we sat beneath. On the last day, in the late-afternoon heat, she rocked him back and forth . . . back and forth . . . back . . . forth . . . back. She came to a complete stop. My mother and I were all that remained of our family."

The drumming had reached a crescendo and then fallen silent, as if it, too, had struggled for life and lost.

"My little brother Ammah was dead," Grandmother whispered. "It is strange how I remember the names of my family but not my own from The Time Before.

"We carried Ammah to the beach to set him on the sand, but by then the many decaying bodies were washing back up onto the shore. Not just our own people but others, hundreds of others with odd clothing and unfamiliar features. My mother and I decided to take his body up the mountain. We took turns carrying him into the edge of the hills. We set him in a shallow grave and covered him with heavy rocks. My mother died the next day, sitting on top of the rocks he lay under."

The drum continued to lie silently in Grandmother's hands.

"I covered her with the faded threadbare cloth that we had used to carry my little brother. I placed stones around the edges to hold it down in the winds that blew across her motionless body. I stayed with her as long as I could, not knowing what to do or where to go. Finally, I retreated farther up the mountain."

Grandmother gazed at Le.

"It was then that I stopped speaking a human language altogether for a long time. Perhaps that is why I don't remember my name from The Time Before; there was no one left to speak it."

Joyce shut the book. She stopped her tears with both hands before they ran down her cheeks. She had to get busy. She needed to get some hours in at the publishing house she worked for. But she couldn't stop thinking about the little girl who couldn't remember her name. *Would I forget my name, too, if there were no one left to speak it?* she wondered.

She put *The History of the World* on the table next to the other books. But, looking down at it, she remembered how it had mysteriously traveled to her daughter's room, so she decided to put several books on top of it. *Maybe that will keep it in its place.* Plato leapt up on top of the pile of books and ran one paw across his face as if to wipe his own expression away.

Joyce read online because that was one of her jobs. She read whatever the publishing company sent her. The pay wasn't great and there were no benefits, but she got to work from home and set her own hours—and she got paid to read. She did it mostly in the mornings, as she also had a second job two evenings a week.

Plato watched from the top of the stack of books as Joyce left the library, then listened as she went up the stairs to her small office, once a large walk-in closet. He heard the clacking of the computer keys as she logged in: *tip tap, tip tap*.

Chapter 4:

ONE HUNDRED
YEARS OF PEACE

Grace came out of her room. She wasn't really feeling better, but she needed to stretch and get out of bed. Still in her pajamas, she wrapped a soft blanket around her shoulders and came down the hallway and into the library. The big purple book was on the chair. She glanced down. It was open to the spot near the end where she had been reading when her mother had so abruptly taken it away. Plato looked at her from his perch on the back of the library chair.

Maybe Mom changed her mind and left it out for me. She considered this for a moment, then decided, *Probably not.*

But she was curious about this book. She knew her mother didn't want her to read it, but she didn't know why. She stood at the bottom of the stairs.

Tip tap, tip tap—she could hear her mother working up in the office. She didn't seem to know Grace was out of her room.

Plato jumped down and padded noiselessly across the floor and arched his back for rubbing. Grace ran a hand along his back and all the way to the tip of his curved tail. She settled on the floor and let the seat of the old leather chair do the work of holding the big book. Tugging the blanket close around her shoulders, she continued to read where she had left off.

"How may I be of assistance?" Gaylord signed as well as spoke. His voice was deep and soothing.

"I am a Speaker," Le replied, "as you saw from my talking stick. I have been sent by the people for the Council Gathering of the Equinox, and of course I am here for the celebration of One Hundred Years of Peace."

"Ahh . . . yes." Gaylord smiled at her, his old eyes twinkling like bright stars in a midnight sky.

"I have been a long time coming," she added.

She was tired, but she had enjoyed the trip. The air was fresh on the sea and she had made many friends, especially in the evenings while playing music on the decks.

"The boat was a great pleasure," she told him.

"To be on the water is a blessing," he agreed.

Le had visited many places she had never been before as the ship with its huge sails moved from port to port, picking up and dropping off travelers. Travel was one of the many pastimes people enjoyed in a world free from threat.

Sometimes her boat had stayed in ports several days, allowing her time to explore new communities. She was filled with joy at the kind reception she received in each place they stopped. She had participated in similar Water Greeting ceremonies upon arrival in every port the ship had come into.

"Perhaps you are hungry or in need of rest," Gaylord proposed. "May I suggest a place near the Council Tents?"

Le nodded in agreement, although she had been well taken care of on the boat.

"My duties keep me here today, but I shall ask some of the younger among us to show you the way," he said, his fingers moving rapidly.

He took a small bell from the pleats of his flowing white cloak and rang it softly. Several children nearby who had been passing out documents and water came running—laughing and smiling, eager to help. They gathered around him as he explained that two guides were needed to take Le to the Traveler's House nearest the Council Tents.

Some of the older children stepped forward, volunteering.

He chose two children for the task with a touch of his hand.

Le glanced down at some of the badges the children wore with deserved pride, indicating they had begun their education in peaceful conflict resolution. If they continued their training, they could gain full status in their community as Mediators. Someday they might even become members of the Board of Elders for Conflict Resolution among the colonies.

"Greetings," the youngsters signed, rubbing the palms of their hands together and raising their index fingers to face each other—forming an arch. All children learned sign language alongside their native tongues.

"Follow us," they gestured.

"May I carry your basket for you?" the first asked.

Le thought of one of the documents in her basket, the Universal Bill of Rights and Responsibilities, now one hundred years old. *It has withstood the test of time.*

"Thank you," Le signed back, bringing her open hand to her chest in the universally understood sign of gratitude, before gesturing that she preferred to carry her own basket but would follow.

The children bounded ahead of her—like most children, running for the sheer joy of it. Le picked up her stride.

They passed open doors from which Le recognized the unmistakable smell of freshly baked bread. Music and laughter floated down from upstairs windows as groups tuned their instruments and practiced for upcoming performances. Large painted banners in bright colors were strung in the passageways between the many tree houses, marking the parade route.

She glided along, buoyed by anticipation of the events to come: carnivals, sporting contests, concerts, games, performances, lectures, and of course the dances. The children ran ahead of her, stopping every once in a while to let her catch up.

Plato's cold, wet nose touched Grace's bare arm again at the sound of her mother's footsteps at the top of the stairs. She abandoned the open book on the chair and raced down the hallway to her room, her blanket fluttering like a superhero's cape behind her.

A few minutes later, when her mother opened the door to her bedroom, she pretended to be asleep.

Chapter 5:

"WE THE PEOPLE . . ."

Plato watched Joyce as she came into the library. From his perch on top of the books she had piled onto *The History of the World*, he eyed her with a look that reminded her of Lewis Carroll's Cheshire Cat. Despite his grin, she was relieved to see the strange book obeying the laws of gravity, its wide purple spine sticking out several layers below Plato's ample figure.

"You've been getting plenty to eat," she said to him as she noted the extra folds of cat draping over the edges of the books.

She continued down the hallway and poked her head into Grace's room—she was sleeping soundly. Joyce let out a soft sigh before returning to the library and her thoughts about the strange book.

It can't really be from the future, she thought again.

And if it is somehow a history book written in 2200, how and why did it land in the middle of my library floor? If it is a sign, what does it mean?

She thought she would do some research later, to try and find out more about it, but she had decided to spend the rest of the day reading a classic novel. Something firmly set in the past.

She went into the kitchen and put a pot of water on the stove to boil, so it wouldn't be too obvious she wasn't doing anything productive. *Just in case someone comes home early and wonders why I'm reading old books in the middle of the day.*

Samuel, Marq's oldest son, was coming home for the holiday, but he wouldn't be here for a few days. And she didn't expect the rest of the family to get home until dinnertime. She would make that pot of water into soup later.

She had just adjusted the heat and set the lid on the pot when there was another clatter in the library!

She rushed in from the kitchen. The book was on the library floor again—but this time it was resting like a white dove with its wings spread open—*faceup.*

Keeping one eye on the book and the other on Plato sniffing it, she reached a shaky hand behind volume XXI of the encyclopedias—nothing. She pulled out volume XXIII and looked behind it—nothing!

She sat on the chair and pondered the book on the floor and the contents of the library for a long moment, trying to remember where she might have hidden another cigarette.

An ancient model of a ship sailed along the top of a high glass bookcase above a locking cabinet. A collection of dry white bones and bird nests was displayed inside. A carved mask of African descent hung on the wall. Rocks, shells, and small carvings were scattered among the shelves, stacks, and rows of books.

Joyce turned her head, contemplating the opposite wall and its collection of antique bottles and figurines of animals: a deer in midleap, a bear cold and hard as the stone it was carved from, a glass miniature of a cat teetering near the edge of a shelf. There was a sculpture of a man, too, seemingly walking away into the distance. He was bent over, balancing on a wooden staff like a three-legged giraffe. She spied a lacquered box of Asian origins. She jumped up and looked inside . . .

Ahh! And matches too! She lit the cigarette and let herself slide into the temporary euphoria of the nicotine release.

After a moment, she turned her full attention again to the book on the floor. She slid down next to it and began to read from the open pages. Plato wedged his nose closer, as if he were reading along with her.

We the People, in Order to form a more perfect Union, establish Justice, ensure Tranquility, protect the Earth, and promote the general Welfare, by securing the blessings of Life and Liberty for Ourselves, our Children, and our Children's Children for all time to come, do ordain and establish this Universal Bill of Rights and Responsibilities.

This sounds familiar. Joyce recognized parts of the preamble to the United States Constitution.[2] She turned back a few pages and saw that she was reading from a section titled "Founding Documents." She leaned in to read the fine print.

Recognition of inherent Dignity and Rights is the foundation of Freedom, Justice, and Peace in the World.

Disregard and contempt for Human Rights and the Environment have resulted in barbarous acts, which have outraged the consciousness of Humankind and brought Life on Earth to the brink of destruction. We are committed to the advent of a world in which

---

2. The unabridged United States Constitution and the preamble are included in the Appendix.

all beings shall enjoy Freedom from fear and want and the Preservation and Restoration of the Natural World. Equality, Respect, and Compassion are our guiding principles. We have determined to promote Social Progress and restore the Earth by providing Protection for Rights through Nonviolent Action and the Rule of Law.

Something happened that caused the world to change course, Joyce realized. *But what was it?* There were several pages of articles. She glanced through them.

Article 1: All Persons are born free and equal in Dignity and Rights. . . .

Article 2: Everyone is entitled to all the Rights and Freedoms . . . without distinction of any kind, such as . . . language, national origin . . . or territory to which that person once belonged.

Article 3: All Persons have the right to Life, Liberty, and Security of Person. No one shall be held in slavery or servitude. No one shall be subjected to torture . . . or degrading treatment.

These ideas made sense, common sense, for a functional world. *Is this the future? A peaceful, just world?*

She turned a few more pages to a hand-colored picture of a large white bear floating alone on an iceberg. It was looking over the edge of its small melting platform into a sea of blue-green water. She leaned in again. The caption underneath read:

The Ice Bear, or the Sea Bear, was the world's largest land predator. They once could be found in the
now-tropical regions of the Arctic, in the former
lands then known as Alaska, Canada, Russia, Green-
land, and Norway.

*Of course I know polar bears are endangered. Every elemen-
tary school child around the world knows they are in trouble. But
is this really what's going to happen? Is it true?* She wanted to
shout her questions out loud.

She wasn't prepared for the finality of extinct. *Won't
science intervene? Save a few in zoos or in a research laboratory
somewhere? Genetically modify them to survive, somewhere, somehow? Or at least save their DNA? Doesn't somebody in the future
think of something to fix the problem!?*

But this wasn't the only illustration. There were pages
and pages of illustrations and captions of animals and plants
that apparently no longer existed in this future world—blue
whales, snow leopards, leatherback sea turtles, black rhinos,
western red cedars, ponderosa pines, mountain goldenrod,
prairie orchids, the baobab tree, Pacific walruses, monarch
butterflies, mountain gorillas, giant pandas . . . the list went on.

She scanned to the bottom.

Between 1850 TTB and 2042 TTB, it is estimated that
more than one million species of plants and animals
went extinct.

Her chest ached. Her heart had grown too large for
the small cave it had been hiding in. She swallowed hard.
What does "TTB" stand for? "The Time Before," maybe? She
couldn't choke down what she was reading. It was stuck in
her throat—a large lump of fear and guilt. Plato seemed to

sense her distress and rubbed against her. Somehow, she felt comforted by this strange cat that had come with the house and adopted her family. She turned back to the book, paging through the illustrations of extinctions.

Can this loss of life be real? Do I just not know it's happening? Why haven't I heard about all of these extinctions? Sure, I've gotten tired of listening to the news. I'm exhausted by one awful report after another. I guess I've stopped really paying attention—out of self-preservation! I can't take any more bad, sad news! And what can I really do about it anyway? she thought.

Hot! Hot! Hot! HOT! The cigarette burning down in Joyce's fingers suddenly brought her back into the room. She put it out in "the brick" behind the encyclopedias and took a deep breath.

She looked back down at the book. She felt like she was caught in a strange psychological thriller. *If this really is a story of a future world, is it going to be like a movie I can escape from? Is there going to be floor lighting I can follow? Neon-green exit signs, back to the comfortable world of not knowing? Back to the place I left a few hours ago?* Plato let out a quietly calming mew, as if in answer to her thoughts.

Then a new reflection occurred to Joyce: *If this is somehow a book from the future, people survive—somehow, somewhere. Someone, somewhere, wrote this book!*

Chapter 6:

MY SECOND FAMILY

J oyce glanced around the corner at the front door. *The rest of the family still won't be home for a while. Zen has a game. Marq is probably cheering him on from the sidelines. Kate is studying at school.*

She quietly tiptoed down the hall and checked on Grace again—she was still sleeping.

Joyce could see the water boiling on the stove in the kitchen. The steam lifting the lid of the pot was making a persistent hissing sound. She ignored it. She wanted to find out about other survivors from The Time Before, and she wanted to know what happened to the little girl with no name.

Plato seemed to be as interested in the book as she was. He jumped up on a dining room chair next to where she had settled with the big book on the table. She turned back to "Survivors' Stories" and continued to read.

The crowd had increased in number. Visitors arrived from other nearby communities as word spread that this would be the last time Grandmother would tell her story. She began to beat the drum softly and went on, and Le continued interpreting with her hands:

"The rains stopped coming altogether for a very long time. I remember many trees standing naked, bleached white like bones in the sun. No leaves. No fruit. No seeds. No shade. Silent reminders of what had been.

"It was cooler up high. A little moisture gathered in the small clouds that sometimes shrouded the top of my mountain, so I stayed there near the little secret spring in the ravine. I began sleeping in the hollow center of the banyan tree that grew there.

"My mother had told me not to return home because it wasn't safe. So I returned only once during that time to bring things up the mountain: the little food that was left, a knife, a few books though I couldn't read well, a bag for gathering things. Our house on the edge of the village was vacant and eerie. Most of our things lay scattered and broken across the landscape as if thrown about by an angry giant.

"I went to the village but only rarely. I was afraid it too was dangerous. When I did go, I collected books from the library and from school classrooms, carrying a few at a time back up the mountain. I just looked at their pictures at first, not knowing how to read well, but over time I began to decipher some of their meanings. Books became my only company besides the birds.

"I wandered alone—never too far from the spring that trickled out of the side of the hill. I washed myself and drank there. The few birds that were left seemed to come there as well. I found little bits of bitter greens to eat. Sometimes I ate grass and even the dirt that clung to its roots.

"I made a pool by piling rocks around the spring. The birds would eat the larvae and insects in the shallows. I learned from them, scooping up the larvae and drinking them with the water in small cups I made of curled dry leaves.

"The spring water flowed in one side of the pool from a lip of rock and then out the other end, over my rock barrier, disappearing from view. The water ran underground from there to the sea. I can still remember the sound of the water falling over that edge and my reflection floating on the black shiny surface of that pool. I remember the water's coolness as I splashed my feet, breaking the reflection of myself—alone in the only world that was left.

"It was there I learned to talk to the birds. I learned their languages and how they communicated with their feathered bodies, relaxing with their wings out to the side and backs turned when they came to trust me. I bathed or sat by the water's edge day after day and mimicked their sounds. At first, I didn't know what they meant, but over time I slowly came to understand the meanings hidden in their calls to one another. Sometimes the birds would alight on my bare arms and shoulders. Their sharp claws clasping me tickled. In time they vied for positions to be closer to me. They shared my pool as they drank, preened, and rested. They became my second family.

"I followed them at first, as they seemed to know where to find the little food there was to be had: seeds mostly and insects, sometimes a ripe papaya or a rotting avocado. There were a few feral chickens, too, that lived in some of the rusting shells of the old cars.

I became friends with the hens, as much as one can be friends with those from whom they steal. For I stole their eggs. I was so thin and hungry, but I never took all the eggs, for I knew they were mothers, like my mother had been. I had learned by then what real loss was. Compassion was beginning to grow in me.

"One day I was at the old schoolhouse, picking out books to take back up to my mountain. Inside, in the hallway through an open door, the sound of footsteps and then the loud voices of two men arguing startled me. I took the book I had in my hands and hid behind a desk. I waited until all was quiet again; then I waited longer. Eventually, I slipped out a back classroom door, trying to move as quietly as I could through the dry leaves and bits of garbage that blew about in the wind. I ran the rest of the way back to the trailhead that led up to my spring. I ducked under the bushes I used to conceal the opening and covered my footprints like my father had done, by sweeping the dust with a dry branch.

"When the birds suddenly became quiet or flew up away from the pool, I knew it was a warning— someone was nearby. I would hide in the rocks, quiet as I could be. My mother had warned me that although most people are good, desperation can make people do bad things. But over time fewer and fewer people came, until no one came at all, and I lived alone on the mountain except for my new family of birds. I think it was during those times that I forgot not only my name but also how old I was.

"I vaguely recall celebrating birthdays with my family. People gathered, and my mother would pre-pare special foods and cakes. Sometimes my father and brothers would roast a wild boar they had captured in the forest. Wrapped in giant leaves and roasted in a pit filled with hot stones, the meat became tender. All our friends and neighbors would gather to feast on the succulent meat.

"My favorite cake was a dark brown color with a rich, sweet taste. The children played games, and sometimes my father brought out a small instrument that he strummed. My brothers and sister and I laughed, danced, and sang along. Even my grandfather tapped his foot to the rhythm of the music."

Grandmother paused here, looking out to the crowd. "Music is one of humankind's greatest accomplishments that survives from The Time Before. May it always be so," she said. And then she continued on:

"We used something called 'calendars' then, which marked the days and the seasons. We had something, too, called 'weeks,' and each day in a week had a name—though I don't remember the names of them anymore. Each day had something called 'hours,' and hours had something called 'minutes,' and adults spent a lot of time tracking these things.

"Of course, we no longer use these systems. They are antiquated now. That was before we understood the real value of time and the real meaning of progress. That world ended, and many of the things we took for granted ended with it. I have forgotten much, but I do remember how everyone was in such a hurry then. I can't recall now or even imagine what we were in such a rush to do, especially as things turned out.

"Alone on my island, I sometimes sang to myself, as my mother once had sung to me. Other than that,

I would not speak a human language again until I met my third family."

Grandmother paused, and Le's arms and fingers came to rest as well. Grandmother took a small sip of water from a bowl, then offered some to Darkness. He ruffled his feathers and tilted his head back to swallow before settling again on her left shoulder. In the firelight his feathers glowed with exaggerated sapphire highlights and his eyelids dropped halfway at her caresses.

"You see how Darkness sits here on my left shoulder? He is my friend, for he reminds me not to fear death but to fear not living well while I have the chance. He helps me remember what is important."

She spoke to Darkness in a series of clicking sounds and calls. He responded in kind before nestling back into her thick gray hair.

"Darkness hails from a long lineage. His distant ancestor was my first real companion after my first family died. His name was Alala. His story is inseparable from my own. I saved him once, but he saved me many times. I will tell you his story next."

Joyce left the book on the dining room table, walked down the hall, and put her ear to Grace's bedroom door—silence. *She must still be sleeping.*

Joyce went to the laundry room. Plato watched as she moved the wet laundry to the dryer and pushed the button to start it. The deep rumble of the clothes tumbling inside filled the small room. She reached behind the detergent, feeling for a cigarette.

Ahh . . . there.

"I haven't smoked more than two cigarettes in a day for as long as I can remember," she muttered to herself.

But then again, I haven't read a book like this for as long as I can remember either. In fact, I've never read a book like this in my life!

She slid down against the wall and lit the cigarette, propping the cat door open with one foot to let the smoke out. Plato slipped outside through the cat door with the smoke, like a genie from a bottle. He returned a few minutes later. He maneuvered past her shoe, then hopped up on the warm dryer, tucking his feet underneath his belly. He looked down at her with one white brow raised. Joyce got the distinct feeling he expected her to do something more than laundry.

Marq and the kids will be wanting dinner, she deliberated. *He'll be tired from his day teaching and in no mood for some hocus-pocus about a history book from the future falling out of nowhere into our house. I'll have to keep this to myself for now. I'm not at all sure what I think about it anyway!*

Joyce took one more puff of the cigarette.

And the kids? Maybe I shouldn't tell them about the book at all. She looked at Plato for confirmation, but he had shut his eyes. She thought she could hear him purring like a small boat motor beneath the sound of the dryer. She chuckled to herself, a little light-headed. Her mind wandered back to the little girl's story. She wanted to find out what happened. *This girl somehow survives. She somehow survives and lives to tell her story.*

Joyce had to know how.

Chapter 7:

ALALA

Joyce got up off the laundry room floor a little stiffly and returned to the dining room table. Plato followed her, as did the smell of the cigarette she had indulged in.

She settled back into Grandmother's story from her childhood.

"I was wandering alone, scavenging at the edge of the water as I did every few days, looking for food or whatever useful things that might have washed ashore. I wore an old red cloth around my mouth and nose to protect me from the stench of the decomposing garbage that came along with the treasures that made my life on the island possible.

"On an earlier trip I'd found pieces of corrugated metal roofing. I'd hauled them back to my little encampment for more protection against the fierce winds and occasional torrential rains that turned my pool of water brown with soil washed down from the mountainside. I also found a large umbrella frame over which I stretched plastic tarps to shield myself from the sun's harshest rays at midday while I bathed or just sat by the pool. On a metal plate on the handle of the big umbrella frame were embossed the strange words 'Guaranteed for Life.' I often wondered what that meant."

Grandmother's drumming paused while she looked out at the people. The crescent moon moving along the horizon looked like a fine china cup about to spill over. Then she began to beat the drum again, and Le's hands began to move as she continued her tale.

"I dragged old boards up the mountainside to make a flat, slightly elevated sleeping surface inside the banyan tree. I washed and scrubbed old pieces of clothing I found, wrapping them around myself for protection from the wind and sun—but perhaps most of all for comfort from the isolation. The worn clothing of others was the only form of human contact I had.

"Floating crates sometimes came ashore, pushed by the winds and the tides. Some of them contained edible food—if I could get the tins inside open. My only can opener was rusted and broken.

"I didn't know where the cans came from. I think now that many of the things I found came from cargo ships that had been abandoned or that had sunk. But to me back then, they simply came from the sea, as did the white plastic chairs, milk containers, wires and fishing nets, bottle caps and eyeglasses, yellowed toothbrushes, pieces of nylon rope, old tires, and plastic bags. The garbage piled high around me, in some places so high I could not see over it.

"Not wanting to dull my knife, I would open the cans with a sharp rock. I never knew what I would find inside. The labels almost invariably had been washed or worn away. Sometimes the cans contained a gelatinous mush I had to abandon at the first whiff. Other times the fresh scent of oranges or even sweet green peas surprised and delighted me, encouraging me to continue the hard work of opening them.

"The big pieces of Styrofoam I found on the beaches I would set aside for entertainment. Sometimes I turned them into sculptures of people. They often lasted for days, but when the wind and weather finally blew them apart, I felt such sadness and loss that I would cry, rocking myself—knees to my chest. After a while I stopped building the sculptures altogether, for the loss of even these effigies of humanity left me feeling emptier and more alone than ever.

"If I carried something back to my banyan tree, I found a use for it. If I found food, I shared it with the birds that fluttered around me as I pounded open the cans. The day I found Alala I was wearing a pair of mismatched rubber boots that I had come across on separate scavenging treks. I was quite happy to be wearing my 'new' boots. I needed something to protect my feet from the strange and unpredictable things washing ashore—sharp bits of rusting metal, broken needles, chemical pools smelling of filth.

"My first boot was lavender colored and had a little sparkling unicorn with wings on the side— though slightly dulled and faded. It came up just below my knee. I found it lying on the shore, separate from the piles of garbage. At first, I used it as a pitcher to bathe in my pool and to bring water to the small green plants that clung to life along my trail. I learned from these little green sprouts that life is tenacious, though I didn't have that word then—only the observation that the life force in the world was strong. It gave me a kind of hope that I could be strong too. That I could survive.

"I found the second boot still occupied, a leg bone jutting out the top, the rest of its former occupant trapped under an overturned broken rowboat. There was no running away in my 'pair' of worn-out sandals, which were as mismatched as the socks I often found, washed up without their mates. Besides, I needed that boot. I managed to look away as I pulled it off its previous owner. I dragged it behind me on a long length of fraying rope, too frightened to carry it, too nauseous to wear it. I rinsed it and placed it upside down on a branch to dry.

"Unfortunately, it was a right-footed boot, like my purple unicorn boot. So I put my right foot in the small, dark reaches of a world where children still dreamed of such things as unicorns. And I wore a dead man's boot on my left foot. Something of a world now gone rubbed and blistered my skin.

"I was scavenging with a slightly awkward gait in my new boots, gathering more cans to add to my collection. I planned to take them back that evening to my camp. But I was hungry. It was the heat of the day, and my right foot squeezed into the purple unicorn boot hurt. I perched on a high rock above the beach and tugged it off, rubbing my sore foot. I was carrying a sharp rock with me, as I always did on these outings.

I was about to open a can that looked promising. It still had a bit of shiny metal on it but of course no label.

"Something caught my eye farther down the beach, in the edge of the surf. Something black and ruffled was tossing about in the waves. Something alive. I had seen too much death. Wincing, I pulled my boots back on.

"As I drew closer, I saw it was a crow—its black wings flapping, trying to stay above the breaking water. The tide was coming in. The crow had become entangled in something on the beach, probably while it was looking for food, just like me.

"The crow was a little too far out to reach without risking getting my legs wet in the putrid water that surrounded the island, but I couldn't let another thing die. I waded in. He was bound up around the neck by a twisted ribbon of plastic. He was frightened and made a sound not unlike a human crying for help, fighting for his life. I began to talk to him in one of the soft bird languages I had learned from my second family. The sounds I brought forth seemed to soothe him. As the water poured in over the rims of my boots, he stilled long enough for me to cut him free with the knife I kept strapped to my yellow boot.

"I didn't attempt to hold on to him any longer than it took to gently set him on a patch of clear sand. Then I retreated back up to my rock, where I quickly removed the boots and my shirt, the latter of which I used to try and wipe the scum off my blistered feet.

"I was still hungry, and it was a long way back up the mountain. Many members of my bird family had gathered on the rocks and dead trees around me.

They knew I would share the feast inside the cans with them. I worked quickly, pounding a hole in the top of one of the cans. The smell that came out of the puncture hole in the first can turned my stomach. The next can, too, proved worthless. I tossed them both aside. But out of the third can came the sweet smell of peaches. I worked my sharp rock along the edge until I could peel it back far enough to let one of the bright orange slices slide out and down my throat. I set more segments on the rocks around me for my bird family. They hungrily ate them in a flurry of feathers. I ate three more slices before glancing back at the sea. I saw that the crow was watching us.

"I walked slowly toward him, averting my eyes to let him know I was not stalking him. I placed a slice of peach on the sand nearby. He had dried a little by then, but his feathers were matted, crusted in salt and sand. I walked back and opened another can. Luckily, it was more peaches. That is often how the cans came to shore, in lots. One time I found ten cans of pinto beans; another time I found eighteen cans of soup. Today there were nine cans.

"The fifth was spinach. I took a small bite of the wet green leaves, then gave the rest to my bird family. As they ate, I looked up to see that the crow had come to join in the picnic.

"He came up next to me on the rock. I offered him another peach segment. He looked at me—directly in the eyes. My grandfather had told stories of aumakua, deified ancestors who appeared in the form of animals to help and guide their descendants. I knew in that moment that this crow would be my friend, and I came to believe in time he was also my aumakua—I was no longer alone. I began to call him Alala.

"That afternoon he followed us back to the pool—flying low, swooping from one rocky outcropping and bare branch to the next along the path. He watched as I washed my swollen feet in the clean outflow and wrapped my blisters in pieces of cloth. I settled under the shabby umbrella and fell into a fitful sleep.

"Over the next few days, I fought through fevered dreams of The Time Before. The faces of my family came back to me, and in moments I remember thinking I almost knew my name.

"When I awoke, I found Alala looking down at me. He never left my side during those dark days. When thirst prompted me to struggle off my sleeping platform and plunge into the water, Alala would swoop down from his post and join me at the pool's edge before returning to his position as sentinel.

"He watched over me for many days. Eventually, I began to heal, and the blisters on my feet closed. Over time I grew thick calluses—as we all do after unrelenting, seemingly impossible hardships.

"I began to eat again from my stockpile of cans with their mysterious contents. In the evenings Alala would move close to me, often settling on my shoulder, like Darkness does now. We would spend the night together looking out at the sky, Orion with his star-studded belt and sword looking over us both."

Grandmother lightly stroked Darkness before resting her gaze on Le.

"Now I will tell you of my third family. For there is no one left to tell their story." Le was listening attentively and signing as Grandmother spoke. Grandmother nodded to her. Le understood she was now the Keeper of these stories as well.

Chapter 8:

THE BOOK
OF CHANGES

Joyce stood up and stretched. She left the book on the table for a moment to peek in at the simmering pot on the stove. It gurgled and hissed. *What am I going to add to this water to make soup?*

She opened the refrigerator for inspiration. She didn't find any; money had been tight lately, and it showed in the fridge's sparse offerings. She shut the door and went back into the dining room. The book was there still, but now it was open to a different page!

Plato was sitting on a high shelf. She looked up at him. She could have sworn he winked at her with one raised eyebrow as he washed a front paw with his pink tongue. *Perhaps he's removing evidence*, Joyce thought.

She looked down at the pages open in front of her. She'd wanted to know what happened in the future, but now she wasn't so sure. This section was titled "The Great Change." She hesitated for a moment—gathering strength, reminding herself, *This is just a book . . . if a strange one. And it might not be true.* She took a couple of slow, deep breaths. Then, like diving into water from a precarious cliff, she began to read from the pages in front of her.

The Great Change

Some cried in pain and anguish, others in thirst and fear, still others in anger and sorrow, hunger, and loss—but mostly people were simply quiet, consumed in their grief and suffering. They came together in great crowds and small gatherings to mourn, to pray, to comfort one another, and to die. Neighbors and families shared what they had, caring for one another to ease the suffering of family members and friends as they passed.

Ceremonies large and small were held to plead with gods and governments alike—to no avail. Churches filled with nonbelievers and believers of every faith as people went in to pray together. Families and friends gathered to hold each other, to ask for forgiveness, and to say goodbye, as it dawned on everyone it was too late for anything else.

Joyce shifted in the chair and glanced up at Plato. *Breathe in*, she told herself. *Be brave.*

Many died of thirst. If they didn't die of thirst, they died of hunger. If they didn't die of hunger, they died of disease. The only blessing that came was the release of death. If they lived, most wished they had not. People took every last pill in medicine cabinets and rampaged through pharmacies in an attempt to escape life. The lucky ones did. The warming atmosphere had melted the permafrost. Great explosions of methane gas, once trapped in the Earth's crust, were released, exponentially accelerating the warming of the planet. The polar caps in the far north and south melted almost completely on a time frame only the direst scientific calculations had predicted. The natural systems regulating the temperature of the planet collapsed.

I am strong, Joyce whispered to herself. She willed herself to keep reading.

People and machines alike perished. There was no power to run the air conditioners and heaters that kept them alive. Most organic life is dependent on the regulation of temperatures in the narrow band between 5°C and 45°C (41°F and 113°F), machines from 0°C to 70° C (32°F to 158°F). The machines that stored all the data of the Information Age simply overheated. The tiny ones and zeros of the era were rendered gibberish—an unintelligible language no one could read, no one could retrieve.

Governments didn't release their petroleum stocks; instead, they saved them for use by their militaries. World markets crashed. Oil and gas ceased to be pumped from the ground. Coal-fired plants stopped supplying electricity. The electrical grid crumbled. Personal as well as commercial computers and cell phones failed without power.

Grocery store shelves went empty. Supply trucks stopped arriving. Employees stopped getting paid. Bank machines stopped spitting out cash. Credit cards didn't work. Bankers closed their doors and locked themselves in their vaults to die among the stacks of worthless gold and currencies.

Joyce reminded herself that she was choosing to read this. *I want to find out what happens.*

Most of the world's populations lived in cities near the oceans. People fled inland in desperation. But the waters rose and continued to rise as the thermal expansion of the sea overtook the lowlands where people once lived and grew their food. Bridges, roads, and buildings collapsed. Huge fires raged as gas lines leaked, ignited, and exploded in fiery infernos. Towering buildings burned like huge roman candles in the night sky. No sirens were heard. No crowds gathered. Skyscrapers stood looking like tall, grotesque, charred skeletons.

Breathe in, Joyce told herself. *Remember, you wanted to know.* Plato jumped down off the high shelf and then onto her lap.

The coasts of the Americas and Asia flooded, as did the low-lying lands of Russia and Europe. The Black and Caspian Seas overran their banks, spreading hundreds of miles inland over croplands. The major cities of the world were located on shorelines and lay below the rising tides, but even the cities of Berlin, Tokyo, Beijing, St. Petersburg, Shanghai, London, Paris, and Rome disappeared in The Great Change. For they were all located less than 230 feet above sea level in The Time Before.

Breathe out, Joyce reminded herself as she found Plato's soft ears with her fingers.

Airplanes no longer took to the sky. Trains stopped running. Vehicles were abandoned. There was no fuel to run them. Ships at sea could not come into ports, for the ports were below sea level. The crews ran out of food and then drinking water. They died in their bunks or jumped overboard. The great tankers and freighters with all their cargo were abandoned and left to float on uncertain oceans. The ships themselves eventually sank or overturned, spilling their contents into the world's seas.

Breathe in. Breathe out. It was becoming a silent chant in rhythm with stroking Plato's head.

The Himalayas, sometimes called the Third Pole, had provided fresh water to the huge populations of people in what was once known as Asia. The Himalayan glaciers melted. The lowland areas of the civilizations once known as India and China in The Time Before went under the salty brine of the sea. The renowned rivers—the Ganges, the Yellow, and the Yang—the life force of cultures and countries, dried up and were no more without the glaciers of the Himalayas to feed them. The only remaining water that flowed were the tears of the countless millions who had depended on these rivers for life.

Plato began to move his claws, kneading her thigh in time with her internal chanting and aggravated stroking.

The Mediterranean Sea swamped the surrounding lands, including the ancient valley of the Nile. Religious hatred and border disputes hundreds and thousands of years old became meaningless as the waters rose and covered all. The once-snowcapped peaks of the Alps poked their rocky heads up to survey the wreckage of the civilizations that had once surrounded them.

Virtually no one and nothing survived The Great Change. A once-powerful nation called the United States, now ununited, consisted of snowless mountains and high plateaus running along the eastern and western coasts. The Rocky Mountains lay like the spine of a half-submerged dinosaur. The great Mississippi River Basin, some of the most productive land the world had ever seen, lay underwater, returned to the shallow sea it arose from. The farmlands in a place once called California became spoiled fields of fruit trees and vegetables lying in watery beds.

Breathe in! Joyce practically shouted in her head as Plato pierced her skin, accidentally drawing blood. She pushed him off her lap reflexively.

All but the highest points of land in Indonesia vanished. The Amazon Basin flooded. Australia developed a new inland sea. People died of yellow fever, typhoid, and cholera, as well as new bacterial and viral strains once confined in the ice at the poles. Only the areas over 230 feet above sea level were left untouched by the oceans, their inhabitants the only witnesses to what would come next.

The text was barely legible now through her tear-filled eyes. But she kept reading.

After the ice melted, the great turning of the ocean currents slowly stopped. The circulation system of the world ceased. The cooling effects of the poles no longer brought life or regulated the heat of the land. The world's oceans lay still like great watery corpses.

Border guards abandoned their posts as refugees swarmed across the imaginary lines that once divided countries. Stockpiles of weapons were deserted, as the futility of fighting became apparent. Gunshots and explosions were fired in some places, but no weapons or guns, no military might, could start the ocean currents moving or make food grow or fresh water flow down mountains without snow.

Joyce closed her eyes briefly. *Breathe out*, she told herself.

In the final months, government leaders, scientists, religious heads, military commanders, human rights champions, and environmental activists gathered. Together they wrote and signed the Universal Bill of Rights and Responsibilities. For most it was their last act.

In the end, the world that is was born not from the flames of fire but from the watery graves of what was. The world's population, estimated at ten billion at its height, was reduced to a few million stragglers.

Breathe in. Breathe in. Breathe in . . . while you can . . . while you can . . . while you can. Joyce's head dropped into her lap as she sobbed. Plato rejoined her, and she buried her face in his fur. What was happening—or had happened, or was about to happen—was beginning to sink in. "Is it too late to do something to stop this?" Joyce asked Plato through her tears. "Can I change the future?"

He stretched and arched his back in reply, punctuated by his tail in the shape of a question mark.

"Do I have a responsibility to try?" she asked him.

She could see her tiny reflection in the vertical black slits in his green eyes. With one paw he reached out and gently touched her face.

Chapter 9:

SECRETS

Through blurry eyes Joyce looked over her shoulder into the library at the clock ticking naively against the wall—*ticktock, ticktock*. She wiped away her tears. Her family was going to be home soon, and they were going to ask her what was wrong.

She didn't know what she would say. Nothing? Everything? *What can I tell them? What should I tell them? Will they even believe me? What do I believe?*

The questions chased one another around the room.

Joyce stood up and carried the big book into the library and put it on the table next to the chair. She placed *Merriam Webster's Dictionary of Synonyms* solidly on top of it. *Not that anything will keep* this *book in place! It seems to have a mind of its own*—she looked down at Plato—*and maybe an accomplice.*

She wandered into the kitchen, thinking about the loneliness of losing a whole family. She thought about her own family—sometimes annoying, often unrewarding, frequently difficult, but the absolute foundation of her life. She loved every one of them, warts and all. She wondered momentarily, *What would my life be without them?*

Still reeling, she stood in the kitchen as if she'd never been in there before.

Just then, Marq and the kids came in the front door. The boiling water had steamed up the windows so much that Joyce hadn't noticed the car in the driveway.

"You surprised me!" she stammered dumbly as Marq entered the kitchen.

He looked at her. "Dinner ready?" he asked hopefully.

The pot of boiling water gurgled and burped.

"Almost," she said in the most cheerful voice she could muster.

Marq cocked his head to one side and looked at her. She realized she probably looked like she'd been chased by a wild animal.

"The game went into overtime," Zen grunted as he came through the doorway behind his dad.

Joyce didn't need to be told they had lost. It was written all over his downcast face.

"How is Grace feeling?" Marq asked.

"Will you go look in on her before dinner?" Joyce said, wanting him out of the kitchen. "She was sleeping last time I checked."

As soon as he was gone, she hurried over to the stove and tossed some noodles into the pot of boiling water, then started rummaging deep in the refrigerator for leftovers to add to the pot. *Hmmm . . . last night's vegetables, most of a can of chicken broth, casserole from three days ago?*

She threw it all in and added some salt and pepper.

It will have to do.

Marq returned to the kitchen. "Are you all right?"

She dumped a bag of salad in a bowl and ripped open the dressing pouch with her teeth. "Yeah, I'm okay," she said, pretending to care about tossing the dressing really well onto the salad greens in an attempt to hide how flustered she felt.

"Hard day at the office?" Marq quipped, glancing into the library at the stack of books on the table next to the chair.

Joyce realized he probably knew her secrets. *Well, at least one of them.*

"Harder day than some," she said. Her eyes followed his to the books piled on the table . . . and she froze. The purple book was no longer under Mr. Webster's tomb! Plato was sitting on the chair licking his paws again.

"Is everything okay?" Zen put his arm around her.

He was just a big kid, really, so sweet underneath the hard helmet of competitive high school sports.

"Yeah, yeah, I'm okay," Joyce stammered. "You must be hungry?"

She forced herself to look away from the library, afraid of drawing more attention with her expression of surprise.

Kate returned from putting her backpack away in her room. "What's for dinner, Mom?" She lifted the lid and poked her nose into the pot, holding her long straight hair back, for once not in a ponytail.

"Soup," Joyce sputtered, forcing herself to focus on finishing the task in front of her: food for her family.

"I'm starving," Marq announced.

"Is Grace going to join us for dinner?" Joyce asked.

"She is—for a bite." Marq started retrieving bowls from the cupboard.

A few minutes later, Grace came down the hall still wrapped in her blanket. She slid up onto the stool in the kitchen.

"Feeling better, sweetie?" Joyce asked.

"A little," Grace offered with a weak smile, pushing her glasses up on her nose, which appeared to enlarge her amber eyes.

Zen ruffled Grace's tangled bedhead as he passed and winked at her. Kate came over and gave her a hug. "Come sit next to me for dinner tonight?" she said.

Joyce put the ragtag dinner of half-cooked noodles and the week's leftovers boiled together into soup on the table next to the overtossed salad.

"This looks kinda familiar," Marq said—but then he put on a patient smile and quickly added, "Thank you for dinner, dear."

Dinner—that was another one of Joyce's responsibilities, on top of laundry and the other two jobs she held down. But these days, no matter how hard she and Marq worked, it never seemed to be enough.

Her eyes wandered from her soup bowl. *Where is that book now?* She couldn't let her family see it. Not yet anyway. She wanted time to think. Time to come up with an alternative history of the future. One where they all lived happily ever after.

She peeked through the open door to the library again. The book had reappeared! But now it was lying on the floor, in front of the chair—*right out in the open!* Her heart skipped a beat.

"Joyce. Joyce. *Joyce!*"

Marq was talking to her. She tuned back into the conversation around the dining room table.

"Are you going to work tonight?" Marq asked again.

Right, it's Friday. She had a shift at the wine bar, behind the counter. "Yeah, yes, late night." *It is finally the weekend.* She felt as if she'd run a marathon that week already, and she still had to go to work. And she had promised to help with the church rummage sale on Sunday.

"I have that college-placement test tomorrow," Kate said. "I'm going to study tonight."

"What about homework for you?" Marq looked over at Zen.

Zen gave him a shrug. "I've got some, but it's not due till Monday."

"Let's get it out of the way tonight. After the dishes?" Marq said. "Then we can spend some time this weekend seeing if we can get that old boat motor in the garage going."

Zen's face brightened, and he passed his bowl for another ladleful of soup.

"Okay," he said. "Thanks, Dad," he added after a minute, casting his father a smile.

Marq turned to Grace. Her cheeks were flushed. "You look like you should go back to bed."

"Hmmm," Grace murmured. Her spoon rested in her untouched bowl of soup. "I was in bed *all day*, Dad. It's boring!"

"I think going back to bed is a good idea for you too," Joyce said. "Maybe by the morning you'll be feeling better."

Grace sat up straight and put a spoonful of soup in her mouth, looking imploringly at her siblings for help.

Joyce gave them a warning look, and they both kept their mouths shut.

It was getting close to time to go. *I have to do something about that book lying on the floor where everyone can see it!* Her stomach was too tight to eat. She looked at the wet noodles in her bowl and tried to make small talk, hoping not to arouse suspicion. After a few minutes, she casually got up from the table.

"I'm going to be late for work," she muttered as she went toward the library.

As she passed the chair, she kicked the heavy book as hard as she could with one foot. It went under the chair. She peeked back over her shoulder. No one seemed to have noticed—except Plato, who was watching from a favorite spot of his on top of a library cabinet. Joyce fixed her eyes on him a moment, considering stuffing the cat and the book *both* in a bag and taking them with her.

No, that would only draw attention—a lot more attention! She really was late. She had to go.

Chapter 10:

MORE SECRETS

The family got up from the table one at a time. Kate started washing the dishes while Zen and Marq cleared the table and wiped the counters.

Grace, still sitting at the table, dabbled her spoon in her soup bowl. She sipped a bit of the now-cold broth but without an appetite. She was putting off going back to her room any way she could. Her brother and dad went up the stairs to Zen's room to work on his school assignment.

Her dad had been clear as he passed her at the table: "Head back to bed as soon as you're finished eating."

Maybe I can just stay here a little longer, Grace thought. *At least the view is different.*

Plato jumped up on the dining room chair next to her.

The dishes clinked together as Kate swooshed them around in the dishpan, rinsed them, and placed them on the rack to dry.

Grace swirled a noodle in her bowl, creating a little whirlpool of soup.

Kate came in from the kitchen to collect the last of the dishes. "What are you doing?" she asked. "If you're not going to eat that now, you can save it for later."

She looked at her sister. "I don't want to go back to my room," Grace said with a slight whine in her voice.

"I understand," Kate said. "I don't blame you. Well, stay at the table as long as you like, then, but when you're done with your soup, go on back to bed like Mom and Dad said."

Grace pushed her bowl away. Her head bobbed and her glasses slid down her nose. She wanted to argue back, but Kate was almost eight years older than her—more like a third parent than an older sibling—so she could grumble all she wanted, but she knew she had to comply . . . eventually. She rested both elbows and her chin on the table, stalling.

Kate finished the dishes. As she passed Grace, still at the table, she kissed her on the top of her head. "I love you. I have to go study now. Go to bed."

Once Kate disappeared up the stairs to her room, Grace and Plato were the only ones left in the dining room. She offered Plato the wet noodle on the end of her spoon. He sniffed it but declined with a twitch of his tail, as if scolding her for making such a ridiculous offer. Then he jumped down and headed to the library.

Grace slid off her chair and followed him, dragging her blanket behind her.

Plato's tail was up in the shape of a question mark, his rump in the air and his nose under the chair. Grace looked to see what he was so interested in. She spied the big purple book.

She looked down the hall to see if she really was alone. She didn't want to go back to her room—and the book was so interesting!

She got down on all fours and pulled it out from under the chair. *Should I tell Kate about it?* She pondered this for a moment. She didn't know why her mother didn't want her to read it. She was afraid that if she asked her sister or her dad if she could read it, they might say no, like her mother, and take it away. So she decided not to ask.

She pushed the heavy book into the corner behind the chair. Plato watched, sitting upright, his chest out and his tail wrapped around himself. Grace thought he looked like a soldier—or a lookout.

She found the spot near the back where she had left off earlier. Wrapping her blanket around her shoulders, she began to read again.

This equinox was special—it marked one hundred years of peace. There would be celebrations all over the world, on every island, in every community, on every continent. One of the largest celebrations would be held here this year, at the meeting place of this spring's Council Gathering of the Equinox.

Le passed stages going up in all the parks. She was excited by the prospect of learning about new scientific advancements and technologies that would be shared in seminars and readings. Much of the literature of the world's diverse cultures from The Time Before had been saved. Archived during The Great Change, it would be available to read, thanks to the foresight of those who came before. Storytelling, too, would go on for days. Tellers, Le among them, had been invited to share the old stories.

Dignitaries from the Parliament of the World's Religions would speak about the Initial Declaration of a Global Ethic they had agreed upon, a document that outlined their common values and which had solidified their shared commitment to caring for the Earth into action.[3] She saw several groups of

---

3. The Parliament of the World's Religions' Fifth Directive: Commitment to a Culture of Sustainability and Care for the Earth is included in the Appendix.

people dressed in costumes, gathering for theatrical rehearsals. Performances would go on all week. But it was the dancing that Le looked forward to the most.

The children Le was following stopped in front of a large tree with a set of stairs extending down from a built structure above. Looking up, Le saw the familiar emblem of a Traveler's House—a bed under a tree was painted on a sign at the entrance. Smiling, she gestured her gratitude to her young guides. They set off at a run again, this time back toward the dock they had led her from.

As Le climbed the steps, she could see the tops of the bright Council Tents set up near the large Mother Tree that occupied the center of the community. In this community, the Mother Tree was an empress tree that towered overhead, its large lavender blooms clustering around light-green leaves.

Le watched the children running through the village, disappearing and reappearing among the tree houses, getting smaller and smaller as they made their way back to the dock. The air up here was filled with the scent of spring. *This is delightful.* She smiled to herself, taking a deep breath in of the flower-scented air. The bees hoovering around the blossoms created a soft humming above the sounds of people preparing for the festivities below.

As she climbed even higher, she looked out across the village from the level of the canopy. This community, like most, was laid out in a radiating circular pattern. The Mother Tree at the center was surrounded by the main public facilities. Le could see what appeared from up here to be libraries, schools, workspaces, parks, markets, and a place of devotion where people of all faiths could go to worship. Gardens were woven in between, on, and over the built structures. She could hardly wait to explore, but she had responsibilities first.

When she reached the top of the stairs, she presented her talking stick to the woman at the entrance. "I am Le," she signed.

After they went through the same greeting ceremony she had done with Gaylord, the woman gestured for her to come in.

"Welcome," she signed. "I will show you your room."

Le followed the woman on a winding path that spiraled around the trunk of the tree. Tree homes provided clean air, fresh water, shelter, even energy. Tree communities like this one often grew together, canopies and roots intertwining like the people who lived in them.

They passed several doorways before entering a small, inviting room high above the ground. Warm light came in through an open window. There was a basin of fresh water to wash in and a comfortable-looking bed in the corner. The woman moved aside as Le entered the room, gesturing that she would return shortly.

Sitting on the edge of the bed, Le took off her shoes and removed her outer cloak. Squeals of delight drifted up from below and floated in through the open window—children playing. Le went to look out. Through the branches and early spring-green leaves she could see piles of garments of many colors and patterns, heaped on the ground where the youngsters had shed layers as they played. Some older children and adults were standing off to the side. Le watched as one of them comforted a child who had fallen.

Le turned at a light knock on the door. A tray arrived with a cup of steaming tea, slices of thick, dark bread, and oil to dip the bread in. The woman set the tray on a table; glancing outside too, she smiled at the sound of the children. Then she signed that Le was welcome to sleep, wash, or join the others in the common rooms.

Le placed both hands over her heart and lowered her head. The woman mirrored the gesture before shutting the door as she left the room.

Le was alone. She moved to the basin and splashed cool water on her hands and face, relieved to have finally arrived. She took off several more layers of clothing, for it was the habit of travelers to carry the clothes they needed on their bodies.

She took a sip of the floral tea and let out a soft, contented sigh. *It has been a long journey—nearly halfway around the world,* she thought.

She let her remaining clothing fall about her feet as she finished undressing. She would leave her soiled garments in the basket. She could ask for them back if she wanted them, but she liked trading in her old clothes for different ones.

She looked through the clothes in the closet. *So many to choose from!* She picked her skirt up from the floor, still warm from wearing it under her cloak, and held it against her body, remembering how it twirled just right when she danced, revealing the blue pleats tucked inside. She looked through the colorful blouses in the closet again but chose a white one with flocks of birds in flight stitched across the billowing sleeves. She held it up against her skirt. *Perfect for tonight's opening dances!* she thought. *Sky-blue pleats with a white cloud blouse.*

She moved to the bed and leaned back, closing her eyes. She only intended to rest a moment, but when she opened her eyes again, rose-colored light filled the room. The sun was low in the sky. Now music came in through the open window along with the coolness of an evening breeze.

Drawn to the deep rhythm of the bass like a magnet, she moved to look outside again. A new group had formed in the field below. She ate the bread, dipping it in the rich, succulent oil, and drank the cool tea as she watched from above. The drums, as always, were placed in the center. Dancers, young and old alike, began to gather and move in unison with the beat. She pulled on her skirt and new blouse and began making her way down to join them.

Le stood at the edge of the field, watching. At first it appeared that everyone was dancing to their own private music. The only unity was the deep bass. But as she watched, groups began to dance in spontaneous synchronized motion. There were no apparent leaders or followers. Instead, small groups formed and then dissolved, only to form anew with a different movement and formation. Le stepped into one of the groups nearest her. As she began to move with the other dancers, a feeling of happiness swept over her. She swirled, and her skirt expanded to display the sky-blue pleats. She swayed, and the flocks of birds on her sleeves seemed to dart among the dancers.

Spinning, she was a white cloud in a whirl of color. A deep feeling of connection welled up in her.

Then one . . . two . . . now three groups began to dance in unison with one another. *I know what is coming next!* she realized. Though she had never seen it, she had heard about this new dance in her recent travels. And then it happened—complete synchronicity was reached by all the dancers! For one long moment everyone danced as one, and Le was transported as if by magic in those fleeting moments to a feeling of complete belonging.

Grace looked up when Plato jumped off the chair. She peeked out from the corner she had squeezed into. Someone was coming. She crawled out from behind the chair and fled down the hallway to her bedroom, her blanket flying behind her.

PART II:
THE WORLD
THAT COULD BE

"True peace is not merely the absence of war, it is the presence of justice."
—JANE ADDAMS, ACTIVIST AND WINNER OF
THE NOBEL PEACE PRIZE, 1931

Chapter 11:

THE BOOK OF GABRIEL

Kate came out of her room. She had finished her homework. It was Friday night, so it was a light evening.
But she had to get good grades and she had a test
to prepare for. She knew her only hope of going to a good
school was to get a scholarship. Her parents would do what
they could to help, but it wasn't going to be much.

She walked into the library and picked Plato up from
the seat of the leather chair. He was sitting on top of a big
plum-colored book. She read the title in large gold lettering:
The History of the World.

"Must be another one of Mom's finds," she muttered.
*She's always bringing home books from who knows where. What's
the point? Everything is online. And honestly, who besides our
family really reads books that much anyway? Mom is weird—but
in a good way.*

But Kate was intrigued. She slid underneath the book.
It was strangely heavy—even for a book its size. The weight
pressed her against the chair with something like a g-force.

Kate sat for a minute with her head in her hands. She
let out a little sigh—as if that somehow would release the

nearly unbearable pressure she lived under. It was a long moment before her eyes refocused. She ran her hand over the cover. *What is my slightly crazy mother reading now?* She opened the book.

Grandmother let out a long, slow breath, and the crowd, not realizing they had momentarily stopped breathing too, exhaled. The fire blazed up, throwing sparks high into the sky, casting a bright light on Grandmother and illuminating Le as she continued to interpret Grandmother's words, moving her hands like a moth fluttering near the flames.

"This is the story of Gabe and his young wife, Mia, and of another woman who would, in time, become as dear to me as my mother. They are all gone now, so I have been the Keeper of their stories. Tonight, I am passing their stories on too."

Grandmother nodded again at Le and began:

It seemed that everything was speeding up. Gabe and Mia both worked long hours. Yet it was hard to pay the rent, the bills. The cost of food kept skyrocketing. Transportation of goods had become very expensive. Port cities around the world tried to cope with the rising tides. Local and world economies struggled. The political situation was uneasy as tensions worldwide were fraying. There were petty wars being fought on nearly every continent among the smaller countries, and there was saber-rattling among the larger nations. Several autocrats had risen to power.

No one could refute it any longer; something had gone terribly wrong with the atmosphere. There were still a few that didn't believe that the change had anything to do with human activity, but the fact that things had changed couldn't be denied. People knew it because they were experiencing it—daily. The world's climate had become unstable, and it had happened much faster than most people had thought it would.

Life had become the living hell prophesied by some religions. Mia's parents, who lived on the other side of the country, suspected it actually was the end-times predicted in ancient religious books. Three of the world's major religions foretold an end to the world as it was known. Some people today still believe that is what came to pass.

In the previous few decades, most people had heard that the climate was changing, but few understood the gravity of the situation. Gabe had studied atmospheric science. He knew it was a difficult concept for people to understand that even a few degrees of average temperature rise could result in air-temperature swings that created heat domes or ice storms—far exceeding normal weather patterns. The sun's energy was being trapped by the carbon dioxide, methane molecules, and rising water content in the atmosphere, and it was as effective as putting a lid on a pot—it boiled.

Gabe had worked for NOAA, the National Oceanic and Atmospheric Administration, before the deep funding cuts came, eliminating altogether the jobs of those who studied the results of a warming world. Carbon dioxide in the atmosphere had exceeded 450 parts per million, the upper end of what most scientists believed the Earth could handle without catastrophic results. Those results were now being felt in food and water shortages and extreme, unpredictable weather.

So Gabe and Mia made a decision. They emptied their small savings account and bought a forty-two-foot sailboat. The rising tides had played havoc with the marinas as the ocean waters crept higher, so they anchored the boat offshore on a chain and locked it to a buoy. It had once had a small motor, but it no longer worked. Even if the motor had worked, fuel was almost impossible to find or afford. The only method of propulsion for them was the wind. They rowed out in a small skiff to provision the boat. It was a constant source of worry whether the boat would be there each time they went to stock it with supplies. Gabe spent many nights there, as they prepared the boat, to protect their undertaking.

Water was their biggest worry. But food, too, might be scarce. They didn't know where or when—or even if—they would make landfall. They would set sail and see what came. They had so little left to lose. Mia was a communications engineer but had been unable to find meaningful work after college. Their lives had become a monotonous struggle to simply get by. There was little to look forward to. Most of their friends and neighbors had given up on dreaming of anything larger than getting through the day. Drugs, alcohol, and electronic gaming had become common escapes.

They had asked Gabe's aunt Ruth to join them, but she had said no. She would stay in the house she was born in. Gabe feared she would die there too. Ruth and her two siblings—Gabe's mother and uncle—had all come from Welsh Gypsy ancestry, now more commonly known as the Romani people. Gabe knew their ancestors had been vilified and sometimes even persecuted for the blood that ran in their veins. But Ruth proudly called herself a Gypsy, as her grandfather had before them.

Gabe knew that Ruth felt the wanderlust in her blood sometimes—an inexplicable desire to be on the move. *But for every action there is an equal and opposite reaction, and this comes out in Ruth as a kind of stubbornness to change,* Gabe thought. *Besides, she loves that old house.* It had been the first house her family had ever really settled into, and her brother had lived next door. *It is practically a museum of family history,* Gabe thought.

But Ruth had been supportive of Gabe and Mia's plan to sail away. She knew the importance of dreams and of following them. Gabe thought back over his years growing up with her after his parents died. He remembered how she often said to him, "If people only knew the power of their dreams. Dreams are important—dreams are the first draft of reality."

Gabe remembered how her black eyes would sparkle and dance as she chanted, "People could change the world . . . they could change the world . . . if they only knew . . . the power of dreams . . . if they only knew . . . if people only knew . . . they could change the world."

Then she would wink, and her mischievous smile would cause the small crow's-feet at the corners of her eyes to deepen as she chanted on, "We could change the world if we only knew . . . All we have to do to start is change our minds. We could . . . we could . . . just change our minds . . ." And then she would wink again.

She has a little magic in her, Gabe remembered thinking as a child. *Both she and my uncle have a little magic in them.*

Mia and Gabe reasoned it would be cooler at sea, and safer as well—fewer people. Water temperatures would change more slowly than land temperatures. The cities had become unbearably hot. Many people no longer went outside at all. They spent time exclusively in their apartments, homes, offices, and the few shopping centers that still were open.

Schools now charged fees most people couldn't afford. So children sat, day after day, in front of screens or in darkened houses, left to entertain themselves as best they could. Both parents worked, often multiple jobs, just to feed their families.

Most of the city's parks had been neglected for lack of water to keep things alive and green, and because it was too hot for people to be outside enjoying themselves anyway. Pets were too expensive for all but the richest, and the richest lived almost exclusively in gated communities or in the underground housing being built to escape the heat. The dusty parks had filled with people who no longer could afford both a place to live and to feed themselves and buy clean drinking water.

Water of any kind was expensive. Traditional sanitation practices had broken down with the diminishment of reliable reservoirs from the winter snowpacks. Most houses still had indoor plumbing, but the water was rarely on. Municipalities had begun to shut it off for weeks, sometimes months, at a time.

There just simply wasn't enough water to be pouring it through pipes into every household. People had to buy drinking water, and water for household use was sold in large five-gallon containers.

People dug holes in their backyards and constructed makeshift outhouses, trying to maintain any form of sanitation they could. It had become unthinkable that fresh water would be used to flush a toilet.

Gabe and Mia watched as charities opened soup kitchens and a few medical clinics in the parks. They hadn't had to go there—yet. The clinics were understaffed and chronically underfunded. If you were poor and you got sick, usually you simply died.

Gabe heard rumors of a new bacteria spreading that no antibiotic could effectively fight—even if you could afford to go to the doctor. Outbreaks of typhoid and cholera were becoming common. Mass burial sites had been established for those whose families couldn't afford to pay for individual burial plots. The sites were located on top of old landfills.

When Gabe and Mia ventured out of their modest house, which wasn't often, the scenes they came across reminded Gabe of images he had once conjured in his head while reading historical accounts of the plague during the Dark Ages. Some people had started referring to this as the New Dark Age. There were similarities, certainly. Education and learning had taken a back seat to survival.

At first the richest bought houses on the northern slopes of the city, where there were still a few trees and there was a little shade to be had. New houses were being built underground—the benefits included coolness and security from the roving gangs of displaced and disenfranchised people that roamed the city at night. But sea levels were rising. Underground dwellings were being compromised by the rising waters, and the ones that weren't were still depressing, dark reminders that no one was going to be escaping the consequences of a changing climate.

There was nowhere to go. There was just one Earth. Just one planet on which human life, all life, depended. A few people talked about colonizing other planets or one of the moons of Jupiter, but the reality was dawning on everyone: even if a few people miraculously managed to set up a sustainable living environment on another planet, most of humankind would be stuck here in this nightmare.

Mia and Gabe boarded up their windows for security and to keep the house as cool as possible. Many people had done the same. The only window left in Mia and Gabe's house was way up high in their bedroom.

The time had come for Gabe and Mia to embark on their journey. One evening they went out for one last walk through their neighborhood—the only time that was comfortable and safe to go outside anymore was dawn and dusk.

Holding each other's hands for comfort and security, they watched as a small child a few blocks from their house wandered out of an open door and sat playing by the steps outside in a few shoots of dry grass, where a lawn had once been. They stood in silent wonder, contemplating the innocence of the scene.

Mia squeezed Gabe's hand. He squeezed hers back. He knew what she was thinking. They had talked about getting married, and they had so wanted a child of their own, but it seemed unlikely that they could afford to give a child the basics of happiness— food and shelter, security and time. Food and shelter were difficult to provide for themselves.

They walked by one of the city's parks. The trees were grubby and mostly bare. There were only a few patches of grass left. They moved closer together as they passed hundreds of people sitting on the ground outside makeshift shelters—old tents, tarps, and cast-off materials hobbled together for protection from the elements. A few people had made signs asking for help, but most had come to accept that no one had anything to spare.

Gabe reached into his pocket; he had only a few coins, but he dropped them into the hand of a young mother. Money had become practically worthless as inflation soared.

Mia leaned against Gabe's shoulder. "Do you remember when we never thought anything about fresh air or green trees? We just took it for granted that the sky was blue and that the seasons would come, one after another."

Gabe looked out across the skyline at the gray haze, vaguely recalling that, once, the sky had been blue.

The air had been filled with smoke from the endless wildfires and dust storms racing across the exposed earth for so long that it was becoming difficult to remember that it hadn't always been this way.

"Did you ever see an empress tree?" Mia asked.

Gabe shook his head.

"Empress trees were one of the most beautiful trees on earth. I walked around underneath some one summer when I was young and we were visiting relatives. They were so amazing. The whole tree was covered with long lavender blossoms. They were called empress trees because it was a custom to plant one at the birth of a baby girl in China. The tree would reach maturity at the same time as the child—they grew very fast. The wood was used for making all kinds of things, including guitars, because it was so light and strong. My mother said they were sometimes called phoenix trees because they would regrow from the stump seven times if someone cut one down. I still have the seeds I collected. I don't know why I kept them. I guess I was fascinated that such a large, beautiful tree could come from such a tiny seed."

She looked down at her dusty sandals. "When people first started talking about the climate changing, I didn't believe it. I guess because my father didn't believe it and still doesn't believe humans caused it. I remember saying I thought a few degrees warmer would be nice. I feel so bad for saying that now. I didn't understand."

Gabe nodded. "Gigatons of carbon dioxide were released into the air. I wonder how our parents and grandparents didn't understand what they were doing."

"I think the sky must have just seemed so big," she said. "There must have been a sense that it was endless."

"It didn't help that the pollutants were mostly invisible to the eye," he added. "I think it made it easier to deny what was being done."

"I wonder if everyone had acted, you know, done what they could?" Mia hesitated. "Maybe it would have come out differently."

Gabe pulled her closer. She leaned into him, one foot turned in. She thought about how different her life was from what she had dreamed of growing up.

He seemed to read her mind. "We still have each other," he said.

They returned home just as the red fiery eye of the sun set on the horizon. It would be their last night before launching into the unknown on the sailboat.

Mia sat on the edge of their bed. They had never married. The money, the time—it had all seemed in short order. Gathering family and friends to celebrate had been impractical with everyone spread out across the country and travel so difficult and expensive. No one traveled for pleasure anymore; it was too dangerous. They had lost contact with many friends and family as phones became more expensive and access to the Internet had become unreliable.

Gabe came and sat next to her on the bed.

"I want to get married," she whispered.

"You know I do too." He put his arm around her. "Let's get married tonight."

"Right here? Who will marry us?"

"Do we really need someone to marry us?"

Mia frowned. "My parents wouldn't like it. Probably wouldn't consider it a real marriage."

"Let's make our own ceremony," Gabe urged. "It may be the only one we ever get. A moon marriage, maybe?"

Mia was silent for a moment. "The moon is full tonight, I think."

Moon marriages were becoming more common. As traditional societies frayed under the pressure of collapse, self-declared vows of commitment, counted in moon cycles instead of years, had become more common.

A single tear traced down Mia's cheek. Gabe caught it gently with his finger, then took her head in his hands and kissed her softly on the forehead.

"Yes, let's get married," he said. "We will do it ourselves, tonight."

"I want some kind of water in the ceremony," Mia said.

A bath was a luxury; even showers were rare. Hair washing mostly took place in a shallow basin, and bathing had been reduced to a damp washcloth.

"Okay," Gabe said. "We'll use the rest of our water. It's our last night, and with the rest of our gear we'll only be able to carry a couple of canteens to the boat in the morning anyway."

He began to heat the water they had left before he poured it into the bathtub. It had to be boiled for safety and then cooled. It would take some time.

Mia brought in the vining plant she had been keeping alive with a few spoonfuls of water a week. She set it on a stool near the head of the tub and wound it around the empty pipe that once had been the shower stand. She lit candles, placing them nearby on the ledges and counters.

They both looked at their remaining clothes. *There isn't much in the way of wedding clothes,* Mia thought, *not much in the way of clothes at all.*

But Gabe had a white linen shirt, and Mia a white blouse with small green embroidered leaves and soft yellow flowers around a low collar. Below their wedding shirts they each wore jeans with obvious worn places.

Mia remembered her mother telling her that worn-out clothes with holes were once stylish. *Clothes were actually made and sold to look worn! Hard to imagine that world, that time,* Mia thought. *Everyone we know would be in high fashion now.*

She combed her thick black hair and braided a crown of sorts onto her head. It was something her mother had done when she was young and times had been happier. Tonight's braid was messier, Mia having done it herself—little strands of hair fell around her heart-shaped face. She gathered a few odd bits of jewelry from the dresser and tucked them into the weave. *I look like a princess—at least from the waist up,* she thought.

Gabe pulled back his hair too. It had grown long in the last few months. After he lost his job, they had been focused solely on preparing the boat, and he had let it grow. He was surprised as it grew longer how it had become lighter from the sun—almost blond.

"What shall we do for rings?" Mia asked.

Gabe looked around. He had been using old rubber bands to keep his lengthening hair out of his face as he worked on the boat.

"These," he said, holding up two rubber bands with a smile.

"Okay, for yours." Mia laughed. "I have an idea for mine."

She went to her dresser where she kept a jade box with a dragon carved on the top. Inside, along with the small seeds from the empress tree, was a ring. Its single stone was an opal, turquoise blue with sunbursts of warm yellow and sage green in the swirling center.

In the darkening room, it glowed. She took it out and showed Gabe.

"It was my great-grandmother's on my mother's side. She married my great-grandfather before she ever met him. That was the only way a woman could come from China to the United States then—if she was already married to a man here."

"It's beautiful!" Gabe said, smiling.

They kissed at the edge of the tub. Mia unbuttoned her jeans and let them slip to the floor. Gabe followed. Wearing only their wedding shirts, they stepped into the water together, holding hands. They stood facing each other, the candlelight flickering around them.

"With this ring, I do thee wed," Gabe said, slipping the opal onto her finger. "I promise to care for you all the days of my life." He kissed her tenderly.

"And with this ring, I do thee wed," she repeated after him, ". . . all the days of my life."

She slowly lowered herself into the water. Gabe joined her. Her wet blouse was soon translucent. The small flowers at her collarbone stood out like a fine china pattern on her skin. Gabe gently began to kiss her, undoing each of the buttons . . . one at a time.

The wind came up. It was a rare evening—the sky was clear. In the sweet hours of the night, the moon cast zebra shadows through the blinds on the small upper window. Stripes fell across the bed and over their bare skin. Half-wild and momentarily free of the world, they joined in a coil of long hair and soft blankets, finding each other's lips again and again and again.

What am I reading? Kate turned back to the cover. She traced "The History of the World" in its gold-leaf cursive with a finger, then moved to the first thin pages:

Published 2200

Nearly seven generations from now? Kate's eyes widened. *Not possible*, she quickly concluded.

She let the weight of the book fall back down on her lap. Plato took this as an invitation to regain his position on top of it. Kate picked him up and snuggled him. She tried to comfort herself by comforting him.

There was so much to think about. Some of the other kids at school were talking pretty hopelessly about the future. But she had held herself together, believing—as most people did—that there would *be* a future. But Gabe and Mia's story told a different tale. The room spun around her. *Could this be my fate too?*

Chapter 12:

THE BOOK OF MIA

K ate set Plato down on the floor and picked up the book again. She wanted to find out what happened to Mia and Gabe.

Standing near Grandmother, Le listened intently, memorizing each part of the story as she signed Grandmother's words to the gathering. Her movement in the flickering firelight held the audience's attention, as if she were almost acting out what happened next.

Grandmother continued on:

As dawn lit the sky in unearthly colors of bruised yellow and purple, surreal and tragic at the same time, Mia carefully removed a picture of herself and Gabe from a frame. In the picture, they were looking at each other as if no one else in the world existed. She placed it inside the cover of a homemade book of favorite poems and songs, alongside a few other photos.

She looked over at Gabe, still sleeping in their bed. *We won't be getting much sleep in the coming months,* she thought, *two people alone on a sailboat. It will be difficult. Someone is always going to have to be on watch.* She let him sleep.

Mia had been awake since before dawn, excited, anxious, maybe even a little happy to be leaving. *Although I don't know for what or to where, it could hardly be worse than here,* she thought.

And now we are married. She twisted the ring with its single stone around on her finger, getting used to the feel of it.

It had been a moment of impulse, but her first thoughts this morning were ones of comfort. *There is a floor, of sorts, underneath us now. Something solid to count on.* She had committed herself to Gabe, and he to her.

She looked back down at the book in her hands. Inside was a small collection of pictures of her family, mostly from when she was a girl. She glanced through them. *In pictures everyone always looks happy,* she thought. *We were so blissfully unaware of what was coming.*

She held up her favorite picture of her father, a religious man, hardworking. "I put myself through school," he liked to say. But he had had the help of the government as an ex-military man. She looked again at the photo, noting his thick, sturdy neck and short-cropped hair, a habit of dress from his time in the navy.

Mia's mother must have taken the picture, for she wasn't in it. But Mia could see her mother's shadow falling across the lawn in front of her father. *Yes,* she remembered, *my mother is just a shadow of my father.*

Grandmother paused in her telling of the story to add, "She wouldn't always be, but Mia didn't know that yet."

Mia's father's gaze was steady, confident—straight into the lens of the camera. He held her in the picture with one strong arm. His other hand extended down to her older sister standing next to them. Mia tucked the pictures back inside the book with the picture of Gabe and herself.

Mia couldn't put off telling her family she was leaving any longer. Phone contact had been erratic at best in the last several years. Occasionally a call would get through and she could hear her mother or her sister's voice saying, "Hello . . . hello . . . ," but the reception was so poor it was rare that a full sentence was exchanged before the connection was lost altogether and silence fell again like a sharp knife between them.

So that morning, in the pale light of dawn, Mia finally sat down and wrote a letter to her parents and one to her sister. She had written these letters a dozen times in her head, but not until now—when it finally came down to actually leaving—had she been able to muster the courage to tell them her plan to sail away with Gabe.

She wrote, informing them, "Gabe and I got married." She didn't mention that it was a moon marriage, that there had been no minister, no license. She continued, "We are taking our honeymoon on a sailboat." She couldn't bear to divulge that she didn't expect to return, that she didn't expect to ever see them again.

She would drop the letters off at the post office on the way to the boat. *If it is open,* she remembered.

I might as well put these letters in bottles and toss them off the boat—the chances of them being delivered are probably about the same. There was no telling what would become of them.

Gabe stirred in bed. She went over and crawled in next to him, reflecting on the night that had just passed—*Our wedding night. It's hard to envision a wedding that could have been sweeter.* The simplicity and honesty had made it more perfect than she could have imagined. Life had stripped both of them of any pretense with each other. They had formed a new kind of bedrock in the last few years, more real than she had witnessed in her parents' marriage.

"Hardships can have unexpected outcomes," Grandmother said, pausing her drumming for a moment while the thought rested in the cool night air. Then she continued:

Mia and Gabe got up as the first true rays of the sun came in through the window. They began the final preparations for their departure. Within a short while, everything was done.

Mia looked around the house. *I am as ready as I ever will be,* she realized.

They would walk away from what was left of their belongings, letting their neighbors take what they wanted. There was little market for anything anyway—outside of food and water, no one had money for anything else. Someone without a home would be squatting there within a week.

"Let's go see Aunt Ruth," said Gabe.

Ruth was their final relative living nearby. It would be a difficult parting. She was almost like a parent to Gabe.

He gathered up the last of their clothes and food, wrapping them in a light blanket and tying it all with a rope. He tucked his harmonica and his pocket-knife in her basket and lifted the heavy bundle onto his shoulders.

Mia took the antique bone comb from the top of the dresser. It had come from her great-grandmother too. She put it inside the book along with the photos. She placed them all in her basket. She had already carefully folded her wedding blouse inside for safe-keeping. She slipped the strap of her small guitar over her shoulder, gathering the last canteens of water as she turned for one last look at the place that had been their home. At the last moment she walked back to the dresser and took out the jade box that had held the ring. The small seeds of the empress tree were inside. She tucked the box into her basket too and followed Gabe into the street—into an unknown future.

Kate thought about Zen and Grace. She didn't want them to see this book. Zen was so sensitive, and Grace was too young to have to think about all this. *We are all too young to have to think about this!*

There were only a few things Kate and Zen couldn't talk with their mom and dad about, but they often shared their worries first with each other. They were the closest in age of all the kids, only five and six when their parents married.

Maybe I should talk to Zen about this book, she thought. *Could it really be a history book from the future? I don't want to tell him about it, but how can I keep it from him either?*

Plato watched Kate put the book on a top shelf in the back of the library, where she figured Grace couldn't see it and Zen wouldn't look.

She went to the kitchen and took down the biggest glass she could find in the cupboard. When she opened the freezer, cold mist rolled out of the open door. She dropped the hard ice cubes in the glass, noticing the sound they made as they hit bottom. Filling the glass to the top with water, she drank it in big gulps. *I have a test tomorrow. I have to go to bed. Will I be able to sleep? Will I ever sleep again?*

She went upstairs to her room, turned off the light, and tried to get comfortable in her bed. She tossed about, haunted by what she had read.

Eventually, though, sleep finally came—as it does even to the most restless minds. She dreamed of Mia and Gabe going to sea. In her dream, she was trying frantically to take Zen and Grace and go with them.

Chapter 13:

THE BOOK OF RUTH

Marq was weary to the bone. He came into the library after checking on Grace and dropped into the chair. Plato rubbed against his legs, holding his tail in its customary position of a question mark, as if asking if he could jump up onto Marq's lap. But Plato didn't wait for an answer to this particular question. He landed in Marq's lap and started purring.

What was going on with Joyce tonight at dinner, anyway? Marq wondered. *She'd looked downright unwell.* She'd been a kind of green color at dinner that reminded him of an olive, her pink mouth the talking pimento.

Marq glanced at the grandfather clock with its long tail rhythmically keeping time in the library. *She won't be home for a while yet.* They would have a few sacred minutes alone at the end of the day, his favorite part—holding his wife before falling asleep.

He looked down at the table. *Something is upsetting her. What is she reading?*

There was a large book on the table next to the chair. It had a purple cloth covering. The gold lettering caught his attention. "The History of the World" was scrolled across the front. *Presumptuous*, Marq brooded. *There isn't anyone who's got time to write all the history of the world down.* As a Black man, he knew that most of what was written in history books left out the real stories, the hard stories. The stories some people would like to forget.

He pulled the hefty book off the table. Plato stopped purring and jumped down. Marq heard him go out the cat door in the laundry room as he turned to the publication date.

"'Published 2200'?" A look of skepticism chased a look of surprise around his face.

He had developed a habit in college of reading books out of chronological order, sometimes starting at the end and reading back to the beginning. *And why not cut to the end and see how things came out? Probably not so good,* he thought.

He opened the book to the back, looking over the index and glancing through the lists. Unconsciously he ran his hands through his hair as he read, one hand coming to rest on his chin in a way that had earned him the nickname "The Thinker" among his students—after Rodin's famous sculpture. Marq skimmed through the index:

Founding Principles . . .
The Time Before . . .
Survivors' Stories . . .
Universal Bill of Rights and Responsibilities . . .

He turned to the Founding Principles at the back:

Disregard and contempt for Human Rights and the Environment have resulted in barbarous acts, which have outraged the consciousness of Humankind and brought Life on Earth to the brink of destruction. We are committed to the advent of a world in which all beings shall enjoy Freedom from fear and want and the Preservation and Restoration of the Natural World . . .

Well, maybe this is worth reading, he thought as he continued thumbing through the documents at the back:

Therefore the General Assembly of the World proclaims this Universal Bill of Rights and Responsibilities as the common standard of achievement for all Communities . . .

"Responsibilities as well as rights; it's about time!" he nearly shouted. He grew more interested as he continued to read backward through the document. There were a dozen articles outlining a future world—he scanned them, gleaning the meaning. Plato returned from outside and jumped up on the open pages. Acting like a public notary he left his wet paw prints across the extensive list of countries that had signed the document. Marq nudged him aside. When he was done reading, he leaned back in the chair. *The future may come out better than I expect,* he thought, indulging in the possibility.

Plato watched Marq, one eyebrow raised, stand up and stretch and go into the kitchen. Marq dug around in the back of the refrigerator until he found a cold beer. He poured it into a tall glass and took a long drink. When he came back, the cat was sitting on top of the book, which was now open to a page closer to the front.

Marq shook his head. *I either need to do more of this or less of it,* he thought, looking at the drink in his hand. He sat down again and began reading from the open pages as Plato wrapped his long tail around himself and looked on.

The glowing fire radiated heat and light for this final Telling. Le stood next to Grandmother, unceasing in her interpretation of the story.

Grandmother continued:

Ruth's house and a few of her neighbors' houses were tucked in between new towering apartments. She had lived in the neighborhood her entire life. It was the house next door to her brother's—well, it had been her brother's once. It was sold after his disappearance. But Ruth had refused the offers from real estate developers over the years to buy her out, no matter what money they offered or how they pressured her—she knew the value of a house was not in money alone. Not if it had been a real home. Her memories were here, and those weren't for sale.

She and her brother had been inseparable before his disappearance, especially after the loss of their sister, Gabe's mother. Ruth suspected her brother had succumbed to their Gypsy wanderlust. She wasn't one to show much soft emotion, but when she spoke of him, a sad air overcame her. There wasn't a day she didn't think of him and wonder if he might come back. That was one of the reasons she stayed where she was too. *You never know,* she'd often think.

Ruth was small in stature, but she was large in spirit. Those who dared cross her learned quickly she could best most people even twice her size with a look. Family, above all else, mattered to Ruth. She didn't have children of her own. With both her sister and her brother now gone, Gabe was her only family.

Gabe knocked but didn't wait for her to come to the door. It was unlocked, as usual. Ruth was standing at the window watching the day come and looking at the first blossoms on the apple tree outside her back door.

Some of the old tree had died back with the droughts, but it looked like a few buds were about to break open. She had taken special care to keep it as moist as she could with the leftover water from washing and dishes. One bucket of water at a time, she had saved the old tree. Now it was rewarding her with a few white blossoms with pink centers and spring-green leaves. The tree was older than she was. Ruth remembered climbing it with her brother and sister when they were children.

She stood still as Gabe and Mia came in the door. She had ignored his many scoldings to lock it; she believed living behind a locked door was no way to live at all. She had had a good life, and when her time came, it came. Until then, she would live as she always had, without fear and in service to others.

Ruth could fix practically anything—and she did. Once she used a bone from a dinner plate to fix the carburetor on an old car. Her basement was filled, floor to ceiling, with parts and tools. It had become the makeshift local hardware supply, after the big stores were boarded up and deserted.

She belonged to an organization that served dinner three nights a week to the homeless and the poor. She regularly marched at rallies to protest the latest government corruption or to promote fairness in the tax code and voting rights for all. Everyone in her neighborhood knew she would help them if they needed her. She often took in children to stay with her, as working parents struggled to find childcare.

Aunt Ruth's most regular companion, though, was a neighborhood cat. A stray, probably cast off when someone couldn't afford to care for him. As he made his rounds about the neighborhood, the cat was a ray of hope and happiness to many in a grim life. So she'd named him Hope.

Ruth looked forward to Hope's visits. They didn't last long, but he always came around for a rub behind the ears and for the small morsels of leftovers she saved for him. She enjoyed the easy companionship of animals. Her worries would lift for a few precious hours in the company of Hope.

Hope seemed to have a sixth sense that helped him know when Gabe was coming for a visit, for he always showed up at some point. He would often jump into Gabe's lap, purring loudly before falling into a deep, contented slumber. Then, as quietly as Hope had arrived, he would depart without notice. *Cats are like that,* Ruth would muse.

Mia and Gabe stepped inside. Gabe smiled as he reached around Ruth's petite, bony, five-foot frame, all muscle and attitude. He looked into her sharp eyes. She didn't smile a lot, and she didn't suffer fools, but she loved people and she loved him as if he were her own son. Mia came closer and Ruth embraced her in the hug as well.

"We have some happy news," Gabe ventured, holding off the second part of his announcement. "We got married last night," he said.

Ruth hugged them tighter.

"I'm so pleased." She smiled at them both, her eyes moistening and the little crow's-feet at the corners expanding. "Well, let's have a celebration!" She poured water from a pan into thin crystal glasses that she had Gabe bring down from an upper shelf. The glasses had belonged to Gabe's mother.

"I offer a toast . . . to life!" Ruth said, raising her glass.

Gabe and Mia drank thirstily, and Ruth refilled their glasses as Mia showed Ruth the opal ring on her slender finger.

After a moment, Gabe continued, "We have come for another reason too. We've come to say goodbye. We are on our way to the boat."

"Yes, I guessed," said Ruth.

She had supported them buying this boat, even though she knew what they were proposing to do—sail away.

There was a long pause . . . Gabe and Mia looked down at their feet, then out the window. The day was already getting warmer.

"I've been thinking about it," Ruth broke the silence. "I've come to a decision. I'm going with you."

Mia and Gabe exchanged surprised looks.

"No matter what comes next, at least we'll all be together," said Ruth.

Gabe couldn't believe his ears. He and Mia had asked her many times to join them as they prepared for the trip. She had always been so stubborn, refusing to consider leaving her house and neighbors. He stepped back, looked her in the eyes, and asked, "You know we may never come back?"

"I know," said Ruth. "That is why I've decided to come. My bag is packed." She nodded at a bulging green canvas duffel bag leaning up against the wall. "I'm ready."

She lifted the bag onto her back; it was almost as big as she was. She knew they needed to be on the move before it got any later—any hotter.

Gabe and Mia went out the door, and Ruth shut it firmly behind her. She didn't plan to look back, but at the last moment, just as they were about to round the corner away from the only home she had ever known, she turned her head. The cat was following them.

Chapter 14:

THE BOOK OF HOPE

"Surprise!" Sam beamed as he walked into the house, three days earlier than expected.

Marq had become so captivated by the book that he'd gone back and read from the beginning, including "The Great Change" and the story of the little girl. The front door opening caused him to snap back into the present.

Plato jumped down off the back of the chair and went toward the door.

"Goodness!" Marq set the book down as Sam stepped into the library.

Sam stood before his father. Marq smiled his easy smile for a moment before running his hand over his head and bringing it to rest on his chin, solemnly studying his son's face. His dark eyes took in his accomplished son, just out of law school, just now reaching his prime. Just beginning to live. Marq ran his hand through his hair again.

"Hey, Dad, you all right?" Sam asked.

Marq stood and, embracing his son, wondered momentarily if he should wait until Joyce got home and talk to her about sharing the book with Sam. But the serious nature of the problems the world faced couldn't be avoided. And whether it really was a book from the future or not, the subject matter was very real—and the book seemed to offer some viable solutions.

He picked it up and handed it to Sam.

"What is this?" Sam asked, turning the heavy book over.

Plato rubbed against Sam's legs.

This habit his father had—resting his hand on his chin after running it through his hair—was familiar to Sam. *This must be serious*, he realized. His dad wasn't one to be overly dramatic, and this particular gesture usually preceded something important.

Like Joyce, Sam read books the usual way, from the beginning. He sat down on the floor next to his dad, who settled back on the leather chair and took a drink from the glass on the table. Sam opened the curious book to the table of contents. After scanning through the list, he turned the thin pages to see when it had been published:

The History of the World

To the Best of Our Knowledge

Researched and Compiled for the Hall of Records by

The World Council Committee for Remembrance

Published 2200

"Wow, strange," Sam said, thinking silently, *Maybe that's why Dad is acting like this. But it can't be true? A book from the future?*

Just then, Joyce walked in the door. A look of surprise, then happiness, then anguish crossed her face like a fast-moving storm.

Sam stood and hugged her. He was more concerned now than ever. *Why are both of them acting so weird?*

Joyce stammered out something about expecting him next week, then said, "You found the book?"—more of an announcement than a question.

"I gave it to him," Marq said.

Joyce turned away.

"It's going to be all right." Marq put his arms around her. "We'll get through this together. Whatever may or may *not* come."

Joyce slumped into the vacant chair.

"Together," Marq repeated. "That is how we get through everything."

"Together," she repeated absently.

Sam sat down on the floor again, and Marq brought in a chair from the dining room for himself as Sam began to read aloud where his father had left off.

Gabe and Mia went out the door, and Ruth shut it firmly behind her. She didn't plan to look back, but at the last moment, just as they were about to round the corner away from the only home she had ever known, she turned her head. The cat was following them.

Ruth knew it was Hope, even from a distance. No other cat she knew held its tail quite like that—in the shape of a question mark.

Chapter 15:

THE BOOK OF SAMUEL

Sitting on the floor, Sam continued to read aloud. Marq rested his chin in his hands and Joyce sat next to him, her feet up on the edge of his chair. Marq reached down and squeezed her foot, then found her hand and held it tightly as Sam read to them.

> Grandmother looked at Le, who was standing next to her. The firelight lit her black hair and her calm, clear eyes. Le poured water and offered it to Grandmother, who shook her head.
> Darkness stirred on her shoulder and then settled back on her cloak again. Le took a drink of the water, looking again to Grandmother, knowing she must remember every word—for now this was her story to Keep. Grandmother continued on, and Le resumed signing, her arms moving like branches in the wind, her fingers supple leaves.

> Mia directed their route past the post office. *I'm slightly surprised it's open,* she thought when they

arrived. It often wasn't. Regular times could no longer be counted on. The doors were unlocked, but the lights were off. Ruth waited outside with their gear while Mia and Gabe went in. A tired-looking man behind a barred window waved her over. He extended his gnarled fingers to take her letters. She hesitated. Still holding on to the letters, she reached deep inside a pocket and gave him the coins for the postage and a little extra for a tip—*A bribe, really,* she thought. She hoped it would help the letters have a better chance of being delivered.

If the letters were conveyed to her family, it might be the last time they would ever hear from her. Mia felt sick in the pit of her stomach, and her knees trembled. Gabe put his arm around her and led her back outdoors. It was midmorning. As they stepped out, they felt a wave of heat blast them in the face.

Ruth was waiting, leaning against her green duffel bag in a bit of shade from the building. She was drinking from one of the canteens. She handed the water to Mia as they approached. Mia drank gratefully, then passed the canteen to Gabe. After a few minutes of rest, he pulled his bundle onto his back. "Better get on," Gabe said, looking in the direction of the boat.

Mia took up her guitar and basket. Ruth, shouldering the green bag, pretended not to notice it was just a little heavier than it had been before.

The cool air off the water brought some relief from the midday heat as they rowed out to the sailboat. Gabe used the rusty key to unlock the cabin door, then a second larger key to release the boat from the thick chain cable that held it to the buoy. They raised the main sail and pointed the bow toward the open ocean. The city's skyscrapers, with their many broken or missing windows, looked like the board of an abandoned chess game. As the tallest buildings sank into the sea behind them, it occurred to Gabe, *This is likely the last time I will see this city.* Each experienced a rush of emotions, a complex mixture of grief and elation. They stood together on the deck, looking in one direction toward the future, while in the other direction they watched their collective pasts disappear on the horizon behind them.

They had been at sea for weeks. Gabe had found his sea legs and no longer had to abandon his post at the wheel to lean overboard with seasickness. Mia had taken to playing the guitar in the evenings, once the heat of the day passed. She sang a verse of an old song she remembered by Hamza El Din:[4]

Water, water, cleanse my mind,
Make me peaceful, make me kind.

She added a new verse of her own, inspired by the clean breeze off the water:

Water, water, cleanse my soul,
Make me peaceful, make me whole.

Mia's voice was untrained. It had a raw, authentic quality. It soared and broke in unexpected movements

---

4. These lines have been attributed to the musician Hamza El Din, but after due diligence the author was unable to confirm their source.

like a bird in flight, leaving her listeners breathless. She had started to play the guitar to entertain Gabe and herself when the electricity was off—which was much of the time in the last year. He would bring out his harmonica, a gift from his uncle when he was young. They played together, making up songs as they went or trying to remember and play the ones they both knew.

Gabe and Mia had taken the boat out a few times before setting off on this journey, but they had never sailed at night, and this was the first bluewater sailing either of them had done. He wished they had more experience. He understood the basics of sailing from a few summer classes years ago on a lake. But sailing on the ocean, out of sight of land—this was new and intimidating.

The name of the boat, *Freedom,* was painted on the stern. It was the name the boat had come with, faded and chipped but still visible in light-blue lettering against the white hull. At first Gabe wondered if it was a fitting name. *Freedom from what?* he wondered. *What does one do with freedom?* He had always been preoccupied with goals and achievements, school and then work. This was really the first time in his life he'd had time—unscheduled time.

Initially all this freedom felt daunting, like a gift he didn't know how to open. Once his anxiety passed, he became bored. But slowly, he began to occupy his own mind, with his own choices, his own desires, his own thoughts.

Gabe liked the open water, especially after he got over the worst of his seasickness. Out here the sky was a clear blue crystal dome, and the air was fresh with the smell of salt and space. This far away from the city, the stars at night were lively points of light in an ink-black sky, like little windows opening to other worlds. *I never really appreciated them before,* he marveled their first night on the water.

With the light from the city and the smoke and dust from the fires, he hadn't really seen them before. Honestly, he hadn't been outside at night very often in his life. It had been too dangerous lately, and as a child, entertainment at night had mostly been on screens of one kind or another—indoors.

The sky, filled with the stars and the changing phases of the moon, came as a revelation and grew into a passion. Volunteering to let Mia and Ruth sleep, Gabe began to take his turn at the helm at night so he could be alone with the sky, to think, to dream.

On Gabe's first night watch, Hope arrived on deck, as if it were the most natural thing in the world that he should be there. The moon rose dressed in hues of amber light on the eastern horizon. Gabe had never before watched the moon rise. It stunned him how large it appeared on the horizon. He was looking out to sea with the light of the moon casting a long golden road on the water when Hope leapt onto the bow from the open hatch above the V-berth where Ruth slept. Gabe's feelings of alarm, and a little annoyance, quickly melted away as the cat bounded into his lap and began purring. *Ruth must be behind this!* Gabe thought.

The nighttime watch soon became "their watch," as Hope began to regularly join him for his evening stargazing. The cat slept most of the day on Ruth's bunk, then spent the nights on deck with Gabe. He came to love the quiet company of Hope. He felt somehow that the cat understood what was happening, what he was thinking about, how things might even turn out. *Silly,* he would tell himself, *surely a cat couldn't know any more than I do.* And yet, Hope's emerald-green eyes with their black vertical slits seemed to hold secrets, like a tear in the fabric of time and space.

Ruth feigned an unconvincing surprise at Hope's appearance, wondering out loud how the cat had gotten there. When Gabe asked her directly, she simply winked and said, "Some things we just can't know for sure."

Mia seemed happy to have a cat on board. She loved animals of all kinds, and Hope was something she could pour her tender heart into as she mourned leaving her family behind.

The three of them took turns at the wheel and at managing the sails. They had only a vague idea of where they were and an even vaguer idea of where they were going. Mia had brought along a hand-cranked radio, though she hadn't been able to get it working. They had a compass Aunt Ruth had given them long before her decision to join them on the journey. They used it and the sun during the day, the moon and the North Star at night, to keep them pointed generally on a westerly course. But they had nothing to guide their latitude north or south. By now the world's global positioning satellites had either stopped working or had been taken over by the military; they didn't know which, but they had no access to them. Mia had read that the ocean currents had been slowing, but those currents should be carrying the boat southwest—at least initially. But precisely how far or exactly where, she didn't know.

Of the three of them, Mia was the most familiar with the night sky, thanks to her childhood camping trips with her parents and sister. The stars and the moon became her best tools for trying to figure out where they might be. Each of them, during their turn at watch, made regular entries in the logbook—noting the date; the phase of the moon, if it was visible; the direction and strength of the wind; as well as how much food and water they had in the hold.

They all marveled at what they had been missing while living in a city. None of them had seen so many stars before. Mia, too, began to regret that she had spent so much of her life indoors. The sky was bejeweled and bewitching. The stars appeared to move across it, arriving where they started the next night to begin the ballet again.

Of course, the turning of Earth explained all this. Gabe vaguely remembered learning this from school, but nothing in his formal education had prepared him for the majesty of the experience of watching the sky night after night.

Gabe began to think he hadn't really lived at all until now. His head became clear and his mind calm on the open sea. Living under a dynamic night sky gave a depth to his spirit and answered a calling he had not known was in him. He felt like he was truly alive for the first time in his life.

He brought out his harmonica most nights and began to play with a new soulfulness he had not known was in him either. He began to live not only in his head but in his whole body. He started to breathe more deeply, see more clearly. His muscles and back grew strong pulling lines and hoisting sails. Food tasted better—even the simple fare of potatoes or rice, the mainstay of their diet.

Mia was often still in bed when he crawled in next to her after his night watch. The warm, sweet smell of her skin stirred his emotions and his body. They often spent several sweet, sacred hours in their berth before he fell asleep and Mia went topside to spell Ruth at the helm.

In the afternoons, in the hottest part of the day, Gabe began a ritual of swimming when he awoke. Mia often joined him. Following one another over the edge of the boat, they frolicked and played in the cool water.

At night, with Hope riding on his lap, Gabe felt life was good. *Maybe we should have left long before we did,* he realized. He began to understand what freedom was, and he knew the boat was aptly named. No matter what happened next, he had finally lived—really lived—for the first time in his life. He began to feel hopeful about the future they were sailing into.

Chapter 16:

THERE'S A LIGHT ON

S am looked up from the book, out the darkened window. *When was the last time I went outside at night? Or looked at the sky—really looked at it?* He noticed the light from the neighbor's back porch was on. It twinkled in the wet branches of an old tree near the house. *Not unlike starlight,* he thought.

"Does that funny older woman that sold you this house still live there?" Sam asked, motioning toward the house with the light on.

Joyce roused herself to turn and look out the window at the ramshackle house across the way.

"Yes," she said. "I think so. We don't keep up with our neighbors like we once did. I guess the last time I saw her was shortly after we moved in, a few years ago." Joyce yawned widely. "I think I'm going to bed," she said, rising all the way out of her chair. She kissed Sam on the cheek. "I'm so glad you're home."

"I'll join you," Marq said, groaning slightly at the effort of rising. He reached down and put his hands on his son's shoulders. "We're both glad you're home, son."

He took Joyce's arm, and they walked together down the hall. Sam heard their bedroom door open and then shut. Then the house was quiet.

Sam stretched and stood up. He moved to the chair, still warm from Joyce sitting on it. *Maybe I'll go out for a walk later tonight, to clear my head—and to look up at the stars, if the sky clears.*

Sam turned back to the book. Plato leapt up on the empty seat next to him and sat looking at Sam with green eyes, as if he expected Sam to continue reading aloud to him.

"Want me to keep going?" he asked the cat.

Plato arched his back, stretched to make a bridge with his body between the chairs, and poked his head into the book. He sniffed the pages with one eyebrow raised. His long whiskers explored the text, as if he were reading braille, taking in the meaning by feel.

Sam continued reading about life on the boat:

Most mornings the sun came up warm and the wind began to blow. They sailed through marine-blue waters. Sometimes whitecaps would break around them or large swells would carry them along. Other times the winds would die down or not come at all, and they drifted as much as sailed.

During the first weeks at sea, Ruth noted in the logbook seeing seals, sea lions, dolphins, seabirds, a few whales. Each entry during their first few weeks included their mutual wonder at the beauty of the ocean. Gabe and Mia dropped trawling lines over the edge and brought in fish to supplement their supplies. But as they sailed and drifted farther from land, they saw fewer birds, fewer marine mammals, and fewer fish on their dinner plates.

What they did begin to see everywhere was garbage, the remnants of human civilization: Plastic bags, bottles, buoys, cups. A plastic doll with missing arms floating like an injured mermaid, her long wet hair trailing on the surface.

Mia began to make a list in the logbook of the things she saw: Parts of hulls, single rubber sandals, deflated balloons, Styrofoam cups, plastic silverware, cracked bucket lids. And lots of unidentifiable parts of things. Plastic bags looked like jellyfish floating just under the surface. The list grew longer as the weeks passed: bottle caps; bubble wrap; straws; toothbrushes; pens; jugs; paintbrushes; half-submerged nets; once a globe of the world floating uncannily on its side, North and South America looking like they had crawled out of the water and draped themselves like helpless swimmers across the top. The garbage was often so thick they could barely see clear water.

One afternoon they hoisted up the weathered spinnaker sail, trying to catch any wind they could. There hadn't been much lately. Nor much rain. They were slowly plugging through the goopy plastic residue of humanity, much of it submerged below the waterline.

"Plastic everything, everywhere," Mia said. "And its cousin, Styrofoam."

"Humankind's legacy," Ruth lamented as she peered over the edge of the boat.

One day the waters appeared a little clearer. A few patches of gray-blue could be seen between the islands of garbage. Ruth spotted a large turtle floating serenely on the surface, but upon closer inspection she saw that it wasn't alive. It had been caught in a ghost net just below the surface. Ruth lowered the dinghy and rowed out to it. She cut it loose and pulled it up close to the boat with a net. The smell was overwhelming, but she set to work cleaning it.

She didn't know herself what she would do with the shell, but she knew that she wanted it. Needed it. She would find a way to honor this ancient creature. She guessed that it had been well over a hundred years old when it died. Keeping a line tied to the big boat, she worked swiftly, cutting away the rotting flesh, scrubbing and rinsing the shell. Mia and Gabe helped her pull it aboard. They tethered the gigantic shell to the deck to dry in the sun.

Neither Gabe nor Mia could imagine what she would do with it. Nor could Ruth explain it herself. She was the one that went swimming that evening.

Ruth stayed out in the water a long time. She tipped her head back and looked up at the sky, floating on the surface like a turtle herself. Gabe and Mia stayed aboard with Hope, who after close inspection took up residence in the empty shell. He looked overboard at Ruth from his new vantage point.

That evening, after her watch, Mia made a note in the logbook: "No wind again today. Giant sea turtle found dead, caught in a ghost net. Should be nearing land again soon."

Mia had brought along a world map, not an official nautical chart. The map had been all she could find. She kept them on a westerly course, but she was beginning to suspect that something had gone wrong. By her calculations, as primitive as they were, they should have already reached the islands off the coast of Asia. But there were no signs that they were getting any closer to land, and the winds had continued to diminish.

One long day passed into the next, over and over, with little or no wind to move them. One night, as Mia tossed in her bed, she finally gave in to no sleep and joined Gabe up top on watch.

"Hey."

"Hey there." Gabe smiled, happy to see her. "Why aren't you sleeping?"

"Couldn't."

She came and snuggled up against him. Hope disappeared inside to take her warm spot in the bed. Mia put her head on Gabe's shoulder. He caressed her head and dark hair. His strong hands worked their way down to her shoulders and the round hills of her topography.

In the starlight, Gabe looked like the Norse god Thor. Opening herself to him in a perfect moment she would remember for a lifetime, Mia watched the constellation Orion over his shoulder.

Grandmother paused here, looking up at Orion, who appeared upside down to her in the sky. "The best and the worst moments of one's life are often tied together. The beautiful and the heartbreaking are as if one thing. Mia believed this was the moment they conceived their first child."

Mia and Gabe held each other a long while in quiet reflection. Finally, Mia broke the silence.

"I think there is something going on," she said.

"What's wrong?" Gabe asked.

"Well, the winds are not as strong as they should be. And although we keep our bow pointed west, we don't seem to be making much westerly progress," Mia told him.

"What could it be?" he asked.

"I don't know for sure," she said, "but I know there are ocean currents at work underneath us. We are essentially sailing on a moving platform. I'm worried we are going in circles."

Gabe listened as Mia explained. She brought out the map and the logbook. She showed him her notes and rough calculations in the back, pointing out where they should be. And then she shared her greatest fear:

With one slim finger she drew a wide, spiraling circle in the Pacific Ocean.

"I think we might be trapped here—in the Great Pacific Garbage Patch."

Sam stood up, and Plato was forced to jump down. He carried the heavy book to the old upright piano in the living room and left it open on top. He let his fingers quietly find a melody. In minor tones he played for a few minutes, improvising a song.

He had a good life compared to many, and he knew how lucky he was, but he wondered, *Am I trapped in my own gyre? In a life I don't actually want? Do I really want to be a lawyer in a corporate office?*

He didn't know what he wanted—or even what he needed. Jet lag, stress, a new job, being home with the family, this crazy book that claimed to be from the future . . . it all swirled in his head. *Maybe I will just step out and get some fresh air.* He put his still-damp overcoat on and slipped into his dad's boots by the door.

Plato glided out in front of him. A few stars blinked through the cloud cover.

"Beautiful," he noted to Plato. But the cat made straight for the old lady's yard with the light on and disappeared.

Chapter 17:

THE WORLD
THAT COULD BE

S am took a couple of deep breaths of the cool, wet air and tried to find a constellation he recognized between the clouds. He hadn't been outside at night very often in his life—as a young Black man, he had to be careful. He walked around the block. Most of the houses in the neighborhood were dark at this hour.

The night air cleared his head and left him feeling peaceful. He stepped back inside. Plato had apparently returned through the cat door, for he was waiting on top of the piano looking at Sam, sitting upright. Sam thought the cat looked like a conductor with a tuxedo on. Plato's tail hung down, twitching like a metronome—back . . . and . . . forth . . . back . . . and . . . forth.

Sam reached for the book, wanting to find out what happened next, but it was no longer open to the story unfolding on the boat.

It was late and Sam was tired, but he was sure the book hadn't been open to this spot when he set it on top of the piano before going outside! Now the book lay open to the "Universal Bill of Rights and Responsibilities."

"Okay," he said to Plato, "let's take a peek at this bill of rights in the future."

> We the People, in Order to form a more perfect Union, establish Justice, ensure Tranquility, protect the Earth, and promote the general Welfare, by securing the blessings of Life and Liberty for Ourselves, our Children, and our Children's Children for all time to come, do ordain and establish this Universal Bill of Rights and Responsibilities.

At law school, Sam had studied the founding documents of the United States extensively. This bill of rights appeared to be based on the United States Bill of Rights[5]—but with some additions.

He read on:

> Disregard and contempt for Human Rights and the Environment have resulted in barbarous acts, which have outraged the consciousness of humankind and brought Life on Earth to the brink of destruction. . . . We have determined to promote Social Progress and restore the Earth by providing Protection for these Rights through Nonviolent Action and the Rule of Law. . . .

He read the first six articles, then continued.

Article 4: . . . All Laws are to be written and disseminated in such a fashion that the common Person is

---

5. The unabridged United States Bill of Rights is included in the Appendix.

able to comprehend their Meaning without need of interpretation or legal aid.

Article 5: Those in Public Office are to be held to the highest Standards of Truth. . . .

Article 6: Henceforth, the Waters, the Sky, Plants, Animals, and the Earth itself shall have Legal Recognition, Protection, and Rights before the Law, including the Right to Legal Representation in Courts and Representation by Proxy in the Governance of the Planet.

His eyes grew wide at the significance of having laws written so that the common person could understand them without need of interpretation. *This is not a new idea*, he remembered. *During the Roman Empire, laws were written and displayed in town squares. The Twelve Tables, as they were known, were posted for everyone to see and written so everyone could understand them.*

As he read, he also recognized roots and remnants of the United Nations' Universal Declaration of Human Rights, written and signed in 1948.[6] Sam paused, thinking about the ramifications of what he'd just read. *Entities other than humans are given legal rights! Is this the way the world is finally saved? Restored? Through the rule of law? Maybe there is a way out of the mess we are in.*

Plato jumped down from the top of the piano. His feet landing on the keys sounded wildly loud in the wee hours of the night, startling Sam. The cat sauntered toward the kitchen with his tail high in its customary shape of a question mark.

---

6. The United Nations' unabridged Universal Declaration of Human Rights is included in the Appendix.

Sam got up and followed him. He was suddenly hungry after his walk. He scrounged through the cupboards. *These are pretty empty for a whole house full of people*, he thought. *Times must be even harder than I realized.* He found the peanut butter and some sticky red jam in the bottom of a jar. He made a sandwich, tearing a bite off and setting it down in front of Plato. The cat sniffed the sandwich.

Sam chuckled. "Yes, I believe Plato, the Greek philosopher, once said, 'Knowledge is the food of the soul.' But he didn't say anything in particular about peanut butter and jelly sandwiches—or cats, as far as I know." Sam finished his sandwich and headed back to the living room.

"Okay, Mr. Philosopher," he said, sitting back down on the piano bench again. "Shall I continue reading?"

Plato licked Sam's fingers with his rough pink tongue. Sam took that as a yes.

Article 7: Everyone has the Right to manifest their Religion or Belief . . . so long as its Practice does not impinge on the Universal Rights of others. The Government shall neither support nor oppress any Religion.

Sam tapped the book. *A person can practice their religion, but only if they don't violate another's rights. That seems so reasonable.*

Article 8: No one shall be subjected to arbitrary interference with their Privacy . . . no Person, Company, or Government Agency shall sell or provide Information to any third party . . .

An individual's private information is now constitutionally protected. Sam let out a little whistle. Looking up, he saw Kate standing in the doorway watching him.

"You're home!" She ran into his arms.

"How long have you been standing there?" he asked.

"Long enough to realize you found the book too," she said.

"Dad gave it to me."

"So . . . he knows about it?" she asked.

"So does your mom," Sam said. "We were reading it together before they went off to bed."

"I've been dreaming about that book," Kate said. "I found it this evening and was reading it. I had a dream about Zen and Grace and what the future may hold. It was uncanny."

"Of course, it's just a book though," said Sam. "How could it really be from the future?"

"But there's something else about it that's strange," said Kate. "It's like it was written just for us. Or maybe it's for everyone, but it's like someone or something wanted to give us a peek into the future—our future. There's one part in the book in particular—"

"About the cat?" Sam interjected.

They both looked over at Plato, who was back in the library, seemingly asleep on the chair. They eyed him suspiciously for a moment. Sam told her how he found the book mysteriously open to a different page when he came back from a walk. "Innocent until proven guilty?" Sam suggested.

"He's just a cat," Kate said guardedly.

"Like every other cat," agreed Sam, but the lilt in his voice didn't match the doubt on his face.

They built a fire in the living room fireplace as Sam told her how in the book the world adopts a new constitution and a Universal Bill of Rights and Responsibilities.

She sat next to Sam in front of the flames with the book open as he told her how the new bill of rights would make it illegal to lie to the public. It had also taken money out of politics and strengthened protections of privacy. It had even given rights to nonhuman entities like the oceans and the sky. Sam was clearly animated by these ideas, but Kate wanted to get back to the stories.

"I left off reading from 'Survivors' Stories,'" Kate told him.

"I've been reading about Gabe and Mia—they think their boat might be trapped in a gyre," said Sam.

"Let's find out what happens next," Kate said.

Chapter 18:

TRAPPED

S am turned to where he'd left off in "Survivors' Stories."
Kate imagined they were in the crowd listening to
Grandmother speak with the sound of the fire crackling
next to them as her brother read aloud.

As more fuel was added to the fire, it blazed up
again and lit the round faces of the people nearest
Grandmother, like little moons orbiting around her
gravitational pull. She lifted her voice so all could hear
her words.

"Humankind is capable of withstanding unimag-
inable hardships, but one of the most difficult is to
have nothing to occupy the mind."

She continued her story:

Weeks passed into months and then more months.
The logbook read like an obituary of hope as they swirled
closer to the middle of the powerful gyre created by the
confluence of the ocean currents. When they reached

the center, the winds died completely. With nothing to propel them out of it, they spun in a giant circle. Gabe began to call it "circling the drain." Neither Mia nor Ruth laughed when he said it.

They tried to think of ways they might escape. When no viable plan emerged, fear and anger took hold. But fear and anger are not stable states. After the initial shock wore away and they realized they might not arrive anywhere other than right where they were, in the ever-present here and now, they each in their own time and way made peace with what appeared to be their fate—they had been given this life for as long as it lasted.

Gabe started keeping his harmonica tucked in a cubbyhole on deck. He began teaching himself to play it more seriously. At night, he'd take it out and experiment with new breathing patterns. Breathing in and out through its hollow teeth, he'd make odd sounds— nothing particularly musical at first. But night after night he played, blowing and humming through this strange little gadget.

At first, he played old songs and tunes he already knew. But over time he invented new sounds, new music. His breath made audible expressed both the fear and growing courage he lived with daily. The harmonica became a part of him, became his voice. Hope seemed to like the music and curled in Gabe's lap, purring, whenever he played. Gabe found himself looking forward to the companionship of this small soulful instrument as well as Hope on his nightly watches.

To pass the time and give focus to something other than worry, Mia began to draw in the back of the logbook and on small scraps of paper. But there was just one pencil. She took great care with each mark she made, studying her subject well before her hand drew a line. As the pencil grew shorter, her skills grew sharper. Mia admired the fine lines of Hope's coat and the patterned interlocking design of the turtle shell he was so fond of sleeping in on the deck.

One afternoon, she drew him asleep in it, curled up, his nose tucked under his white paws.

Ruth looked over her shoulder. "You've captured him!" she said. Then she added with a wink, "As much as anyone can capture that cat!"

Ruth had taken to whittling with the pocketknife she kept on a string around her neck or slipped into her pocket. She had a small stone she pulled from her duffel bag to keep it sharp, and she gathered carving materials from the debris that drifted by the boat. She fashioned useful things from pieces of wood or plastic—small cups for drinking, spoons for stirring, a clip for the logbook.

One long, quiet evening, Ruth pulled a deck of cards out of her green canvas duffel bag. They all began to play at night after dinner—gin rummy, hearts, blackjack. Ruth's favorite when she was alone was solitaire. Over time, the cards showed signs of wear at the corners from the countless games. The faces of the kings and queens faded—no match for this duty. Even the jokers weren't laughing, having been pressed into use as other cards fell from service. Ruth scribbled new numbers and symbols over their once-smiling faces.

The only one of them that seemed unfazed by the lack of things to do was the cat. Hope did not seem to have a care in the world and contentedly napped most days away in his turtle shell or on Aunt Ruth's bed.

The sun beat down relentlessly. Ruth's tan skin became leathery brown, while Gabe's fairer skin burned, despite all his attempts to stay covered up from the sun. His clothes were ripped and ragged or worn so thin they no longer offered much protection. Mia collected many types of seaweed and began experimenting with cooking them as well as creating sunblocks, particularly for Gabe. He sat on the deck as she applied green strips of wet seaweed to his bare skin. It felt funny at first, but he came to anticipate the cool relief of a green second skin when she came in from one of her harvesting trips.

"You're getting a very special spa treatment," she would tell him.

"You're married to a green monster," he'd chuckle.

The food supply was limited and growing smaller. Water was scarce. They conserved every drop they could. When rain did fall, it was just a drizzle. Ruth devised a clever way to catch more water. She rigged the sails into huge funnels that directed the water right into empty jugs she brought up from the hold. Gabe laughed out loud when he first saw the contraption Ruth had built. Using her system, the rain that did fall kept their jugs partially refilled.

When boredom or sadness overcame Ruth, she would go out rowing in the skiff; sometimes Hope went with her. Mia watching them from the deck was reminded of a favorite childhood poem by Edward Lear. She copied it into her small book. And one night after dinner, she sang on deck:

The Owl and the Pussy-cat went to sea
In a beautiful pea-green boat,
They took some honey, and plenty of money. . . .

The Owl looked up to the stars above,
And sang to a small guitar,
"O lovely Pussy, O Pussy, my love. . . .
What a beautiful Pussy you are!"

. . . They sailed away, for a year and a day
To the land where the Bong-Tree grows. . . .

And hand in hand, on the edge of the sand,
They danced by the light of the moon,
The moon . . .
They danced by the light of the moon.

Ruth laughed for the first time in a long time that night.

They each began to take turns out rowing. They gathered and tied bits and pieces of ropes together they found floating so they could venture farther and farther out and still be tethered to the boat, extending their range on each outing. It was the only time alone any of them had besides sleeping or their turn at watch.

Grandmother stopped talking for a moment. Looking only at Le and speaking softly, almost in a whisper to her alone, she said, "There are gaps in the story here. Something happened at sea during the long wait that followed. I only know a little of it. There was a child born at sea. That part of their story went unspoken of for a long time. Much later, I came across entries that had been torn out of the logbook. It is part of another story I shall tell you later."

Grandmother turned back to the shimmering faces of the crowd. Le's thoughts were on the story Grandmother wasn't telling her—yet.

The throng of people had not heard what Grandmother had said to Le, but they had seen the look of sorrow on her face.

Grandmother went on:

Mia soothed herself with her music—her sweet voice eased them all. Her singing took on an ethereal quality. She sang to the sky, the water, the stars . . . to the child that she had born. She sang of loss and longing. She sang of hope. Her voice reached new highs and lows as she wrote new songs and added new verses to old ones. She persevered through dry, peeling lips, using one of the seaweeds she gathered to mash into a paste to soothe her skin.

Months added onto months, long past the time any of them thought they could have endured. Being trapped, with little hope for the future, they learned to live with the knowledge that they wouldn't likely have one.

But they had the present. And within the confines of the moment, they learned to live. Thinking about the past and worrying about the future began to recede. They lived in a state of suspended animation. Slowly, what was once a burden to bear became a practice in living meditation.

Chapter 19:

THE GYRE

K ate stood up and went to get more firewood. After adding more wood, she leaned in close to Sam's shoulder, shutting her eyes while she listened as he continued reading aloud.

Gabe, Mia, and Ruth had survived on the food stores they'd brought, augmented by the occasional fish they caught. They also ate the shellfish and seaweed that grew on the undersides of the large floating pieces of garbage. They were running low on stove fuel and had decided they would save the last canisters, so they ate what they had uncooked.

Twilight became one of their favorite times. The heat would pass, and a slight breeze off the water gave them temporary relief. They prepared for the evening meal together, the meal the three of them always shared. Well, the four of them—Hope never missed it either. It usually consisted of canned beans and, a few times a week, a bit of fish. The potatoes were gone now—used up along with the dried fruit and vegetables that had been stored under the floorboards, in the coolest part of the boat. Seaweed that Mia collected out rowing now made up for the lack of fresh fruits and vegetables.

They sat on deck one twilight after the sun went down, enjoying the coolness after dinner. Ruth shuffled the cards, getting ready for their nightly game of gin rummy. Mia was picking out a new tune on the guitar after making her daily entry in the logbook. Gabe sat with Hope on his lap, his harmonica in hand.

"It has been twenty-four moons, nearly two years, since we set sail," Mia noted.

"Feels like a decade," Gabe said.

"We should throw a party," Ruth said without looking up from what she was doing.

"A party? To celebrate what?" Gabe grumbled.

"Life," Ruth said simply.

"I think it's a great idea," Mia said, brightening. "It is our twenty-fourth moonversary too."

"Okay," Gabe laughed, "but how do we celebrate out here?"

"Celebrations always start with food," Ruth said.

"And dressing up," Mia added.

"Music and maybe decorations?" Ruth said, thinking out loud.

"Tomorrow night?" Mia asked.

There was suddenly excitement in the air.

"I better practice," said Gabe, taking his harmonica and moving to the bow of the boat. Other than the logbook, there was really no tracking time on the water, so he hadn't realized their anniversary was approaching. Time had taken on a new dimension for all of them—an ever-present now without the constant future planning he remembered from The Time Before. He blew a melody through the harmonica, a new song he had been working on. His tongue fluttered across the small, shiny instrument in rhythm with the tapping of his foot. He would play tomorrow night for Mia—his gift to her.

Gabe practiced a long time, looking out at the sky and the empty horizon. *What if we never escape the gyre? Will we die here on this boat? Eventually run out of food and water? Will we go insane one by one, trapped circling the drain in this sea of garbage?*

Gabe pushed these thoughts out of his mind and blew into the harmonica again—for Mia. *I made a vow to love and care for her. That is a reason to live, to go on trying to do my best, regardless of this seemingly hopeless situation—and for Ruth too. She has always been here for me, and I will be here for her too,* he vowed silently. *To the end.*

Mia went below deck to the small berth she and Gabe shared. She had been collecting bits of cloth she found floating, with the thought of making a new shirt for Gabe. She uncovered the pieces of material she had hidden in the bottom of her basket. *There isn't time now for sewing a new shirt, but I can make the small pieces of fabric into banners for the party.*

She brought the materials for sewing and went up and sat with Gabe and Hope on their watch. He reached out and found her hand, then kissed her fingers one by one, pausing on her ring finger, which he kissed twice.

"Thank you for everything. Thank you for making my life whole. We've been through a lot together. I'm so sorry it has been so hard," Gabe said.

"Hard, yes, but I have had you by my side the whole time." She smiled. "Thank you," she said, gazing deeply into his eyes. She slept outside on the deck that night, in Gabe's arms until morning.

Mia got up early to go out in the rowboat and collect more seaweed. She had a special dish in mind for the party. She also gathered nylon fishing line and thin rope. Ruth produced a needle and thread from her green canvas duffel bag, and, during their afternoon watch, Mia and Ruth sewed the brightest material to the line and hung it like streamers above the deck. Gabe slept in the morning but spent the afternoon perfecting his song for Mia on the harmonica.

Ruth was looking forward to the party. She, maybe more than the others, knew the power of living fully in the moment. She knew she could not always control what happened to her, but she knew she always got to decide how she would act within the boundaries of the circumstances that presented themselves. Even now, even while trapped on a boat, happiness was a choice.

As evening approached, Mia pulled out her wedding shirt from a bottom drawer. She slipped it on over her head. The embroidered green vines and soft yellow flowers circled her neck. She untangled her long black hair with the antique comb she had brought along. Ruth helped her braid it and pin it up on her head with bits of sticks and plastic straws they had found floating in the sea around them. They poked little bright, shiny buttons in her hair, clipped from a worn-out blouse of Ruth's. Mia looked in the small mirror above the dry sink. She was dressed much like she was on her wedding night, but it was not the same young woman that looked back at her two years ago. A lot had happened.

As the sun set, Gabe and Mia could smell something good wafting up to them on the deck. Aunt Ruth was in the galley cooking, whistling to herself as she worked. Hope sat nearby, seemingly supervising the meal.

"Happy anniversary," Gabe said as they sat hand in hand, watching the glassy water reflect the evening parade of colors in the sky.

"You're a day late," Mia said, throwing Gabe a mischievous smile. Gabe laughed.

"So I am, but that means we are in our third year of marriage now, our twenty-fifth moon, I think."

"So we are," said Mia, looking up at the full moon rising on the eastern horizon like an invited guest.

"You look beautiful in your wedding shirt. You haven't worn it once in all this time?" he remarked.

"I guess I was saving it for a special occasion," she said.

Gabe took his harmonica out of his pocket and began to play the song he had composed for her. The harmonica had almost become a part of him. The music that he created was strong and expressive—a reflection of his growing inner life these last two years. When he finished, he set the instrument down and pulled her close.

"I love it," Mia said. "I love you." They kissed a long time, forgetting everything around them.

Ruth appeared at the top of the stairs from the galley with steaming bowls of rice with mussels. She had used a little of the fuel to make a hot meal. Excusing herself for a moment, she slipped inside and dug around in the green canvas duffel bag that was never far from her reach.

She arrived up top again and said, "Ahhh . . . this might add a little variety to our dinner." She twisted the top off of a bottle of fiery red hot sauce and passed it around.

"Woo-hoo!" Gabe shouted with a big smile. "Now *this* is a party!"

Mia grinned. They each took just a few drops, wanting to make it last as long as possible.

Ruth served Hope his own dish of mussels, but without the hot sauce. He purred contentedly. A light breeze stirred the banners as they ate until they were full—not something they regularly indulged in.

Their stomachs satisfied, the mood was festive. Gabe slipped the harmonica from his front pocket and began to play a cheerful tune. Ruth and Mia playfully danced on the deck. As the light waned, Mia took out her guitar and began to strum and sing. Her enchanting voice drifted on the salty air . . .

Water, water, cleanse my soul,
Make me peaceful, make me whole.

Then she added a new verse, looking at Gabe and then Aunt Ruth, feeling grateful for both of them:

Love, oh Love, you carry me,
Without you I could not be.
Love, oh Love, you married me,
Without you where would I be?

As twilight reached toward darkness, the sky came alive again with stars. They sat together on the deck, Hope curled among them, happy in one another's company. As the stars began their dance across the night stage, they sipped little glasses of water, more precious than wine.

And then—everything changed.

Chapter 20:

THE ESCAPE

It was late. The fire in the living room had died down to coals. Kate moved to the chair in the library and, curling up with Plato, took a turn reading. Sam joined her, stretching out on the floor.

Grandmother's drumming picked up in pace, and Le began to move in rhythm with the words, almost dancing as she continued to relay the story:

Based on the entries in the logbook, they were in their third year on the boat when it happened. Gabe was asleep below deck after his night watch. Ruth was on duty, though there was rarely much to do with no wind. But someone had to be on watch in case it started drizzling so they could refill the water jugs, which were now dangerously low. And there was always the thin hope of rescue.

Mia came in from rowing. She called out to Ruth as she came up alongside the sailboat. "The sea is changing. Something is different lately. I'm seeing bigger and bigger clear patches of blue ocean."

"Yes, I've noticed it too," said Ruth. "The garbage seems to be spreading out."

Over cards that night, they all talked about the possible reasons.

"Maybe we are moving again?" Ruth suggested, laying down a tattered queen of hearts.

Mia looked overboard at the clear patches, now reflecting the stars' light. "I wonder . . ." She let her sentence drift off as she looked at the cards in her hand, deciding on her next move and her next words at the same time. "I don't want to get my hopes up or anyone else's," she said after a long pause, "but I think it's possible we might be able to sail out of the gyre on the next big wind . . . if we ever get one." The winds had begun to stir again, which gave her hope.

"If the ocean currents were to stop or even just slow enough, the garbage would begin to spread out, like what we've been seeing," she said. "And if the currents started up again after this lag, that would affect the wind. If that's what's happening, there may be a window long enough for us to break free of the gyre—maybe."

Gabe sighed. "I don't know what to think or hope for anymore."

"Our food stocks are low. Our water jugs are nearly empty," Mia said, immediately regretting stating the obvious.

"I'm afraid of what will become of us if we can't escape," Gabe admitted.

"I try not to think about it," said Ruth.

The following weeks, the skies remained clear and mostly calm, but the clean blue patches of water grew larger. One afternoon while Mia was on watch, she saw storm clouds on the horizon—clouds unlike the occasional ones that had provided a drizzle of rain.

She called out to Ruth excitedly, "Come look!"

"Oh my!" Ruth exclaimed as she hurried about the deck, gathering and setting the water jugs under the funnels and adjusting the sails to use them to collect the rain that looked imminent.

The sky darkened. The wind hit them with unexpected force, sending the boat momentarily on its side before pulling the sail loose, leaving it flapping loudly in the wind. The rain came moments later—hard and fast.

Mia helped pull the thrashing sail into place as Ruth directed the sudden torrent of water into the jugs.

Gabe joined them on deck, woken by the heaving boat and the sound of the pounding rain as well as the women's excited voices. Jug after jug filled, spilling over as the rain continued, and soon all the jugs were overflowing. The main sail was still full of water, and it hadn't stopped raining yet! Gabe looked up at Ruth as he hoisted the last jug into the hold. She directed the stream of water at him, laughing and soaking him.

"Take the spout," Ruth directed Gabe. She slipped below deck for a moment before reemerging with a bar of soap from the green canvas duffel bag. She tossed it to Mia. "You first," she said.

Gabe aimed the funnel of water into the air, creating a shower that came down over Mia. She pulled off her wet clothes, grinning naked on the deck. She rubbed the slippery bar of soap over her skin and through her hair, doing a little hopping dance. Then Mia grabbed the funnel, and it was Gabe's turn with the bar of soap.

Ruth, too, stripped down to almost nothing for the shower of fresh water, catching the last bit before the sail was empty.

"Let's get the sails rigged back up and catch this wind while we can!" Gabe shouted.

Working together, the three of them set the sails. Mia brought out the compass, and Gabe took the helm. They pointed the bow to the west. For the first time in years, they were on the move.

Mia reveled in the feeling of the boat in motion and the smooth feel of her body, washed of the crust of salt that had encased her. Her skin felt soft and her hair silky as it blew around her face.

She broke into song:

Rain, oh rain, come down on me,
Wash my body, set me free.

It was a strange feeling to have the sails up and be heeling over, the heavy keel pushing into the sea with its full weight. They had gotten off the merry-go-round that they had nearly resigned themselves to. Gabe grinned, and Ruth quietly said a prayer.

Weeks passed. Not every day was as windy as the first, but there was enough wind to keep them moving most of the time. Gabe sat on the bow with his harmonica and let the fresh air blow on his face. He sometimes just played with the harmonica, holding it up in the wind, causing it to hum an undulating sound all its own. The wind itself became the music. One afternoon, a pod of porpoises played in the wake of the fast-moving sailboat. Gabe blew into the harmonica, making joyful music for them.

They began to see birds in the sky and on the water. The ocean changed color from deep blue to turquoise green.

And then one morning they spotted something on the horizon—land.

PART III:

THE FUTURE
OF THE FUTURE

"A society grows great when old men plant trees whose shade they know they shall never sit in."

—GREEK PROVERB

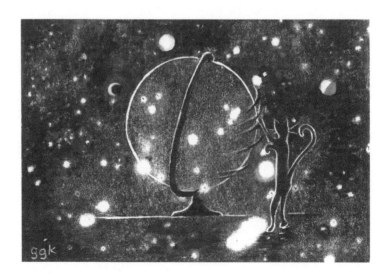

Chapter 21:

THE RULE OF LAW

" L et me read you something," Sam said to Kate. He flipped the pages to the Universal Bill of Rights and Responsibilities and read aloud the first articles. Kate listened, trying to understand and imagine this new world.

She had taken American history in her junior year of high school. She was currently in a civics class. "Do you think this is possible?" she asked. "Could we change our Constitution?"

"Well, it wouldn't be easy," Sam said. "But we could hold a Constitutional Congress or add amendments to the Bill of Rights. The Constitution has had many amendments in its history. That's what the Bill of Rights is—a list of the first ten amendments to the Constitution. We have continued to make amendments, about thirty altogether."[7]

He continued, "If this wild book is somehow truly from the future, the world adopts a constitution and a set of rights and responsibilities based on the Universal Declaration of Human Rights that was drafted and signed by most of the world's nations after World War II. It's already the basis of considerable international law."

---

7. The unabridged amendments to the United States Constitution are included in the Appendix.

Sam paged backward through the book, showing Kate what he had been reading.

Kate could hardly stand to tear herself away from the book—or Sam. But she had to get some more sleep before her test. She stood up and stretched. Hugging Sam, she asked, "Do you think we should tell Zen about the book?"

Sam thought a moment. "I don't know."

Kate hugged him again. "Let's talk about it tomorrow."

"See you in the mornin'."

Plato jumped on the back of the chair. He arched his back and formed his tail into a wide question mark, as if he were listening to their conversation, as if he, too, wondered if they should tell Zen about the book. They both looked at the cat and then each other, before Kate disappeared down the hallway.

Sam sat down and continued reading. *The articles that make up the framework of this future constitution appear to have been ratified by the whole world—or what was left of it, sometime in the twenty-first century,* Sam realized. He scanned through the next articles:

Article 9: Everyone has the Right to an effective Remedy by a competent Tribunal for acts violating their fundamental Rights. . . . No one is above the Law. . . . Everyone is entitled to full Equality and to a fair and public Hearing. . . . Those charged or found guilty shall be treated with Respect and Dignity while making Reparations to those whose rights they have violated.

This worldwide constitution provided legal protection from unfair imprisonment and guarded against torture and mistreatment; it also held those found guilty of abusing the rights of others accountable, using nonviolent means. *What an enduring concept.* Sam smiled to himself, remembering Martin Luther King Jr., Nelson Mandela, Desmond Tutu, and Gandhi before them.

Article 10: No Entity private or public shall levy usury fees. . . . Free access to Education at all levels is a right of the People.

Sam practically shouted out loud when he read this—no more unfair student loans then! Education would be available to everyone. Lending money at unreasonably high rates of interest would be illegal and unnecessary, and public funds would be set aside for the benefit of the people.

He was so excited he kept skimming the articles, though exhaustion was starting to set in.

Article 11: Everyone has the Right to Free Speech, freedom of Opinion and Expression. . . . However, it is everyone's Responsibility to be truthful in the dissemination of Information and to adhere to the guiding Principle of Nonviolence in Speech as well as Action.

Sam immediately understood the importance of this article. *Free press and free speech are protected but also held to standards of truth and nonviolence.* He read on:

Article 12: The Will of the People shall be the basis of the authority of the Government. This Will shall be expressed in periodic and genuine Elections. . . . Voting is a Responsibility of all People. . . .

Sam's eyes felt heavy, but he wanted to read what happened to Mia, Gabe, and Ruth after they escaped the gyre.

Chapter 22:

MY THIRD FAMILY

S am turned back to "Survivors' Stories," telling himself he would read just one more page.

The crowd grew quiet as Grandmother began to speak again. Le's hands leapt in the light from the fire, interpreting Grandmother's words:

I was bathing in the stone pool, as I did multiple times a day, both to get clean and to cool off. That morning several of my little family of feathered friends had joined me along the edges. They splashed water over their backs and onto me as well, making me giggle. Alala was watching over us, high in the banyan tree. He began to call in a way I had never heard before. Something unusual was happening. I got up and pulled on an old dress with a faded flower print. No need to towel off—it was another hot day, and the wind was blowing. I was dry in moments.

I climbed partway up the tree until my head was higher than the surrounding rock ravine. I looked in the direction Alala was gazing. On the horizon I saw the cause of his alarm. The white sail of a boat was visible in the distance. I had not seen a boat for a long time. I had not seen a human being either. I had a strange rush of emotion, fear and longing all mixed up together.

I stayed in the tree, Alala nearby. We watched as the boat neared the entrance of the bay and then sailed past it. Could it be that whoever was on that boat would come to the island? Would they hurt me? Would I be happier in the company of others? I had little to steal that couldn't be found again in the piles of rubbish on the beaches. And water? I had plenty to share.

The boat sailed out of sight, and I climbed down from the tree and returned to my little camp. It was late afternoon when Alala called again. I climbed back up into the tree. The same boat was approaching the entrance again, but this time it sailed in. I pulled on my mismatched rubber boots and put a tattered cap on my head to shield my eyes and protect myself from the sun. I slipped my knife into its makeshift carrier, strapped on the outside of my yellow boot. I quietly slipped out of camp. Alala followed overhead, pausing to wait for me on the bleached white trunks of the standing dead trees along the trail.

I knew every outcropping and beach on this end of the island. I chose a spot to watch from behind a tangle of dead branches.

In the last few months, the beaches had begun to be more pleasant. Much of the organic garbage that had once washed ashore had decomposed. I no longer had to wear a cloth around my face when I was out scavenging, and patches of sand had been washed clean by the tides.

I watched as the sailboat neared and dropped anchor. The boat bobbed gently up and down. Three people climbed in a skiff. I could hear their voices and the sound of the oars as they worked their way to the beach. Alala, perched a few hundred feet up, kept a watchful eye on them too.

The man had a deep voice that carried over the sound of the waves on the beach. He and the younger of two women pulled the rowboat up high on the beach above the tide line.

The older woman adeptly swung a green duffel bag out of the boat and over her shoulder, setting it against a log. A cat with a curved tail popped out of the open bag and began exploring. The man and the younger woman began gathering armfuls of wood before joining the older woman in building a fire.

She piled dry leaves and slivers of wood she was making with a pocketknife into a tower. She reached into the duffel bag and pulled out a piece of glass, holding it so the light from the sun was concentrated to a single point. A little wisp of smoke rose up, and then a small bright flame burst from the pile. They smiled and talked as the flames grew larger.

The young woman began laughing and dancing in little circles around the campfire, which was beginning to crackle and pop.

The older woman cleaned a striped bright silver fish, feeding the innards to the cat. She sharpened a stick and speared the filleted fish, setting it over the fire that was now blazing. The cat seemed to be supervising the whole affair, as if it were all meant for its enjoyment.

I watched in amazement from behind the bushes. I hadn't seen fire in years. My eyes were drawn to the moving flames. As dusk came on, the firelight appeared to grow brighter. The smell of cooking fish drifted in the air. I had not eaten cooked food since I was with my first family.

I listened to the strange sound of human voices. I did not speak their language yet. I couldn't understand what they were saying, but their voices were kind. The younger woman began strumming an instrument like the one I remembered Papa playing. The laughter and the softness with which they talked to one another and the cat put me at ease.

Alala was braver than me. He was the first to approach them. He flew down from his perch in the tree and landed on the driftwood near the man.

The man looked at the crow sitting just a few feet away, and he slowly took a small piece of fish and put it on the log between them. Alala moved closer and took the fish. Then the man put another piece of roasted fish on the log between them.

This time, Alala did not take the fish but began calling to me. It was a particular call. One I knew. He was asking me to come to him. He was asking me to come get the fish, but I was too afraid to come out from my hiding place.

After his calls did not bring me forth, he picked up the piece of fish in his beak and brought it to me, setting it before me, feeding me as I once had fed him. Still behind the bushes, out of sight, I slipped the tender fish into my mouth. I wanted more—I wanted more fish, I wanted to be seen, I wanted to be with people again. All of these feelings struggled against my habit of hiding. Alala returned to the spot next to the man and called to me again. Through the overlay of fear, the deeper impulse for belonging prevailed. I stepped out from behind the bushes—into the ring of light.

Sam's eyes felt heavy. He shut them and drifted off into sleep, dreaming of the world that could be, with Plato in his lap.

Chapter 23:

THE RULE OF LOVE

Joyce tried to go back to sleep. She pulled the covers over her head. She was exhausted. Her feet and legs ached from standing behind the counter at the wine bar. She turned over, nesting against Marq like a spoon in a drawer. But nothing helped. She got up.

She opened Grace's bedroom door and smiled to herself. *At least she is sleeping.* She shut the door and wandered toward the kitchen. Sam was asleep in the library chair, the big book lying open over his chest. Joyce quietly lifted the book off of him, replacing it with a warm blanket. She went on into the kitchen and began rummaging in the cupboards.

The cat appeared, his tail curled into its customary question mark, and let out a plaintive mew. *What do you have for me?* he seemed to ask with his one raised eyebrow.

Joyce bent down and ran her hand along his ample sides. He rounded his back, meeting her hand as she stroked his fur. He let out another mournful meow, a little louder this time.

"Did you think I didn't hear your request the first time?" she asked him. She opened a can of his favorite cat food and gave him the whole thing. "Life might be short," she whispered, patting him again along his back. He purred and ate at the same time, making funny little wet licking noises that made her smile.

She found the end of a chocolate bar for herself and moved to the dining room table, where she had left the book. It was open to the pages Sam must have been reading as he dozed off. *Maybe*, she thought, remembering that the book seemed to have a life of its own.

She began to read while sitting at the table. She liked the part that did away with unreasonable interest on loans. *That would change our lives.*

She closed the book and ran her hand over the deep purple cover with its gold lettering. *Where did this book come from, and why did it come to me? If it's a sign, does it mean I can influence the future?*

Plato joined her in the dining room, cleaning his face with one curled white paw on a chair next to her. She turned the pages, searching until she found the part again about the girl on the island. She read on, nibbling the chocolate.

It was getting late, but the crowd instead of decreasing had grown as more people heard that this would be Grandmother's last Telling.

The drum in her hands was still as she recalled the moment long ago when she first found the people who would become her new family:

I stood in the ring of light, trembling. I didn't know their names or the meaning of the words they spoke, but I could hear the kindness in their voices. When I glanced up from the ground, I saw the expressions on each of their faces. The young woman's soft brown eyes smiled at me. The young man glanced back and forth between Alala and me, beginning to comprehend that there was a bond between us. The older woman looked at me, seeing the frightened child that I was— in need of a mother.

The man stood, looking around to see if there were others accompanying me. I must have seemed too young to be there alone. I learned later that this was the second time they had come ashore. They had landed earlier in the day and explored the deserted village, determining that no one lived on the island anymore. They had moved to this bay for better moorage.

The older woman gazed hard into the bushes from which I had stepped before she approached me.

Love is a universal language. It finds its way directly into our hearts. Pools of tears formed in my eyes and ran down my face. They were absorbed by the dry sand at my feet. My knees buckling, I dropped to the ground. The older woman gently put her arms around me. The younger woman began to sing to me. Though I didn't understand the words, the music soothed and com- forted me. The older woman's arms around me was the first human touch I had known since my mother died. My body melted into hers. In the flickering light of the campfire, in the presence of other humans, I closed my eyes and floated on the younger woman's beautiful voice. I had been found by my third family.

Joyce let the chocolate sit on her tongue as long as it would before dissolving, savoring the moment.

Life is so unpredictable, she thought. *The hard parts and the sweetness come all mixed up together, impossible to separate— loneliness from love, hunger from its satisfaction, the present from the future.* She took another bite of the chocolate, letting these ponderings play in her mind as she read on.

In the morning, using hand motions and a mixture of birdcalls, Alala and I led the young man to the freshwater spring. I helped him fill and carry jugs of water back to the beach.

He started calling me Little Bird that day because I talked to the birds. He taught me his name, Gabe.

That afternoon, I led the two women to my pool to soak. They taught me how to say each of their names, Mia and Ruth. I remember the strange feel of the sounds in my mouth and on my tongue. That night I asked Ruth, in a series of gestures, to sleep with me inside the banyan tree.

I slept in her arms that night and every night to come on the island. She became Mama Ruth to me. I felt secure in the world that she seemed to create by her very presence. She snored a little in her sleep. To me it was not much different than the sound of the cat purring, curled at our feet. Alala watched over us all from his perch in the tree.

One night as we watched the stars together, I pointed to the night sky and the one star I had noticed that did not seem to move, a star that all the other stars seemed to revolve around. Later, when I understood more, Mama Ruth told me it was called the North Star, the star sailors use for navigation. What I didn't say, but I think she knew, was that she had become my North Star—the person whom my life now revolved around.

Safe in her embrace, I slowly began to tell her in gestures and broken words about my life, about my first family. About living on the island alone except for my family of birds. Sometimes I would wake up in the night and think for a moment that I knew my old name, but before I could bring it to full consciousness, it evaporated, much like the passing clouds that now occasionally graced the sky. And so I became Little Bird.

We began to expand the living spaces near the pool to include a separate area for Mia and Gabe. We regularly scavenged the beaches together, wandering farther afield than I had dared to go alone. We gathered and washed clothing and shoes. We found ropes, tarps, and buckets, among other supplies.

But still the one thing we looked for the most was food. Mama Ruth pulled a can opener out of her green duffel bag on the second day, and I watched with appreciation as she quickly and deftly opened one of the cans I offered my new family. Canned goods now became easy to access, but there were also more of us to feed.

One morning, Gabe and Mia stayed behind to work on their shelter and Mama Ruth and I went out alone to the shore to see what had washed in on the latest tide. As we walked, we looked out to the east and saw a great cloud on the horizon. I had not seen a cloud like this before. It was approaching fast. The wind picked up and began to blow the sand and dry leaves into little twisters.

"Come here, Little Bird," Mama Ruth gestured, pulling me close under a large rocky outcropping up away from the beach near a grove of trees. I was frightened. I snuggled in her lap as we watched the wind whip the tops of the trees. We could hear the dead branches as they came crashing down.

As the storm front passed, a soft, cool rain began to fall. I felt a sense of joy rise inside me. We nestled together in speechless awe at the simplicity of gentle rain. The small, shriveled plants that had survived the long drought were washed of their dusty coats and glowed vibrant colors of green. The birds, which had followed us, began singing happy songs in accompaniment to the rain. Alala found a small, clear puddle of rainwater from which to drink and then splashed big water droplets all about as he bathed.

Feeling giddy, I pulled my old dress over my head. Leaving only my mismatched boots on, I ran out from our rocky shelter and pranced in the puddle too.

When Mama Ruth and I reached home, we were soaking wet. Gabe and Mia were sitting together under the shelter they were building, watching the raindrops slide off the roof into the pool. Hope sat happily in Gabe's lap, seemingly as content and grateful as they were for the new shelter.

Mama Ruth and I joined them. Mia was untangling her long black hair with a bone comb. When she finished hers, she went to work untangling mine. She worked slowly from the tips up until the comb passed smoothly through my hair.

Together we watched as the beads of water fell into the pool, sending out perfect little concentric circles that widened and joined one another. Then, almost as swiftly as the rain had come, the clouds passed and the sun broke out and shone brightly in a clean blue sky. The banyan tree twinkled with thousands of tiny stars as the sun winked through the droplets that gathered on its outstretched leafy arms. The birds preened and called joyfully.

The world was suddenly dazzling. I felt safe in it with Mama Ruth and my new family. I had not known such happiness in a long time. A deep and pervasive contentment in living settled in me. It wouldn't last. I was only beginning to understand that nothing lasts forever—neither happiness nor sorrow. But I had learned how deeply people need one another. We are meant to live in flocks, in tribes, in community with one another.

Joyce closed the book. She carried it back into the library. Sam was still sleeping soundly in the chair. He knew about the book, but she wasn't sure about sharing it with Kate or Zen.

There was an old cabinet in the library that had a lock on it. She put the book inside. Stretching with one hand and feeling along the top of the cabinet, she found the key. She locked the book inside. Dropping the key into her bathrobe pocket, she thought, *Maybe that will keep it in its place.*

Chapter 24:

THE BOOK
OF BELONGING

Kate woke early. Her alarm was going off. She rolled over, hoping for a few more moments of precious sleep. But remembering the test, she stretched and swung her feet over the side of the bed. She tugged a sweatshirt over her head and pulled her jeans on. She passed Zen's door on her way down the stairs to the kitchen. The house was quiet. Light was just beginning to show in the windows.

It was too early for anyone else to be up on a Saturday morning, but Kate wanted to study more before her test. Sam was asleep in the big green library chair with a blanket over him. She tiptoed past him. Plato jumped down from the top of a library cabinet at the sight of Kate on her way to the kitchen. She started the water for a cup of strong black tea, then decided to treat herself to hot chocolate instead.

The cat rubbed against her legs as she waited for the milk to warm. She picked him up and hugged him before pouring a little of her warm milk in a saucer for him. She fixed a piece of toast to go with the hot chocolate as he lapped the milk—purring at the same time, making her chuckle.

She had planned to study, but at the sight of Sam she started thinking about last night and reading the strange book together. The book suddenly seemed more important to her than any test she would take that day. She slipped inside the library and looked around for it. It wasn't on the side table or on the floor near Sam. She didn't see it on any of the bookshelves. *It's a big book, and with its purple cover it shouldn't be hard to find,* she thought. Then she noticed that the locking cabinet was slightly ajar. She peeked in. The gold cursive title on the deep plum background caught the light. *There it is!*

She hauled it out as quietly as she could and carried it back to the kitchen. She propped the book on the counter, reading while she waited for another piece of toast to pop up. Kate found the part where Grandmother was telling her story:

Early on, we communicated a lot with gestures and expressions. Then Mama Ruth started teaching me signs for simple words.

"Sky," she said, moving one arm in an arch and looking up. I copied the motion and the word at the same time. "Wind," she said next, swaying her arms in unison like a piece of cloth blowing side to side. "Wind," I repeated, pursing my lips and pushing my breath out to make the sound while I copied her arm motions.

"Rain," I repeated after her, wiggling my extended fingers.

"Love," she said, pointing to herself and crossing her arms over her chest before pointing at me. I mimicked the action, pointing first at myself and then at her as she had done. I understood immediately what we had said to each other: "I love you."

In the evenings after dinner, I taught Mia and Gabe what Mama Ruth had taught me in the morning.

It was practice for me, and I felt proud I could teach them something.

"Bi . . . i . . . ir . . . d," I awkwardly voiced and made a beak opening and shutting with my fingers. Mia giggled, recreating the gesture. Gabe moved his fingers like a beak opening and shutting in front of his mouth and then pointed at Alala. *He wants to know Alala's name,* I realized.

Talking out loud to other humans still felt funny. I opened my mouth, saying his name slowly in my native language. Gabe repeated the sounds several times before getting it right.

"Awe . . . Law . . . La . . . Awe . . . Law . . . La . . ." It was my turn to smile as he struggled to make the unfamiliar sounds. I understood them asking me my name many times, but I could not bring it to mind. So *Little Bird* it became. It wasn't long before we came to understand each other for basic needs—at least most of the time.

Mia, Gabe, and Mama Ruth continued to marvel at my ability to talk to the birds. I taught Gabe a few sounds so he could talk with Alala. We laughed again as he tried to make the guttural sounds in his throat and clicking movements with his tongue. Alala wore a look of amused patience. But I think he came to love Gabe as much as I did. Hope and Alala even developed an affinity for each other—as long as the cat didn't try and get too close, though Alala with his beak was plenty able to defend himself if needed, and he always had the advantage of flight.

The rains began to come more often. On the far side of the mountain where the most rain fell, the island was beginning to stay green. We made plans to plant a garden there. We gathered seeds from old plots and found feral plants from which we ate and gathered more seeds for sowing.

One day as we were planting the garden, Mia brought out the small box with the dragon carved on the top. She opened it to show me the seeds inside.

"They will grow into big trees," she signed and spoke at the same time. I held a tiny seed in my hand, almost in disbelief that such a large tree as she described could grow from it.

Here, Grandmother paused in her storytelling.

"I was too young to realize then that most big things—trees or ideas—start small. Ideas and trees grow from seeds we water and tend. The world that is grew from the seeds of love and peace planted during The Great Change. And remember this," she said, looking first at Le and then to the gathering around her, "we choose the world we live in and the one we leave for the next generation by the choices we make every day. What we tend and care for grows. Whatever we give our energy to grows, be it hate or love."

We planted five seeds of the empress tree that morning around the garden. I would never see them grow into trees, but we planted them, and I think perhaps they grow there still.

With my nose in the fresh dirt and my fingers nearly black with rich soil, I couldn't remember ever being happier. On the wet side of the island, the earth responded to the rain and the long rest from intensive farming. It broke into bud and bloom. Plants long dormant and trees thought dead began to sprout. Roots below the surface came forth in a carpet of life. Mushrooms bloomed from unseen mycelium below. Flowers now decorated the island in variations of bold purples, crimson reds, brilliant yellows, and translucent oranges. Rain was the secret. I wanted to gather the flowers up, but I had learned to let things be. I did not need to possess in order to love. So I admired the flowers where I found them, in the cracks and crannies of rocks and old roadbeds where water gathered, and in the wide, wild fields that had once been pastures and farms.

One day Mama Ruth sent me with food to be delivered to Mia and Gabe, who were working in the late-afternoon sun in the garden on the far side of the mountain. On my way back, I decided to pass through my old village and by my first family's home. I wandered into the yard. It no longer felt as scary as it once had. Time had passed.

Grandmother glanced up at the large crowd. "Though I do not think time heals all wounds, it does make them easier to bear." She continued:

The horrific memories of the final days there had begun to recede, and the many more happy memories of my first family began to come to the forefront of my mind. As I stood in front of my old house, I thought about my sister and my older brothers and how we had once slept under the big tree in our yard.

Now there was a thick green vine climbing up into what had once been the canopy of the tree. Alala flew about in the dappled light, casting the shadow of his wings around the base like a giant butterfly. Small butter-colored flowers and bright grass had begun to creep back under the tree like a living carpet. I slipped off my sandals and padded around. The bouquet of the earth beneath my feet perfumed the air. I laid down under the tree, looking up at the cobalt-blue sky with a dash of white clouds. I thought of my mama and my papa, and I was glad for the life they had given me. What had they called me? I could almost hear it and their voices. But Little Bird was the only name that came to me now.

I looked in the broken windows of the house. Green shoots were coming up through the floorboards. I saw a doll in a corner tucked behind an overturned chair. I remembered her! Once a favorite of my sister's, she had been passed down to me. I was getting too old to play with dolls, but I didn't want to leave her on the floor. I ducked inside, carefully picking my way to her. I wiped off her face with the corner of my dress and straightened her clothes. Tucking her under my arm, I began the trek home.

It was getting late, nearing dusk. Mama Ruth, Gabe, and Mia had continued to honor this time of the day as they did on the boat. I wanted to be home for the quiet hour, for dinner and for the blessings that would be given for our food, and for the songs we would sing as Mia and Gabe played music after we ate. I wanted to tell them about my adventure to my old home.

As I reached the trailhead to our camp, I saw by the sun that it was later than I'd realized. I hurried up the path, Alala close overhead. When I arrived I saw that Mama Ruth was just putting our food on the makeshift table around which we all gathered for meals. The stumps and mended chairs we used for dining were already set in place. Mia and Gabe had beat me back and were bathing in the pool after the hot work of their day in the garden. I came close to Mama Ruth for the hug I knew would envelop me.

"There you are!" She smiled. "I was beginning to worry."

I held out the doll to show her. She took it in her arms along with me.

"Well, who do we have here?" she asked.

I gestured to her that it had been my sister's.

Mama Ruth found a place at the table next to her for the ragged doll. No one was ever turned away from her table. I knew we would wash and mend the doll's clothes in the morning. Mia and Gabe joined us at the table with wet hair and clean clothes.

"Bless this meal before us," Mama Ruth said. She continued, "We are grateful for the things we have, for each other, for fresh water to drink and clean air to breathe. Blessed be the rains and the sun, the trees and the birds. May we always be grateful for the earth, upon which all life depends."

"Have you been adventuring? Finding new companions?" Gabe asked, looking at the doll sitting between Mama Ruth and me as he served us all from the pot she had set on the table.

In gestures and words I told them about returning to my old home, of the yard and the tree full once again of leaves—if not its own. Of the flowers in the yard and of finding the doll inside and how I couldn't leave her behind.

After we had all eaten, Gabe raised the bowl he used for his food and water. We all had a single bowl—or a large cup, in my case—that was our own to look after.

"I have an announcement," he said.

Mia looked at him and smiled.

"We have an announcement," he corrected himself. "We are going to have a baby."

Chapter 25:

THE BOOK OF ZEN

K ate made another cup of hot chocolate. She was headed for her room with it and the book, but this time, as she was about to pass Zen's door, she paused. She hesitated a long moment before knocking softly.

Not waiting for a reply, she went in. He was still asleep. She put the book on the end of the bed and slipped in next to him, sipping the hot cocoa. Zen stirred and turned over, looking at her with one questioning dark-brown eye. The other eye was still deep in his pillow. His thick, curly black hair and the blankets obscured most of his sleepy face, but a fleeting smile crossed his lips. She took another sip of the hot chocolate before offering the cup to him.

"Isn't it a little early for breakfast in bed, Kat?" Zen asked. His words were muffled by the pillow, but Kate caught his amused tone. He regularly called her "Kat" when they were together.

He didn't seem surprised by her presence. They often talked in each other's rooms—just not usually this early in the morning. They were the closest in age of all the kids—just six months apart. Kate had been seven and Zen six when their parents married. Now, a decade later, they were inseparable.

"I have something I want to show you," she said.

He turned over and propped himself up on one elbow, taking the offered cup. "What is it?"

Plato had followed her into the bedroom and was sitting on top of the book at his feet. Even Plato seemed reluctant to let Zen see the book. Kate had to pick him up off of it to get him to move.

She leaned against Zen, the big book between them.

"What is this, Kat?" he asked.

"Well, I don't know for sure," she said. "This book just appeared in the library yesterday. That's what Sam told me anyway. He came home late last night."

"Sam's home already?" Zen asked.

"Yeah, but he's still sleeping," she said.

"So was I," he said, with a sideways glance and a little smile on his lips.

Kate turned to the first pages and placed her finger under the words as she read aloud.

THE HISTORY OF THE WORLD
To the Best of Our Knowledge
Researched and Compiled for the Hall of Records by
The World Council Committee for Remembrance
Published 2200

She tapped the date with one finger. "The publishing date is 2200! That is like seven generations from now!"

"So?" Zen shrugged. "It can't be true. You don't think that it really is from the future . . . do you?"

"I don't know what to think. On one hand, of course, how could it be? But there are things in here I've been thinking about . . . and reading it . . . it seems . . . well, very possible. Maybe it is from the future?"

Zen sat up a little straighter and looked at her. "Kat, you're crazy."

But they thumbed through the pages together, the book in their laps between them, sharing the hot chocolate back and forth. They paused at some of the illustrations, maps, and documents. She told him about the section titled "Survivors' Stories." And about Little Bird, Gabe, Mia, and Ruth, who seemed to have lived during something called The Time Before and through something else called The Great Change.

Kate began reading aloud to Zen where she had left off.

Grandmother looked out at the many faces gathered for the Telling, but her gaze landed on Le again. Le nodded. She was listening. She would remember.

Grandmother continued:

Gabe was like a big brother to me. He loved fishing. We got some of our meals that way out in the rowboat together. But the days of a plentiful bounty from the sea had passed and the world had not yet recovered, though in time it would.

Back then we were lucky to bring home enough for a thin fish soup. But Gabe and I loved going out together in the rowboat, whether we caught anything or not. Leaning over the edge and looking into the water was like peering into another world. The waters had continued to clear of garbage, and life was stirring down there.

Gabe liked to tease me. Sometimes he pretended the boat was about to tip over. He rocked it back and forth as I giggled.

As we neared shore one day, he said, "Here, take the oars," and he motioned for me to trade places with him. I sat facing him. He reached out with large hands and pushed the oars through the water as I pulled on them.

"Let me do it," I said in broken words.

He snickered as the boat turned in a little circle, but he also coached me. "You can do it," he encouraged me.

I looked over my shoulder toward the shore. One of the things about rowing is the person doing it is sitting backward, facing away from the direction they intend to go. After a few circles, we began to get a little closer to the beach.

The next day we went out rowing again. After I got better at rowing, he dove overboard and swam toward shore, letting me practice getting the boat in while he held onto the long line wrapped around his waist.

"This way!" he shouted, while I struggled to synchronize the oars. Eventually the boat scraped against the sand, and I got out, proud to have made it back.

Later that day, Gabe wanted to go in the water and swim. He and Mia both went while I stood on shore and watched. Mia waded back in to me. Her belly was growing thick around the middle and her wet shirt clung to it, emphasizing her rounding figure.

"Do you want to come with us?" she asked.

"Yes!" I loved water, but I had never learned to swim. I could always touch the bottom in the rock pool by our camp.

"Take my hand," she said.

I kicked off my boots and took Mia's hand, and we walked out into the surf. It reminded me for a moment of the time I found Alala. I hadn't been in the ocean since then. The water was much clearer now, but I looked back toward the shore for Alala.

"Don't worry. We won't let anything happen to you, and we are not going out over your head," she assured me.

Alala was, as always, looking out for me, this time from one of his perches on a piece of driftwood near the beach. He was unconcerned. So I relaxed too.

The waves in the bay were not large, but it was a new experience for me to play in them. "This is fun!" I yelled above the sound of the water rushing up and down the beach. We began jumping over the breakers. In between waves, I let go of Mia's hand. The pull of the breaking waves washing in and out was exhilarating. Mia and Gabe took turns holding me up and showing me how to hold my breath and dive into the waves just before they broke on me. Standing up on the other side, I shouted, "I did it!"

When we finally came out of the surf, Mama Ruth was waiting for us all. "Here you are." She smiled at us, handing out towels for everyone and dry clothes for me.

That day she was mending clothes on the beach while we played in the waves, patching holes in a pair of pants for me as she watched us. She wore her graying hair pulled back with a piece of rope she'd found on the beach to keep it out of her way. She had strong, steady hands. She was always working on something.

As we toweled off and put our clothes on, she continued sewing, her head tilted to one side. She had only one pair of glasses, and one of the lenses had fallen out. She had to tip her head to one side and tuck her chin in to see what she was doing. It reminded me of some of my birds who turned their heads to one side to see what was in front of them, and it gave her an inquisitive look that I liked.

We ate dinner on the beach that night. Mama Ruth built the fire using that lost lens from her glasses to magnify and focus the sun's heat, just as she had done the first time I saw her.

Gabe and I had brought back three small fish for dinner. We ate a few greens that we had coaxed from the garden along with the fish. As we watched the sun go down and the moon rise, I reminisced about the evening I first met my third family. It seemed like so long ago.

Mia sang and Gabe took out his harmonica and played as we hiked up the path to our camp at dusk.

> Love, oh Love, please come with me,
> Without you where would we be?
> Love, oh Love, my life with you
> Gives me purpose, meaning too.

As I tucked myself against Mama Ruth to sleep, I could hardly imagine a world anymore without them all in it. I fell asleep that night surrounded by love, looked over by Alala, Hope curled at our feet.

Chapter 26:

LITTLE BIRD

Zen and Kate both looked up as his bedroom door opened with a slight squeak of old hinges. Sam slipped into the room and onto the end of the bed.

"Hey, man, I heard you were home!" Zen said, leaning forward.

"Yeah, I got in last night. Thought I would make the most of the time we have." Sam gave him a bear hug. "So you know about the book now too?" he asked.

"Kat just brought it in this morning," Zen said. "Early," he added, poking her with his elbow.

Kate caught Sam up with the story.

"Let's find out what happens next," Zen said.

Sam joined them on the bed, and Kate shifted the heavy book on her lap as she continued to read aloud.

The expressions on Grandmother's face told as much about the times she was recalling as the words she spoke. She went on:

We spent many happy days playing in the waves. Mia showed me some basic swimming strokes, holding me in the water, and Gabe showed me how to move my legs as I learned to propel myself. Sometimes Mama Ruth would join us. I would go with her outside the breakers toward the open sea. She liked to float out there on her back, and she taught me to do the same.

As I tipped my head back, the water would rush into my ears, hushing the sounds of the world. I would enter into the silence of the sea—just me and the clear blue water under me, the bright blue sky above. In those moments I felt a oneness with the world—a thin slice of girl pressed between the ocean and the sky.

As my skills and confidence grew, I swam farther and farther out. One afternoon, Mia and Gabe rowed to the anchored sailboat. They had been trying to fix the old radio. I waded out confidently into the water, dove under the breakers, and swam toward the boat. I floated on my back for a long time.

Finally lifting my head, I bobbed up and down. I looked back. I couldn't see the beach. I had floated past the boat! I tried to swim back, but the tide was taking me away from the island, away from my family and everything I knew. I hadn't told Mama Ruth I was going swimming because I was just going out to see Mia and Gabe. I shouted for help.

I remember thinking, *No one can hear me. No one can see me.*

A rising sense of panic started to take hold, but, remembering what Mama Ruth had taught me about floating, I laid my head back in the water and rested in the great silence. I shut my eyes, and an odd peace came over me as I accepted what might come.

Grandmother looked up at the night sky as if she were looking back in time to the moment she was describing.

I had seen too much in my short lifetime to be surprised by death—even my own. I opened my eyes again after a long time and looked around me. I couldn't see the island at all now. I took another big breath and tipped my head back. I was suspended again in the silent world, held precariously between the water and the sky.

I thought about my sister, who had chosen to go below the surface. I wondered if we would meet again in a watery world under the sea. I looked up at the clouds, letting the tide carry me where it would. Surrendering was surprisingly easy.

Grandmother paused again, seeming to remember that day as vividly as if it had happened yesterday, not decades earlier. "It was the first time I remember thinking, *Maybe fighting death is not always the answer.*" She continued:

I floated for a very long time, belonging to neither water nor sky but to a world I can only describe as "between."

A black silhouette with wings began crossing over me and circling around and around. Alala. Watching him was enough. I was not alone. I was content to accept whatever came next. Then, suddenly, the water around me churned, and four strong arms pulled me out of the sea.

Mia held me as Gabe rowed against the tide to bring us back to the island. Alala overhead called and called in a raspy high tone intermixed with a deep chortle that I understood to mean I had been found. I was coming home. When the rowboat finally scraped against the shore, Mama Ruth was waiting there for us, her face a mixture of sternness and loving relief.

I tried to explain that I hadn't intended to go out so far. It was an accident. Mama Ruth just looked me straight in the eyes and said nothing. Instead she took me in her arms—exactly what we both needed.

We ate in silence that night around the table except for a few words from Gabe of gratitude that we were all safe. I fell into a broken sleep in the banyan tree.

I dreamed I was still floating on the water, Alala above me, but in a night sky filled with stars.

I had no words at the time to explain that I was no longer afraid of death. I had no words for the tranquility I felt at its acceptance.

Grandmother stroked the iridescent feathers of Darkness on her left shoulder. Le, looking intently at her, could almost see the little girl she had once been.

"Death is not always our enemy," Grandmother continued. "It, too, can be a friend." She took a small book from the folds of her cloak. "This is the book your great grandmother Mia always carried," she said to Le. "She gave it to me on the night of her passing." Grandmother opened it up and read aloud:

"The Uses of Sorrow"

(In my sleep I dreamed this poem)

Someone I loved once gave me
a box full of darkness.

It took me years to understand
that this, too, was a gift.

"That is from the great poet Mary Oliver, who lived in The Time Before." Grandmother handed the book to Le and said, "This is yours now for safekeeping. There are many more treasures inside."

Grandmother's drum lay silent in her lap. She picked it up now and began to rub it softly before resuming the story and a heart-like beat, *boom-boom, boom-boom.*

In the morning I bathed in the pool and rested in the shade. I occupied a different world now, a place I remember as halfway. Halfway between sleeping and dreaming. Halfway between lightness and dark. Halfway between knowing and not knowing. Halfway between childhood and maturity.

I began to spend more time in the pool alone. And it was there that I first felt the stirrings of my young body. My breasts began to swell, and my hips slowly widened. My monthly flow of blood began. And I felt a new longing in my body and my heart, though for what I did not know.

Mama Ruth and Mia guided me in caring for myself and understanding the changes that were happening to my body, but I felt alone in ways I didn't understand. Something inside of me had changed.

Chapter 27:

THE SIGNAL

"Will you read for us, Sam?" Kate moved the heavy book over Zen, toward Sam, and reached for the last sip of hot chocolate. Zen teasingly held it out of her reach until she jabbed a finger in his ribs, causing him to almost spill the last of it.

Sam smiled at his brother and sister and rolled his eyes as he said, "You two!" But he was glad to be home. He loved his crazy mixed-up family, every one of them. Sam began to read:

Grandmother had a faraway look on her face. Le listened carefully as she translated, knowing she was responsible for remembering the story for those who would come next. Her movements had a natural grace and helped fix it in her mind.

Mia had been spending hours a day tinkering with the hand-cranked radio on the boat. Gabe usually joined her, turning the handle as she tried to get it working. Occasionally she would get wisps of fuzzy sound on it.

One afternoon she shouted and gestured wildly to Mama Ruth and me on the beach. "Listen!" she yelled.

She had found a station that was broadcasting a signal. Others had survived The Great Change!

The signal was weak and intermittent. It sounded like a nest of bees trapped inside a box. But as Mia tuned in, we began to understand that it was a regular broadcast. We could comprehend some of what was being said. The broadcast was in many languages. In each language, there was an invitation to come to one of the refuge centers.

Coordinates were given for locations around the world. Mia consulted the map she had brought with them, contemplating and adjusting the latitude and longitude lines they had drawn on by hand. Mia explained that if we could get close enough to one of these refuge centers, we'd be able to get a signal from something called a Radio Direction Finder, or RDF—the signals were being transmitted to help guide survivors to the camps.

Many evenings Mama Ruth, Gabe, and Mia sat up late together talking. I couldn't hear everything they were saying as I drifted in and out of sleep, but they were listening to the radio. Sometimes Orion would be well on his way along his nightly march across the sky before Mama Ruth would come to bed. One evening she came in early. I was still awake. She put an arm around me.

"I think it is nearing time for us to leave the island," she whispered and gestured with her hands.

I caught my breath, holding it.

She told me, "Mia and Gabe particularly want to go because of the baby coming."

I had thought that someday maybe we would leave the island. I just wasn't prepared for that "someday" to become a "today."

"I have never been anywhere else," I murmured, uncertain how to sign the complicated thought and the emotions that it was loaded with.

But Mama Ruth somehow seemed to understand me anyway. She drew me close, and I let her hold me for a long time.

She explained, "We hope to find one of the refuge centers we hear about on the radio. A place with a regular food supply, a doctor or a nurse, a community for us all to be a part of, a school for you, perhaps."

I was happy on the island with my birds. And now that I had a human family too, I didn't want to leave.

"We will all stay together," she signed.

I understood that. And for all the changes going on inside of me, I knew I wanted to be with them.

I would go.

I wasn't able to sleep much that night, wondering what new life lay ahead for us. I felt a little stir of excitement along with fear at the thought of leaving the island.

Grandmother picked up the drum again that had been lying silent near her, and she started to tap it rhythmically.

We began to make preparations for our departure. Using large heavy thread and needles that Mama Ruth pulled out of her green duffel bag, we reinforced the main sail of the boat. When that project was done, we sewed together a spare sail out of old tarps, a sail we hoped we wouldn't need. We also repaired the rainwater catchment system Mama Ruth had devised. We gathered and stowed all the food we could and filled water containers, stocking the boat with as many supplies as possible in preparation for our departure.

One of us would often turn the crank on the radio as we worked. The broadcast Mia found sometimes played music as well as listing coordinates to the refuge centers.

The music coming across the radio was fuzzy and often interrupted, but the sound made the work lighter. Sometimes Gabe would stop right in the middle of a task just to swing Mia and me or Mama Ruth in his arms. Mia said they were breaking international rules by playing music, but Gabe just grabbed her midsentence and spun her around. She laughed and said maybe some rules should be broken when it came to music.

The plan was to sail south, finding our way in daylight by the eastern and western arc of the sun across the sky and the compass Mia and Gabe had brought—originally a gift from Mama Ruth. We would hope to find an RDF signal, a beacon to a refuge center.

We visited our garden one last time, bringing armfuls of produce to be stored in the coolness under the floorboards of the sailboat. We left markers to indicate where water could be found, should anyone come to the island after us.

We were carrying the last of our things to the boat early one morning, in preparation for the tide that would carry us out of the harbor. Before we left camp for the final time, I said goodbye to the pool and the birds that I could not expect to follow me this time. Mama Ruth was there. Her hand was on the umbrella pole, fingering the words "Guaranteed for Life" inscribed on the attached metal plate.

"Whose life?" Mama Ruth said, talking to Hope, who was winding himself around her feet, more than to me. "No life is guaranteed," she said with a small smile that for once didn't light up her eyes.

Alala called and circled overhead as I watched the only home I had ever known recede into the distance, until all I could see was the top of the mountain near our little spring. Gradually, like the setting of the sun, the mountain that had been my home for so many years disappeared too. I stood for a long moment on the stern, looking out across the empty skyline behind us. Alala, finally perching on the mast, must have been the last one of us to see our island set on the horizon.

With four of us now to take turns at the wheel, Mama Ruth and I started spelling Gabe of the night watch.

"You are too young to be out alone on watch all night," she said.

"But I like it," I insisted. "I want to. I want to do my part." I stomped my foot.

"Okay," she finally relented, "we'll compromise. You can take the helm as the sun goes down, and I'll sleep nearby on the wide bench seat."

And so it was. Alala perched on the deck during my watch—and Mama Ruth snored. Hope wandered between sleeping in the huge turtle shell still on the deck and curling up with Mama Ruth on the bench.

I was alone—well, almost. Enough to take pleasure in my own company.

It was easy to stay awake the first half of my shift. But eventually, sometime in the night, when I could hardly keep my eyes open, Mama Ruth would wake up, stretch, and suggest I just shut my eyes for a moment on the warm bench. Usually, the sun coming up over the horizon was the next time I would open my eyes. Then I would wander down below to the V-berth I shared with her and sleep until the sun was high in the sky.

We sailed many days, and I watched as Mia marked a full cycle of the moon in the logbook with one of the charcoal pencils she made while we were on the island.

We took turns cranking the handle, and Mia tuned into the radio multiple times a day, hoping to catch an RDF signal that would lead us to a refuge center. Sometimes the winds would push us so hard we would have to take down some of the sail we had up to keep from being blown over. Other times we would float placidly with no wind at all and only the current to carry us.

One night after dinner as Gabe cranked the handle and Mia tuned the radio, we heard a new kind of signal.

"It's the RDF signal!" she announced breathlessly.

We began crisscrossing back and forth in front of the signal, changing tack when we went out of range and crossing back again to find it, like Mama Ruth's zigzag seams on the sailcloth. We were all excited.

How long would it be before we found other people?
Cross-stitching a path, we sailed toward the future.

As the sun set one evening and I took the helm as
usual, I noticed that Mama Ruth didn't snore even
though her eyes were shut as she lay on the bench
nearby. Mia stayed by the radio, and Gabe moved
about the cabin and deck in a fit of anxious activity. It
was getting late. Finally we found the RDF signal again
after crossing outside its range. But now the wind
died completely as darkness settled deeply around us.

"I have to get some sleep," Mia said.

"There is nothing to do but wait for the wind,"
Gabe said. "I might as well join you."

Ruth was finally snoring on the bench with Hope at
her feet. I was getting groggy but had managed to keep
my eyes open, alert enough to notice that something
was afoot. The air felt too still. Too heavy. It was as if
the wind was holding its breath, waiting for something.

Alala stirred in the strange, thick air, shaking himself and fluffing out his feathers. He flew up to the top
of the mast from my shoulder. Suddenly the sea began
to toss, and the wind came at us from all directions
at once!

Mama Ruth awoke at the sudden change. Together
we heard more than saw the storm's approach. The
water hurled itself in angry waves against the sides
of the boat.

The sail we had up flapped violently. I was unable
to control the boat with the winds shifting directions.
The sound of thunder rolled in the distance. Mama
Ruth took the helm and sent me down to wake Mia

and Gabe, but they were already on their way up the stairs. They joined us on deck. We watched as the skyline and the stars disappeared altogether, melting into the sea.

"I've never seen anything like this," said Gabe.

Mia took hold of his arm and nodded in agreement.

In the blackness that ensued, we could not discern water from sky. Huge lurching rollers buffeted the hull. We moved about the deck, gathering everything we could in our arms and taking it into the cabin of the boat. Then the storm engulfed us.

"Go down below!" Mama Ruth ordered me, the wind ripping the words from her mouth. I didn't argue this time.

The boat rocked brutally. Mia and I fastened down cupboards and put away belongings as best we could, but she lost her footing as the boat tossed wildly. She banged hard against the counter at waist level. She gasped with the impact. Holding her round belly with one hand and my hand with the other, she pulled me into the bunk she usually shared with Gabe. We lay there breathing hard for a moment, bracing against the sides of the boat to keep from toppling out of the bed.

"Hand me the pillows!" she yelled above the roar of the storm.

We packed them around ourselves. Mia lashed a sheet over the top of us to help hold us down as the boat rose and fell fiercely in the cresting waves and deep troughs. Pressed against Mia's back, I could feel more than hear her humming under her breath:

Love, oh Love, please comfort me,
Without you where would I be?

Gabe came down to check on us.

"Are you both all right?" he asked breathlessly.

"We're okay," Mia said. A forced smile crossed her face briefly.

I looked at her, knowing she was not.

"I love you," he said as he kissed her on the head and tussled my hair before careening off back topside to help Mama Ruth.

PART IV:

THE ALPHA
AND THE OMEGA

*"We cannot solve our problems with the same thinking
we used when we created them."*
—ALBERT EINSTEIN

Chapter 28:

THE PAST IS
A MAGIC BOX

T he rustling sounds of preparations for breakfast could be heard coming from the kitchen through the floor below them.

"Let's just read a little longer," Zen said. "Here, I'll take a turn."

Kate and Sam exchanged surprised looks. Zen wasn't usually interested in reading. He cleared his throat and pulled the large book onto his lap. He had a beautiful deep voice.

Slowly Grandmother began to pass her rough hand over the drum's surface, as if she were rubbing an injury that had never quite healed. The sound issuing from the hollow of the drum was uncannily similar to a stifled cry. "I could not have imagined I would have survived, let alone lived to be so old on that terrible day," she said, and Le translated the words through her fingers.

Grandmother began beating the drum, increasing the tempo until it was nearly deafening. Then the drum was suddenly silent in her gnarled hands.

As morning broke, an eerie light began to show in the porthole. The boat was still tossing up and down, but the wind was beginning to subside. The waves were not as big. I unlashed myself from the bed. Mia didn't look well. She stayed behind.

Holding on as I moved, I poked my head out of our room. Things were heaped and scattered everywhere. Water sloshed underfoot. Cupboard doors flapped like broken wings, and drawers gaped open like astonished mouths. I moved toward the stairs and up the ladder.

Mama Ruth was at the helm. She looked grimmer than I had ever seen her. She motioned for me to stay below. I backed down the ladder and crawled in with Mia again. Slowly the wind fell off and the sea calmed more.

Mama Ruth appeared at the door and said, "Go up and take the helm. Stay the course." She hugged me quickly and then sent me out with a look.

I was alone on the deck. The water washed about in the cabin below.

The boat rode low, close to the surface of the ocean. I looked around. Gabe was nowhere in sight. Neither were Alala or Hope.

I called out into the emptiness around me, in more of a whisper than a shout, "Gabe . . . Alala . . . Hope."

Had the storm taken them all? I felt a hole opening in my chest where my heart had been.

I untied the rope and stick Mama Ruth had rigged up to keep the boat pointed at an angle to the waves while she ducked below. I looked around, stunned by the destruction the storm had wrought. A ragged sail waved in the wind like a white flag of defeat from the mast, which was broken off partway down. The top of the mast was missing altogether! Lines of rope trailed into the sea. There was a hole in the deck, probably where the mast landed as it fell. The small sail we'd made before leaving the island was rigged to the stub of the mast. A shiny object caught the light and my attention as the boat swayed back and forth. Gabe's harmonica was wedged in a crack along a split seam.

Mama Ruth stayed below with Mia for a long time. I had only a little steerage with such a small sail, but it was enough to keep the boat from going sideways to the waves.

Finally, Mama Ruth reappeared in the doorway. There were no words, only a long aching cry that came out of my mouth. She came to me and held me as I wept. I may have begun to accept my own death, but I was still crushed at the loss of those I loved. Those I depended on.

I know now the depth of Mama Ruth's strength that day, for she carried not only Mia's loss and mine in those awful hours but her own as well.

"What happened?" I was finally able to ask through my shock and disbelief.

"The mast cracked in the fiercest moments of the storm. It hung at an angle like a shattered limb. We couldn't steer the boat. We were afraid it would capsize in the waves." She paused, silent for a long moment, a mournful look on her face before she went on, "Gabe climbed up and cut away the old lines. He attached the new sail to the standing mast that was left."

The crow's-feet at the corners of her eyes deepened.

"As he was making his way down, the end of the mast that was still hanging was caught by a gust of wind and tore all the way off. As it crashed down, Gabe became tangled in the lines. He was pulled overboard."

Mama Ruth was silent again, her gray mouth turned down as she looked out to sea. "There was nothing I could do," I heard her whisper, above the waves. Her stonelike face was a study in pain.

I pressed against her, unable to get my breath.

"And Alala?" I asked.

"I don't know," Mama Ruth answered. "Hope is missing too."

I looked across the bow where he had slept so many times in the great turtle shell. It was no longer lashed to the deck.

The sun rose the next morning on an improbably quiet day—as if nothing at all had happened. We drifted.

Mia stayed in the berth she had shared with Gabe. I could hear her crying through the door. I went in and curled up next to her, hugging her back as I had the night before, both of us taking and giving comfort at the same time.

Mama Ruth and I used a cracked orange bucket to bail out the galley. She would scoop the water in and hand it up to me at the top of the stairs. My job was returning the water back to the sea from which it came. With each bucket I tipped over the edge, I looked down and thought of Gabe, then peered up at the sky and thought of Alala. I wondered in a fanciful way if Hope was riding in the turtle shell like a little sailor in a tiny boat.

When I told Mama Ruth, she just smiled faintly and said, "You never know with that cat."

She and I worked all that first day to get the water out of the boat, patch the hole in the deck as best we could, and put away the scattered belongings that littered the floor.

By evening we were exhausted and hungry. We had only one partial canister of fuel left, the one they had saved for emergencies long ago, before they reached the island. She managed to get the stove lit and make a hot meal.

"Take this to Mia," she said, handing me bowls of steaming taro for both of us.

Mia was lying with her back to me, looking out the small port window, when I came in. She turned over. Her eyes were swollen and red, but she managed a little smile for me before tearing up.

"I don't know how I'm going to do this alone," she said.

"You're not alone," I said softly, trying to reassure her.

I helped her prop herself up. She took a few small bites of food. I was hungry and gobbled mine down despite my grief.

"Would you like the rest of mine?" she asked, holding her bowl out to me.

Grandmother looked up from the drum she had been rubbing. "I ate hers as well as mine, and I was reminded once again of the tenacity of life. Life would go on—someday without me too."

After dinner I helped Mia rise slowly out of bed. She was bruised and battered, but she climbed the few steps up to the deck where Mama Ruth was at the wheel.

We sat in silent contemplation for a long time, the three of us touching but not talking.

It was Mia who finally spoke. "Did the radio survive?" she asked.

"Yes, but it got wet," Ruth said, looking exhausted.

"Ruth . . . Ruth . . . go on down to bed. I can take the wheel for a while. I can't sleep anyway," said Mia.

"I'll stay up here with you," I offered.

Mama Ruth disappeared below deck to sleep. The last thing I remember before my eyes shut was Mia at the wheel, silhouetted against a faint light on the horizon.

When I opened my eyes again, the sun was up but close to the skyline. I had slept for nearly an entire day. Mama Ruth was at the helm, though there was little to do but let the current take us, as the water was calm. Hardly a breath of wind rippled the surface. Mia brought dinner up, and we ate in the silence of shared anguish.

I cleaned the dishes with a bucket of salt water lowered down over the edge, thinking of Gabe and Hope the whole time. One day followed the next. I felt suspended in time, but then reality would break through the numbness and I would remember in my body the echo of loss and sorrow.

I helped where I could. Mama Ruth continued to make repairs to the boat, and Mia slept much of the time. When all was done that a girl could do, I spent the rest of my days on the bow looking up at the sky. *Maybe you never know with that bird either,* I thought.

On the seventh day after the storm, we held a service for Gabe. Mama Ruth used a piece of the sailcloth that had weathered the storm to bundle up his clothes and the harmonica. She tied it all together with a length of frayed line. We gathered as the sun set in colors of bruised and battered purple.

The ocean surrounded us, and the bowl of the sky above us began to light up with stars. *Gabe's favorite time,* I remembered, realizing that Mama Ruth had chosen it perfectly.

She was quiet for a long time as the stars shone brighter and brighter against the black sky. Then she uttered these words in a dreamlike state.

Grandmother cleared her throat, emotion still caught in it after all these years:

The past is a magic box into which we can only peek
It keeps our most precious memories safe,
Locked forever in time and place.

It holds our greatest achievements
On a shelf supported by our biggest disappointments
Regret resides there too,
Alongside our deepest loves, beside our perfect moments, together with our eternal grief.

She handed the bundle to Mia, saying, "You will know in time what to do with these."

Then Mama Ruth sank down on her knees and wept. It was the first time she had really cried since the storm. Mia and I held her, wrapping ourselves around one another as we mourned the loss of a husband, a nephew, a friend, and a father-to-be. I cried for the loss of Gabe but also for my companion, my friend, my family—Alala. And for Hope.

I had started to make a habit of sleeping with Mia so she wouldn't be alone. Later that night, I awoke to the sound of the door opening. Mama Ruth came in and sat on the bed next to us. Mia tossed uneasily next to me and opened her eyes. Mama Ruth had been up on deck, but there was no wind. We were only drifting.

"I can't sleep. I keep waking up—dreaming of Gabe and of Alala," I told her.

Mia rolled over, her hair an unruly cascade of black. She sighed deeply. "I can't sleep either."

Mama Ruth held me like she once had when I was young, when we first slept together in the banyan tree. She stroked Mia's head with her other hand. Then, clearing her throat, she repeated the words she had recited earlier that evening for the ceremony. But this time there was more . . .

Our secrets lurk in the corners
Of the magic box we call the past
Among our missed opportunities,
Always just out of sight.

We peer in occasionally,
Eye to the keyhole,
Too close to focus,
Too filled with tears to see,
All but a blurry image
Of the truth that resides in thee.

Mama Ruth gently brushed a long strand of Mia's black hair off her face, where it lay like black cursive writing on her wet cheek. Then she added these final words:

Some of us don't look at all
Keeping *that* box in the darkest corners
Of the attics of our minds
Where we never go by day
Where we cannot be coaxed to stray.

But like sleepwalkers at night,
In our dreams we creep,
Up the stairs, and through
The narrow keyhole of memory we peep.

I fell asleep in Mama Ruth's arms and slept deeply, pressed against Mia. For the next few days, I continued to move in a state of suspended being, mechanically going through the motions of my daily chores—my eyes always on the sky. Gabe was gone. But maybe, just maybe, Alala would return.

One night after dinner, Mia joined Mama Ruth and me on deck.

"Bring me the radio, please," Mia asked.

I found it and brought it to her. I cranked the handle as she operated the controls. There was a long moment of silence. Would the bees in the box buzz again? We held our breaths.

Chapter 29:

THE BREAKFAST TABLE

Joyce was pouring coffee when Sam, Kate, and Zen all came downstairs to the kitchen. Sam gave his dad a hug where he stood at the stove flipping pancakes. She set her cup down, embracing Sam. Then she squeezed Kate and Zen, but when she saw the big plum-colored book Sam had set on the counter, her eyes darted between it and the children. Grace was at the dining room table sipping milk from a mug with Plato in her lap.

Sam's and Joyce's eyes locked.

"Kate and Zen know about the book," Sam said.

"But I locked it in the cabinet!" Joyce practically screamed, accidentally causing everyone in the kitchen to turn and look at her.

"We've been reading it together in Zen's room this morning," Kate said.

Joyce handed Sam her coffee cup and made a wide circle around the book, eyeing it suspiciously as she made her way out of the kitchen toward the library. She felt for the key in her bathrobe pocket. *It is here, but the cabinet is unlocked!* She peered inside. Nothing but a catnip mouse of Plato's with one ear missing. She looked back over her shoulder. Plato had followed her into the library.

Joyce pitched the mouse to him. "Are you playing games with me?" she asked.

Plato arched his long tail into a question mark, as if giving her a playful reply.

She went back to the kitchen and helped Marq carry out pancakes, syrup, and plates. Sam brought the book in and set it on the table. Grace climbed in his lap smiling, seemingly happy to have her oldest brother home. Zen and Kate brought the silverware and big glasses full of milk, sitting down next to each other as usual. Joyce sat as far as she could from the book. Plato settled on her lap. *As if to make amends*, she speculated, petting him despite her consternation.

"So, Mom, you found this book?" Kate asked.

"Well, *found* isn't quite the word I would use. The book seemed to fall out of time and space. It landed in the middle of our library floor yesterday morning!" Joyce's voice was a little shrill. *I'm probably alarming the kids*, she worried for a moment before her thoughts went directly to wanting a cigarette. She shook her head as if to vanquish the thought. Her oldest daughter was looking at her sideways when her attention returned to the room.

"Where did you 'find' the book this morning?" she asked Kate.

"It was in the cabinet in the library. The door was ajar, and it was inside."

"Well, I'm not quite sure what is going on with that book"—Joyce pointed an accusing finger and looked suspiciously at it again—"or this cat." She looked down at Plato in her lap.

"What do you mean?" Zen asked.

Joyce recounted for them in detail the strange clatter in the library the day before and going in to find the book in the middle of the floor. And how it had a propensity to *move*—seemingly of its own accord.

Marq leaned back in his chair. Despite her distress, Joyce noticed Marq seemed to be enjoying having the whole family together around the breakfast table.

"Well, I'll have to say that it is a strange book and a strange story. We've all read parts of the book it seems?"

Grace, with a little white mustache of milk, piped up, "Me too."

They all turned and stared at her. "I don't know why everyone is trying to keep it from me," she said innocently. "I like it!" She recounted to her family the future she had read about—a future when the earth is green and people live in peace.

Kate and Zen started talking about what they had read—about Mia, Gabe, Aunt Ruth, and Little Bird. Then everyone at the table started talking at once about the book—how it moved, how Plato seemed to be weirdly connected to it, about the stories inside and the future world that it told of.

Sam was animated. "In the back of the book there is a Universal Bill of Rights and Responsibilities. Rights are given to other entities besides humans." He picked up the book and turned to the end.

He handed it to his dad to show him, but Marq passed it back to Sam. "Read it to us," Marq coaxed.

Sam began to read aloud:

Henceforth, the Waters, the Sky, Plants, Animals, and the Earth itself shall have Legal Recognition, Protection, and Rights before the Law . . .

"Is this the way the planet is saved?" asked Zen.

"Restored?" Kate probed.

"It will take more than that, but the rule of law seems to be the foundation," Sam said.

Joyce could see Sam was excited to share what he had been reading with his family. He continued to read aloud:

It is decreed that from this day forth, acts of war and aggression are outlawed. It is the Responsibility of every Person and all government agencies at all levels to resolve conflicts through Nonviolent means.

"Wow, war outlawed?" Marq said with a question in his voice.

"Could it be done?" asked Kate.

Joyce leaned forward. Her voice was clear and steady now. She knew her history. "War *was* outlawed," she said with authority. "After women got the right to vote in the United States in 1920, many women turned their attention to world peace. The Treaty for the Renunciation of War[8] was drafted and signed by all the major world powers, including the United States, in 1928."

"Well, it didn't exactly work out last time," said Sam.

"If we did it once, maybe we can do it again," said Kate. "Maybe world peace is possible."

"If the book is right, that *is* what happens in the future," said Marq.

"A detailed plan was devised to reach world peace again in the 1950s after World War II," Joyce said, and she looked over her shoulder toward the library. "There is a book in there, *World Peace through World Law*.[9] It was a complete plan to disarm and establish peace in the world. It was written by two professors and reviewed and expanded on by thousands of citizens and experts—including military leaders."

---

8. The unabridged Treaty for the Renunciation of War is included in the Appendix.

9. Clark, Grenville, and Louis B. Sohn. *World Peace through World Law*. Cambridge, MA: Harvard University Press, 1958.

Marq said, "Why does it seem to take so much destruction for people to come to their senses? Think what we could do for people and the planet if we used all of our resources together with all our brains to solve the issues we are facing."

Joyce let out a deep breath. *Maybe there is a way out of the mess we are in,* she thought to herself, hopeful about the future for the first time in as long as she could remember.

Joyce saw Kate and Zen share one of their looks. Kate spoke first: "We were just reading in the bedroom, and we want to find out—"

"—what happens next on the boat," Zen finished her sentence, as they often did for each other.

Sam passed the book to Kate. Zen got another helping of pancakes. Marq brought more coffee from the kitchen, filling the empty cups.

"Can I stay and listen too?" Grace pleaded.

Joyce looked over at Marq. "We're all in this together, I guess," she said, repeating Marq's words from the night before.

Kate began to read aloud to her family assembled around the table.

The crescent moon had nearly completed its journey around the perimeter of the gathering and now looked like a cat's sharp claw tearing at the horizon as it began to sink below the skyline.

There was still a large crowd that wanted to hear more, but Grandmother needed rest, and she had a few last preparations to make.

"I must go soon, but first I will tell you the end of this story."

Each night Mia would ask for the radio to be brought to her. I would crank the handle, but no more bees sounded inside. There was no sound of friendly voices. No music. No signal.

The radio had been too damaged by the salt water in the storm.

For days I laid on the bench looking up at the sky or out to sea. I took my turn at the helm and helped Mama Ruth with the daily chores of cleaning and feeding ourselves. But the storm had blown us off track. Without the radio and signal to follow, we had no way of finding a refuge center.

Then one morning, my eye caught a glimpse of something moving on the horizon. It was winged. I sat up. It was moving toward us!

My heart leapt as I recognized Alala. I watched as his winged silhouette moved closer. I squealed with happiness when he landed on the broken mast and then dropped down to the deck and perched near me on top of the damaged radio.

Mama Ruth poked her head out of the cabin and said, "Well, look who is here!" She smiled as broadly as I had seen her smile in a long time.

Mia came up top too, and we all talked at once, happy and surprised to have Alala back.

Mama Ruth wondered aloud, "Where could he have been?"

"Hard to imagine he survived this long at sea!" Mia marveled.

Alala accepted water and food. I stroked his back, running my hands along his silky feathers. After our reunion, he flew up to the top of the mast again and began to caw loudly. He flew away and then circled back, landing once again on the stub of the mast, calling loudly. He did this three times as we watched.

"He is telling us where he has been," I said, "where land is. He is calling us to follow him."

Chapter 30:

ARRIVAL IN NEWLAND

K ate passed the book to Marq, who took a turn reading to the family still gathered around the table.

Grandmother continued, a brightness in her voice as she told this part of the story, her drumming somehow echoing her mood. Le interpreted with a reflected lightness in her movements:

Mama Ruth and Mia set the sail as I stood on the bow of the boat watching Alala. We began to follow him. He would fly out of sight, but before long he would reappear from the same direction, land on the mast, call, and then fly away in the direction he wanted us to go. We traveled many days this way, Alala coming back to sleep with us on the boat each night.

One late afternoon, Mia gave a shout. "Land in sight!" she called.

Following Alala, we approached a sheltered harbor. At the entrance a single flag was flying—a

picture of Earth set on the deep blue-black background of space. Below it was a large sign welcoming
all in many languages. As we set the anchor in the
harbor, a small flotilla of boats surrounded us.

The people in the crowd around Grandmother
whispered to one another. They knew that this part of
the story was a historic account of this refuge center
and the village that grew up around it, now known as
Newland. It was one of the first communities established on the basis of the Universal Bill of Rights and
Responsibilities after The Great Change.

The first boat came alongside our own. We were
instructed to stay aboard, but we were asked if we
needed food, water, or medical assistance. We were
given fresh water, and a nurse came on board to exam-
ine Mia. I would realize later how courageous these
people were. They were risking their lives to welcome
strangers to a new land.

It was explained through an interpreter that this
was a nonviolent colony. Under international treaty,
it could not harbor weapons except for defense.
Disputes were settled by tribunals, with mediators
trained in peaceful nonviolent reconciliation.

We were given the choice to stay on our boat in
quarantine or move on if we chose to. In either case,
we would be given food, water, and medical supplies.
I would learn later that this was the practice throughout all the colonies.

If we chose to stay, we would be allowed to come
to the refuge center after our quarantine. If we wanted

to join the community, we would go before a council to pledge our allegiance to these principles.

Grandmother reached inside her cloak and produced a scrolled piece of paper. Le could hear it crackle with age as Grandmother unrolled it.

"This is the actual document that was handed to us that day," she explained. "I didn't understand all of it then, but I have come to know its wisdom. I have carried it with me all these many years. It contains the founding principles of the world in the time now known as The Great Change.

She began to read from the yellowing scroll, which seemed to glow with its own light:

Recognition of inherent Dignity and Rights is the foundation of Freedom, Justice, and Peace in the World.

Disregard and contempt for Human Rights and the Environment have resulted in barbarous acts, which have outraged the consciousness of Humankind and brought Life on Earth to the brink of destruction. We are committed to the advent of a world in which all beings shall enjoy Freedom from fear and want and the Preservation and Restoration of the Natural World. Equality, Respect, and Compassion are our guiding principles. We have determined to promote Social Progress and restore the Earth by providing Protection for Rights through Nonviolent Action and the Rule of Law. . . .

Therefore the General Assembly of the World proclaims this Universal Bill of Rights and Responsibilities as the common standard of achievement for all Communities. Thus, keeping this Declaration constantly in mind, we shall strive through Education and Nonviolent Action to promote its universal and effective Recognition and Observance.

Grandmother passed the scroll to Le and said, "Be sure, as Keeper of these stories, to care for this document as well. Without it, I think life on the planet as we know it now would not exist."

She looked out at the crowd and continued to speak:

"For many years, 'The Great Change' referred primarily to the collapse of the world that was, but in the last fifty years, it has taken on a new meaning. 'The Great Change' now, of course, is used to reference the rise of a just, peaceful, verdant world. Humans evolved to understand the difference between a want and a need, the value of cooperation and the meaning of compassion."

She continued, "After that day, Mama Ruth, Mia, and I were safe. We joined the colony here in Newland."

Grandmother looked at Le and told her, "Mia gave birth to your grandmother here in Newland. It was the beginning of a new life for all of us."

Then she addressed the crowd: "This is the end of my story of The Time Before and The Great Change. I have lived a long life. I understand now what my grandfather said to me when I was a child, just before he died—'I have had more than my share.' I now, too, have had more than mine."

She looked to Le and said, "Please walk me home and stay with me awhile. I have more that I shall tell you along the way."

Grandmother returned her focus to the crowd and gestured, "May peace and love surround you."

Darkness rode on her left shoulder as the crowd parted to let her pass. There was the sound of weeping. Many bowed their heads. Then, from the back, a clear voice began to sing:

Love, oh Love, you carry me,
Without you where would we be?

Grandmother and Le could hear others joining in the singing as they walked home one last time.

Chapter 31:

THE OMEGA

M arq looked up. Joyce caught his eye. She smiled. He passed the book to her. She took a sip of her coffee and cleared her throat before she took the next turn reading.

Though she would see it but briefly, Grandmother knew the sun would rise above the horizon in the morning for the first time in many moons. Its rise would mark the time known among the people as the Alpha and the Omega—the beginning and the end.

The first rays of the sun would mark the start of a new year, the end of the old—both equally important. The season of darkness would be over. Light would again come to the people of this land, once known in The Time Before as Antarctica. The Alpha and the Omega would touch, and the cycle of life would begin again.

She was ready, as ready as anyone ever really is, for the end of one thing and for an unknown next.

After she said her goodbyes to Le, she had gone to sleep for a few hours, thinking she might want to do things differently in the morning—knowing it would be her last. But upon waking, she found herself savoring the little rituals born of a lifetime.

She lit the fire. The heat felt good as she warmed her hands in front of it. The light of the flames cast her shadow in sharp contrast against the stone walls. Grandmother moved about, quietly performing the small rites of morning—washing her face, dressing, combing her long gray hair with the same comb Mia and Mama Ruth had used to untangle it long ago, when she was known as Little Bird.

To Darkness, the only witness of the scene, she appeared to be dancing on the walls and ceiling, defying the laws of gravity and age. He flew down off his perch near a window. She offered him a piece of water-soaked bread. She would not eat. She had, by her own choice, eaten her final meal at a dinner in her honor almost a full moon cycle before. Darkness refused the offering. Instead, he flew up to sit once again upon her left shoulder. She caressed his inky black feathers and chortled to him in their shared tongue, thanking him for his companionship. He would not leave her until she was gone—and maybe not even then.

She took out her drum and began to move her hand across its surface, producing a sound like a great wind moving through a long valley. The fire flickered. Then her hands began to move in a steady pulse, and the room was soon filled with a deep rhythm as if from her own beating heart. The din echoed off the walls, creating a cacophony of sound, as if many hearts in fact were beating as one.

She took a final sip of water and began to sing in a low voice just under her breath:

> *Water, water, cleanse my mind,*
> *Make me peaceful, make me kind.*[10]
> *Water, water, cleanse my soul,*
> *Make me peaceful, make me whole.*

The energy in the room could not escape as the noise grew louder. Finally, Grandmother threw open the door and stepped outside. The sound rushed out with her. Her voice and the drumming trailed off into silence. The only sound she could hear was that of her own heart beating slowly, echoing in her ears alone.

She had prepared her place ahead of time. One handful of thin earth and hard rock at a time, she had over many months scraped a shallow grave into the ground.

In the dim light before the dawn, she saw that many people had come in the night and lined the inside of the open grave with beautiful cloth, herbs, and dried flowers. They had left small gifts of gratitude and remembrance, shells, polished stones, and notes.

Candles flickered on the edge where each night visitor had placed one. Many dozens of little lights shone brightly around the grave, mirroring the stars above. She knew it was time for her to take her place among them.

---

10. These lines have been attributed to the musician Hamza El Din, but after due diligence the author was unable to confirm their source.

Grandmother stepped into her own grave and curled up in the arms of the earth. The first rays of light from the rising sun touched the wings of Darkness as he circled overhead. She closed her eyes. She could feel her own wings now along her back and shoulders, just below the skin. And in that moment, she remembered her first name, the one her mama and papa and her first family had called her:

Ku'l' 'anela li'ili'i.
Little Angel.

Chapter 32:

THE ALPHA

Joyce looked up at her family gathered around her at the table, listening as she read.

"The part I read was at the back," Grace said. "There was more about Le."

"Let's see what happens to Le, then," said Joyce. She turned to a page near the end.

Firsthand accounts, let alone images from The Great Change, were extraordinarily rare. Le's conscience and history demanded they be archived. She had been a featured Teller last night on the eve of One Hundred Years of Peace. She had told the old stories again for a new generation to hear, perhaps to learn from—but now it was time to let go of the artifacts too.

She pulled the ancient logbook that she had been carrying out of her basket and placed it on the desk in front of her. As she waited for a clerk from the Hall of Records to come catalog and make notes regarding this donation so it could go on display, she took one final look at the drawings tucked inside the front cover, drawings her great grandmother Mia had made during The Great Change. There were several pictures of a cat sleeping in a giant turtle shell on the deck of a sailboat. Her great grandfather Gabe standing at the wheel of a sailboat. An older woman, Ruth, she assumed, fishing from a small rowboat. A dozen drawings of a swaddled baby, sleeping.

Le dug deeper to the bottom of her basket and took out the carefully wrapped pages that had been torn from the logbook, and she placed them on the desk too. These pages were given to her by Grandmother, Little Bird, on the night of her passing.

The edges of the paper where they had been ripped out of the logbook had softened with age. *As all things do,* thought Le. It was time to let them go too. She fingered the ragged edges as she read the first entry in the logbook in her great grandmother's hand: "January 2042. Weather clear, still no rain or wind."

Le glanced at the entries up and down the first few pages. Simple words were repeated time and time again:

No wind.
No rain.
No wind.
No rain.

And then this in a different hand: "February 3, 2042: Mia gave birth to a baby boy this morning. We named him Gaylord, after my brother." *This must be Ruth's handwriting,* Le thought.

She scanned the entries that followed. "Food and water running dangerously low" was interspersed again with "No wind" and "No rain." For month upon month. Then:

August 11: We spotted a boat on the horizon today. It must have a motor, for no wind again. We waved and tried to attract its attention to no avail.

August 12: We saw the same boat again today. Perhaps they did see us. It is keeping a distance though.

August 13: The boat is slowly circling us. All of us are afraid and hopeful all at once. This could be the last entry.

August 14: The boat came close enough for us to shout to one another across the water this morning. It is a family! We are all a little anxious and elated at the same time."

Le remembered the night of Grandmother's death. The story she had told Le after they left the Telling suddenly loomed up in her mind:

Ruth waved a white shirt tied to the end of an oar. The boat seemed to take no notice. She shouted to Gabe and Mia. Gabe came up from the cabin holding the baby against his chest. But the boat had passed out of sight. It was not the first time they had seen someone in a boat from a distance. Gabe went back to playing the harmonica to entertain the baby.

The sighting of the boat had momentarily lifted their spirits, but the day had passed without seeing it again. Mia was cooking a thin gruel for their second and last meal of the day. Rations were so low that the adults had gone to eating just twice a day.

Mia held Gaylord in her lap, feeding him from a small spoon Ruth had fashioned with her knife from a floating piece of wood. Gabe was the first to see the boat again over Mia's shoulder. He pointed, and they all turned to look. Gabe and Ruth stood as the boat slowly approached and began circling them.

Gabe shouted a greeting: "Friends, we have little food and little water, but we will share what we have with you."

The boat circled closer.

A deep voice carried over the water: "We haven't much either."

Aunt Ruth called out now: "Come, we shall share a meal and news—be it as little as it is."

The boat came alongside. Mia saw a young man and woman about her own age and a younger teenage girl.

Le turned to more of the entries that had been torn from the logbook: "August 15: We have new friends. Such a celebration and dinner we shared together despite the meager ingredients."

Then the log entries missed almost two weeks besides quick dates and short notes about the pleasures of company. Le recalled the rest of Grandmother's story:

It was getting quite late. Ruth was holding the baby, who was wrapped in a soft piece of blanket they had

fished from the water, washed, and sewn. It had practically become a part of him. He never slept without
it. His eyes were half shut, and she smelled the top of
his head and his sweet baby breath.

Almost asleep, thought Ruth.

She held him tightly, envying his naivete as to what
was coming. When he was fully asleep, she gently
pulled the blanket free from his fists. Ruth took out
her needle and thread to continue work on the blanket.
She had been embroidering it with trees, colorful birds,
and flowers in green foliage, so perhaps they wouldn't
be unfamiliar to him should they someday reach land.
But the last few nights, after she was able to gently
take the blanket from his clenched little hands, she had
begun to sew his name and lineage along one edge of
it. She was almost finished: "Gaylord, son of Mia Lu
and Gabriel Thomason." The only record he might be
left with.

Both boats were small. They were tethered
together so they wouldn't drift apart and so everyone could climb back and forth easily. They had been
together almost two weeks. Mia and Gabe climbed
back in their boat to sit with Ruth before they all
turned in for the night. Mia held the baby while Gabe
looked at Ruth's handiwork. A troubled smile distorted
his face. Mia looked away. The time would come soon
enough. She couldn't bear to think about it.

Ruth had shown their new friends her method for
catching rain when it fell, and Gabe helped them rig
up a water catchment system with a tired but functional piece of faded blue tarp pulled out of the sea.
Mia took them in the rowboat, showing them how

to reach under the larger pieces of floating foam and gather the small purple-and-blue clams that attached themselves to the undersides. She also showed them the seaweeds best for eating. Each day together was a gift.

On the tenth night, as they began to make plans to leave, Mia and Gabe asked for a moment with their guests. They all sat on the bow of the boat.

Gabe, holding Mia, began, "There is no easy way to say this . . ."

"We don't want you to leave," Mia said, tears already running down her face. "But if you go . . . when you go . . ." Her voice broke.

"Will you take our baby?"

Gabe was unable to hold back his own tears now, hearing the words they had only whispered spoken aloud.

"It may be his only chance," Mia said.

Mia watched the dawn's rose light reach out and brush the world with color. She got out her short pencil and began another drawing of the baby as he slept innocently beside Gabe, her tears smudging the image and wrinkling the paper. But she caught something of his nature in her delicate lines. In careful lettering, she copied Ruth's embroidered words showing at the edge of his blanket.

"Gaylord, son of Mia Lu and Gabriel Thomason," she wrote at the bottom of the drawing.

The clerk arrived. Le hesitated a moment before passing the logbook and all the drawings across the table. Another long moment passed. As the clerk waited, Le carefully took the scroll of the original Universal Bill of Rights and Responsibilities from her basket. Her eyes lingering on its brittle yellowing surface, she wondered, *Is it time to let this go too? It will be safer here, and more people will see it.* She carefully unrolled the paper and scanned the document again. It was dated exactly one hundred years ago, 2042. *The timing is perfect,* she realized, and she gently handed the scroll to the clerk.

Le set her basket down and rested under the Mother Tree in the center of the village. The cool green air enveloped her. She took the bottle of water she had been given upon arrival and poured a little out at the base of the tree, reciting as she did, "For the earth, to which we all belong."

Then she took a long drink herself. She took off her shoes. The ground felt cool under her feet. She wiggled her toes and lay down on the ground, looking up into a cobalt sky.

Le was relieved to have faithfully performed her duties. She had shared the old stories she had been entrusted with and donated almost all of the documents to the Hall of Records for display and safekeeping. Now she just wanted to rest in the quiet shade. She felt as light as her basket. Her lungs filled with the oxygen-rich air under the tree. She watched as a few white clouds floated silently overhead, smiling at the soft hum of insects and the songs of birds. The rustling of the leaves was music to her ears. Circles of lemon-yellow light filtered down through the cool blue shade and fell on her bare arms. *It feels good to be alive,* she thought. *Today is the actual equinox itself, marking one hundred years of peace on earth. The world over is experiencing exactly equal amounts of daylight and darkness today, as it has twice a year for as long as Earth has been circling the sun.* She remembered, *This day was chosen long ago because the equinox's very structure represents equality and justice—the bases of the peace we now celebrate.*

Le was looking forward to the dances that would be held again that night, in remembrance of the day, when the Constitution and the Universal Bill of Rights and Responsibilities were signed by the world's leaders from The Time Before.

In ceremonies around the planet, leaders through The Great Change and the founders of many of the colonies will be recognized and remembered for their parts in helping build a peaceful, just, and verdant world.

There had been many who didn't think peace was possible. This was understandable, for there was a time it had seemed quite impossible. It hadn't been easy. Those stories would be remembered and told also. Tonight, there would be more Tellers sharing stories.

Le turned on her side, her head on her arm. Someone was walking toward her. Le recognized the three-legged gait. The silhouette in motion moved closer.

As Gaylord approached, she felt the stir of recognition again. The cat that had accompanied him when they first met at the dock was following close on his heels.

Her mind flashed to the drawings she had donated to the Hall of Records. Suddenly, she realized what was so familiar about him. He looked like her great grandfather Gabe in the drawings her great grand-mother Mia had made.

Le had never met her great grandfather. He had been swept overboard when the family was en route to the refuge center. At least, that was the story she knew. *It certainly can't be him,* she thought. *Besides that, though Gaylord is old, he is still too young to be my great grandfather. He is closer to my grandmother's age, if she were still alive.*

Great grandmother Mia and great grandfather Gabe were both born in 2016 TTB. Le remembered things like that. She thought again of the pages torn out of the logbook and the story Grandmother, Little Bird, had told her on the eve of her passing.

"A child born at sea," Le recalled.

Could Gaylord somehow be that child? she pondered.

Le stood as Gaylord approached. He paused before her, greeting her with the more elaborate hand motions of someone she had met before, rekindling their acquaintance. Then he opened his cloak to reveal the inner lining. There, just inside, a tattered scrap of old cloth had been sewn. It was faded, but Le could read the stitched lettering:

"Gaylord, son of Mia Lu and Gabriel Thomason."

Gaylord's eyes, the color of long-held secrets, looked directly at Le. "I shall be telling my story tonight," he said. "I came to invite you. I sincerely hope you come."

Suddenly Plato leapt down from Grace's lap, where he had appeared to be listening to the story alongside the family.

Joyce looked up from the book as the cat went to the front door and began meowing loudly, insisting he be let out.

"That cat!" Marq said.

Zen got up and opened the door for him.

Marq shook his head. "Why doesn't he use the cat door?"

"He doesn't think he's a cat," Joyce quipped.

The day was warm. Spring was coming. Zen stood at the open door and watched as Plato sprinted across the space between the houses and climbed up into the apple tree outside the home of their neighbor, the woman they had bought their house from. Apple blossoms floated up on the breeze, as if for a moment they had broken free of the laws of gravity around the tree where Plato was perched.

The screen door opened, and a small, dark woman called up into the tree, "Hope . . . Hope."

Kate joined Zen in the doorway. Grace slipped down and went to look too.

"Hope," the woman called again.

This time, Plato came down out of the tree. They watched as his tail, in its customary shape of a question mark, disappeared through the doorway to her house.

They all looked at one another, and this time their own eyebrows lifted high. They looked a bit like Plato themselves! One at a time they turned back to the breakfast table.

Joyce looked down at the book again. She thumbed through the pages. But they were all blank!

Waiting to be written, she thought. "Hope," she whispered under her breath . . .

Marq looked over at the book, and his eyes widened. "This whole thing just keeps getting stranger and stranger, doesn't it?"

"Why are the pages blank?" Grace asked, looking around the table at her siblings and back and forth between her parents.

"Maybe," Kate ventured softly, looking at Zen and Grace, "it's that the future is up to us to determine."

Grace's brow furrowed. "How do we do that?"

"I think the book is trying to tell us," Sam said.

Marq picked the book up and turned a few more blank pages, then brought his hand up to his chin. "I think we're going to have to figure out how as we go along. But if I've learned anything from this book, it's that the future, and the world, are in our care." He gazed around the table at his family.

"And," Joyce added, "no matter how bad things may get . . . there's always hope if we are willing to dream—willing to try."

FALLING UP

G.G. KELLNER

We are falling through history
Slowly,
One generation,
One lifetime,
After another
Strung together
like beads

Each of us,
With a hole,
In our centers,
Through which
the invisible thread
of Time
passes

We are falling through history
Slowly,
Too slowly,
to comprehend,
We are falling,
Up

IMAGINED UNIVERSAL BILL OF RIGHTS AND RESPONSIBILITIES (2042)

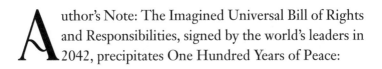

uthor's Note: The Imagined Universal Bill of Rights and Responsibilities, signed by the world's leaders in 2042, precipitates One Hundred Years of Peace:

We the People, in Order to form a more perfect Union, establish Justice, ensure Tranquility, protect the Earth, and promote the general Welfare, by securing the blessings of Life and Liberty for Ourselves, our Children, and our Children's Children for all time to come, do ordain and establish this Universal Bill of Rights and Responsibilities. Recognition of inherent Dignity and Rights is the foundation of Freedom, Justice, and Peace in the world.

Disregard and contempt for Human Rights and the Environment have resulted in barbarous acts, which have outraged the consciousness of Humankind and brought Life on Earth to the brink of destruction.

We are committed to the advent of a world in which all beings shall enjoy Freedom from fear and want and the Preservation and Restoration of the Natural World. Equality, Respect, and Compassion are our guiding principles. We have determined to promote Social Progress and restore the Earth by providing Protection for Rights through Nonviolent Action and the Rule of Law.

Article 1: All Persons are born free and equal in Dignity and Rights. They are endowed with Reason and Conscience and must act toward one another in a spirit of Kindness and Compassion.

Article 2: Everyone is entitled to all the Rights and Freedoms set forth in this Declaration, without distinction of any kind, such as race, color, gender, identity, language, religion, political or other opinion, national or social origin, property, birth, or other status. Furthermore, no distinction shall be made on the basis of the political, jurisdictional, or international status of the country or territory to which that person once belonged.

Article 3: All Persons have the Right to Life, Liberty, and Security of Person. No one shall be held in slavery or servitude. No one shall be subjected to torture or to cruel, inhuman, or degrading treatment.

Article 4: Everyone has the Right to Recognition as a Person before the Law. All are equal before the Law and are entitled without any discrimination to equal

Protection of the Law. All Laws are to be written and disseminated in such a fashion that the common Person is able to comprehend their Meaning without need of interpretation or legal aid.

Article 5: Those in Public Office are to be held to the highest Standards of Truth. They must renounce all payments, goods, or services offered that might influence the performance of their Duties. Public officials must take a Vow of Austerity so they can serve in Sympathy with those that have the least among us. Any Public Official or Servant accused of accepting money, gifts, or lying to the public will be brought before a Truth and Reconciliation Commission and if found guilty shall immediately be removed from Office and barred from further Public Service.

Article 6: Henceforth, the Waters, the Sky, Plants, Animals, and the Earth itself shall have Legal Recognition, Protection, and Rights before the Law, including the Right to Representation in Courts and Representation by Proxy in the Governance of the Planet.

Article 7: Everyone has the Right to manifest their Religion or Belief in Teaching, Practice, Worship, and Observance so long as its Practice does not impinge on the Universal Rights of others. The Government shall neither support nor oppress any Religion.

Article 8: No one shall be subjected to arbitrary interference with their Privacy, Family, Home, or Correspondence. All have a Responsibility to Respect one another's Privacy—no Person, Company, or Government Agency shall sell or provide information to any third party without the fully informed Consent of the Person whose Information is being shared.

Article 9: Everyone has the Right to an effective Remedy by a competent Tribunal for acts violating their fundamental Rights granted here. No one is above the Law, but neither should anyone be subjected to arbitrary arrest, detention, or exile. Everyone is entitled to full Equality and to a fair and public Hearing by an impartial commission in the determination of their Rights, Responsibilities, and Obligations for Reconciliation.

Anyone charged with an offence has the right to be presumed innocent until proven guilty by a public commission at which they have the guarantees necessary for their defense. Those charged or found guilty shall be treated with Respect and Dignity while making Reparations to those whose Rights they have violated.

Article 10: No Entity private or public shall levy usury fees. Public Funds shall be made available to all for the acquisition of Housing, Businesses, and other large expenses. Free access to Education at all levels is a right of the People.

Article 11: Everyone has the Right to Free Speech, freedom of Opinion and Expression, and a Free Press. This Right includes freedom to hold Opinions without interference and to seek, receive, and impart Information and Ideas, including full and free Access to all current and future Communication Forms. However, it is everyone's Responsibility to be truthful in the dissemination of Information and to adhere to the guiding Principle of Nonviolence in Speech as well as Action.

Article 12: The Will of the People shall be the basis of the authority of the Government. This Will shall be expressed in periodic and genuine Elections, which shall be universal and equal through free Voting Procedures. Voting is a Responsibility of all People and a mandatory requirement in Self-Governance. No individual Right to Vote shall be removed for any reason. No one who has reached the voting age of sixteen shall be denied the Right to Vote.

Therefore the General Assembly of the World proclaims this Universal Bill of Rights and Responsibilities as the common standard of achievement for all Communities. Thus, keeping this Declaration constantly in mind, we shall strive through Education and Nonviolent Action to promote its universal and effective Recognition and Observance.

DISCUSSION QUESTIONS

These questions are intended to bring about thoughtful reflections and discussions. The questions can be read and discussed or written about in any order.

1. What does it mean to live a "good" life? Note: Consider defining "good life" first. It may take a while.

2. Do you believe humans have innate rights? If so, what are the most important ones and why?

3. Read the United Nations' Universal Declaration of Human Rights at the back of the book. They were proposed in 1948 and adopted by many countries around the world. What rights might be added now, over seventy years later?

4. Read or skim the United States Constitution and the Bill of Rights. What do you think are the most important provisions of these documents? What changes, if any, or additions (amendments) do you think are needed to make the Constitution functional in the twenty-first century?

5. What actions could to be taken by humanity to move the world toward peace, justice, and verdant sustainability?

6. After women in the United States got the right to vote in 1920, many turned their attention to the cause of world peace. Read the Treaty for the Renunciation of War in the Appendix. How does it make you feel that the world's major powers signed this in 1928? What conditions would be required for war to be made unnecessary? Do the genders view this issue differently? What if women held the dominant positions of power when it came to declaring war?

7. What would your own life and the life of your children or grandchildren be like in a future world where peace, justice, and sustainability were achieved?

8. Read the Parliament of the World's Religions' fifth directive in the Appendix. What might the role of religion be in obtaining a peaceful, just, verdant world?

9. Does anything else besides human life have innate rights? If so, what might those rights be? Whom or what should have them and why?

10. Do you believe in destiny?

11. What changes, if any, are you willing to make personally to leave the planet a better place for future generations?

APPENDIX OF ACTUAL HISTORICAL DOCUMENTS AND PHOTOGRAPHS

CONSTITUTION OF
THE UNITED STATES (1787)

A uthor's Note: After the Declaration of Independence was signed in 1776, the Revolutionary War followed. In 1787, the Constitution was drafted. The following text is a transcription of the Constitution as it was inscribed by Jacob Shallus on parchment. The actual document is on display in the Rotunda at the National Archives Museum. The spelling and punctuation reflect the original.

The procedure for amendments to the Constitution are outlined in Article V.

The Bill of Rights, the first ten amendments to the Constitution, would not be written until two years later and would not be ratified until 1791. Twenty-seven amendments have been made to the Constitution as of 2021.

THE CONSTITUTION OF THE UNITED STATES
(UNABRIDGED)

We the People of the United States, in Order to form a more perfect Union, establish Justice, insure domestic Tranquility, provide for the common defence, promote the general Welfare, and secure the Blessings of Liberty to ourselves and our Posterity, do ordain and establish this Constitution for the United States of America.

Article I.

SECTION 1.

All legislative Powers herein granted shall be vested in a Congress of the United States, which shall consist of a Senate and House of Representatives.

SECTION 2.

The House of Representatives shall be composed of Members chosen every second Year by the People of the several States, and the Electors in each State shall have the Qualifications requisite for Electors of the most numerous Branch of the State Legislature.

No Person shall be a Representative who shall not have attained to the Age of twenty five Years, and been seven Years a Citizen of the United States, and who shall not, when elected, be an Inhabitant of that State in which he shall be chosen.

Representatives and direct Taxes shall be apportioned among the several States which may be included within this Union, according to their respective Numbers, which shall be determined by adding to the whole Number of free Persons, including those bound to Service for a Term of Years, and excluding Indians not taxed, three fifths of all other Persons. The actual Enumeration shall be made within three Years after the first Meeting of the Congress of the United States, and within every subsequent Term of ten Years, in such Manner as they shall by Law direct. The Number of Representatives shall not exceed one for every thirty

Thousand, but each State shall have at Least one Representative; and until such enumeration shall be made, the State of New Hampshire shall be entitled to chuse three, Massachusetts eight, Rhode-Island and Providence Plantations one, Connecticut five, New-York six, New Jersey four, Pennsylvania eight, Delaware one, Maryland six, Virginia ten, North Carolina five, South Carolina five, and Georgia three.

When vacancies happen in the Representation from any State, the Executive Authority thereof shall issue Writs of Election to fill such Vacancies.

The House of Representatives shall chuse their Speaker and other Officers; and shall have the sole Power of Impeachment.

SECTION 3.
The Senate of the United States shall be composed of two Senators from each State, chosen by the Legislature thereof, for six Years; and each Senator shall have one Vote.

Immediately after they shall be assembled in Consequence of the first Election, they shall be divided as equally as may be into three Classes. The Seats of the Senators of the first Class shall be vacated at the Expiration of the second Year, of the second Class at the Expiration of the fourth Year, and of the third Class at the Expiration of the sixth Year, so that one third may be chosen Every second Year; and if Vacancies happen by Resignation, or otherwise, during the Recess of the Legislature of any State, the Executive thereof may make temporary Appointments until the next Meeting of the Legislature, which shall then fill such Vacancies.

No Person shall be a Senator who shall not have attained to the Age of thirty Years, and been nine Years a Citizen of the United States, and who shall not, when elected, be an Inhabitant of that State for which he shall be chosen.

The Vice President of the United States shall be President of the Senate, but shall have no Vote, unless they be equally divided.

The Senate shall chuse their other Officers, and also a President pro tempore, in the Absence of the Vice President, or when he shall exercise the Office of President of the United States.

The Senate shall have the sole Power to try all Impeachments. When sitting for that Purpose, they shall be on Oath or Affirmation. When the President of the United States is tried, the Chief Justice shall preside: And no Person shall be convicted without the Concurrence of two thirds of the Members present.

Judgment in Cases of Impeachment shall not extend further than to removal from Office, and disqualification to hold and enjoy any Office of honor, Trust or Profit under the United States: but the Party convicted shall nevertheless be liable and subject to Indictment, Trial, Judgment and Punishment, according to Law.

Section 4.
The Times, Places and Manner of holding Elections for Senators and Representatives, shall be prescribed in each State by the Legislature thereof; but the Congress may at any time by Law make or alter such Regulations, except as to the Places of chusing Senators.

The Congress shall assemble at least once in every Year, and such Meeting shall be on the first Monday in December, unless they shall by Law appoint a different Day.

SECTION 5.

Each House shall be the Judge of the Elections, Returns and Qualifications of its own Members, and a Majority of each shall constitute a Quorum to do Business; but a smaller Number may adjourn from day to day, and may be authorized to compel the Attendance of absent Members, in such Manner, and under such Penalties as each House may provide.

Each House may determine the Rules of its Proceedings, punish its Members for disorderly Behaviour, and, with the Concurrence of two thirds, expel a Member.

Each House shall keep a Journal of its Proceedings, and from time to time publish the same, excepting such Parts as may in their Judgment require Secrecy; and the Yeas and Nays of the Members of either House on any question shall, at the Desire of one fifth of those Present, be entered on the Journal.

Neither House, during the Session of Congress, shall, without the Consent of the other, adjourn for more than three days, nor to any other Place than that in which the two Houses shall be sitting.

SECTION 6.

The Senators and Representatives shall receive a Compensation for their Services, to be ascertained by Law, and paid out of the Treasury of the United States. They shall in all Cases, except Treason, Felony and Breach of the Peace, be privileged from Arrest during their Attendance at the Session of their respective Houses, and in going to and returning from the same; and for any Speech or Debate in either House, they shall not be questioned in any other Place.

No Senator or Representative shall, during the Time for which he was elected, be appointed to any civil Office under the Authority of the United States, which shall have been created, or the Emoluments whereof shall have been encreased during such time; and no Person holding any Office under the United States, shall be a Member of either House during his Continuance in Office.

Section 7.

All Bills for raising Revenue shall originate in the House of Representatives; but the Senate may propose or concur with Amendments as on other Bills.

Every Bill which shall have passed the House of Representatives and the Senate, shall, before it become a Law, be presented to the President of the United States; If he approve he shall sign it, but if not he shall return it, with his Objections to that House in which it shall have originated, who shall enter the Objections at large on their Journal, and proceed to reconsider it. If after such Reconsideration two thirds of that House shall agree to pass the Bill, it shall be sent, together with the Objections, to the other House, by which it shall likewise be reconsidered, and if approved by two thirds of that House, it shall become a Law. But in all such Cases the Votes of both Houses shall be determined by Yeas and Nays, and the Names of the Persons voting for and against the Bill shall be entered on the Journal of each House respectively. If any Bill shall not be returned by the President within ten Days (Sundays excepted) after it shall have been presented to him, the Same shall be a Law, in like Manner as if he had signed it, unless the Congress by their Adjournment prevent its Return, in which Case it shall not be a Law.

Every Order, Resolution, or Vote to which the Concurrence of the Senate and House of Representatives may be necessary (except on a question of Adjournment) shall be presented to the President of the United States; and before the Same shall take Effect, shall be approved by him, or being disapproved by him, shall be repassed by two thirds of the Senate and House of Representatives, according to the Rules and Limitations prescribed in the Case of a Bill.

SECTION 8.
The Congress shall have Power To lay and collect Taxes, Duties, Imposts and Excises, to pay the Debts and provide for the common Defence and general Welfare of the United States; but all Duties, Imposts and Excises shall be uniform throughout the United States;

To borrow Money on the credit of the United States;

To regulate Commerce with foreign Nations, and among the several States, and with the Indian Tribes;

To establish an uniform Rule of Naturalization, and uniform Laws on the subject of Bankruptcies throughout the United States;

To coin Money, regulate the Value thereof, and of foreign Coin, and fix the Standard of Weights and Measures;

To provide for the Punishment of counterfeiting the Securities and current Coin of the United States;

To establish Post Offices and post Roads;

To promote the Progress of Science and useful Arts, by securing for limited Times to Authors and Inventors the exclusive Right to their respective Writings and Discoveries;

To constitute Tribunals inferior to the supreme Court;

To define and punish Piracies and Felonies committed on the high Seas, and Offences against the Law of Nations;

To declare War, grant Letters of Marque and Reprisal, and make Rules concerning Captures on Land and Water;

To raise and support Armies, but no Appropriation of Money to that Use shall be for a longer Term than two Years;

To provide and maintain a Navy;

To make Rules for the Government and Regulation of the land and naval Forces;

To provide for calling forth the Militia to execute the Laws of the Union, suppress Insurrections and repel Invasions;

To provide for organizing, arming, and disciplining, the Militia, and for governing such Part of them as may be employed in the Service of the United States, reserving to the States respectively, the Appointment of the Officers, and the Authority of training the Militia according to the discipline prescribed by Congress;

To exercise exclusive Legislation in all Cases whatsoever, over such District (not exceeding ten Miles square) as may, by Cession of particular States, and the Acceptance of Congress, become the Seat of the Government of the United States, and to exercise like Authority over all Places purchased by the Consent of the Legislature of the State in which the Same shall be, for the Erection of Forts, Magazines, Arsenals, dock-Yards, and other needful Buildings;—And

To make all Laws which shall be necessary and proper for carrying into Execution the foregoing Powers, and all other Powers vested by this Constitution in the Government of the United States, or in any Department or Officer thereof.

SECTION 9.

The Migration or Importation of such Persons as any of the States now existing shall think proper to admit, shall not be prohibited by the Congress prior to the Year one thousand eight hundred and eight, but a Tax or duty may be imposed on such Importation, not exceeding ten dollars for each Person.

The Privilege of the Writ of Habeas Corpus shall not be suspended, unless when in Cases of Rebellion or Invasion the public Safety may require it.

No Bill of Attainder or ex post facto Law shall be passed.

No Capitation, or other direct, Tax shall be laid, unless in Proportion to the Census or enumeration herein before directed to be taken.

No Tax or Duty shall be laid on Articles exported from any State.

No Preference shall be given by any Regulation of Commerce or Revenue to the Ports of one State over those of another; nor shall Vessels bound to, or from, one State, be obliged to enter, clear, or pay Duties in another.

No Money shall be drawn from the Treasury, but in Consequence of Appropriations made by Law; and a regular Statement and Account of the Receipts and Expenditures of all public Money shall be published from time to time.

No Title of Nobility shall be granted by the United States: And no Person holding any Office of Profit or Trust under them, shall, without the Consent of the Congress, accept of any present, Emolument, Office, or Title, of any kind whatever, from any King, Prince, or foreign State.

SECTION 10.

No State shall enter into any Treaty, Alliance, or Confederation; grant Letters of Marque and Reprisal; coin Money; emit Bills of Credit; make any Thing but gold and silver Coin a Tender in Payment of Debts; pass any Bill of Attainder, ex post facto Law, or Law impairing the Obligation of Contracts, or grant any Title of Nobility.

No State shall, without the Consent of the Congress, lay any Imposts or Duties on Imports or Exports, except what may be absolutely necessary for executing its inspection Laws: and the net Produce of all Duties and Imposts, laid by any State on Imports or Exports, shall be for the Use of the Treasury of the United States; and all such Laws shall be subject to the Revision and Control of the Congress.

No State shall, without the Consent of Congress, lay any Duty of Tonnage, keep Troops, or Ships of War in time of Peace, enter into any Agreement or

Compact with another State, or with a foreign Power, or engage in War, unless actually invaded, or in such imminent Danger as will not admit of delay.

Article II.

Section 1.

The executive Power shall be vested in a President of the United States of America. He shall hold his Office during the Term of four Years, and, together with the Vice President, chosen for the same Term, be elected, as follows:

Each State shall appoint, in such Manner as the Legislature thereof may direct, a Number of Electors, equal to the whole Number of Senators and Representatives to which the State may be entitled in the Congress: but no Senator or Representative, or Person holding an Office of Trust or Profit under the United States, shall be appointed an Elector.

The Electors shall meet in their respective States, and vote by Ballot for two Persons, of whom one at least shall not be an Inhabitant of the same State with themselves. And they shall make a List of all the Persons voted for, and of the Number of Votes for each; which List they shall sign and certify, and transmit sealed to the Seat of the Government of the United States, directed to the President of the Senate. The President of the Senate shall, in the Presence of the Senate and House of Representatives, open all the Certificates, and the Votes shall then be counted. The Person having the greatest Number of Votes shall be the President, if such Number be a Majority of the whole Number of Electors appointed; and if there be more than one who have such Majority, and have an equal Number of Votes, then the House of Representatives shall immediately chuse by Ballot one of them for President; and if no Person have a Majority, then from the five highest on the List the said House shall in like Manner chuse the President. But in chusing the President, the Votes shall be taken by States, the Representation from each State having one Vote; a quorum for this Purpose shall consist of a Member or Members from two thirds of the States, and a Majority of all the States shall be necessary to a Choice. In every Case, after the Choice of the President, the Person having the greatest Number of Votes of the Electors shall be the Vice President. But if there should remain two or more who have equal Votes, the Senate shall chuse from them by Ballot the Vice President.

The Congress may determine the Time of chusing the Electors, and the Day on which they shall give their Votes; which Day shall be the same throughout the United States.

No Person except a natural born Citizen, or a Citizen of the United States, at the time of the Adoption of this Constitution, shall be eligible to the Office of President; neither shall any Person be eligible to that Office who shall not have attained to the Age of thirty five Years, and been fourteen Years a Resident within the United States.

In Case of the Removal of the President from Office, or of his Death, Resignation, or Inability to discharge the Powers and Duties of the said Office, the Same shall devolve on the Vice President, and the Congress may by Law provide for the Case of

Removal, Death, Resignation or Inability, both of the President and Vice President, declaring what Officer shall then act as President, and such Officer shall act accordingly, until the Disability be removed, or a President shall be elected.

The President shall, at stated Times, receive for his Services, a Compensation, which shall neither be encreased nor diminished during the Period for which he shall have been elected, and he shall not receive within that Period any other Emolument from the United States, or any of them.

Before he enter on the Execution of his Office, he shall take the following Oath or Affirmation:—"I do solemnly swear (or affirm) that I will faithfully execute the Office of President of the United States, and will to the best of my Ability, preserve, protect and defend the Constitution of the United States."

SECTION 2.

The President shall be Commander in Chief of the Army and Navy of the United States, and of the Militia of the several States, when called into the actual Service of the United States; he may require the Opinion, in writing, of the principal Officer in each of the executive Departments, upon any Subject relating to the Duties of their respective Offices, and he shall have Power to grant Reprieves and Pardons for Offences against the United States, except in Cases of Impeachment.

He shall have Power, by and with the Advice and Consent of the Senate, to make Treaties, provided two thirds of the Senators present concur; and he shall nominate, and by and with the Advice and Consent of the Senate, shall appoint Ambassadors, other public Ministers and Consuls, Judges of the supreme Court, and all other Officers of the United States, whose Appointments are not herein otherwise provided for, and which shall be established by Law: but the Congress may by Law vest the Appointment of such inferior Officers, as they think proper, in the President alone, in the Courts of Law, or in the Heads of Departments.

The President shall have Power to fill up all Vacancies that may happen during the Recess of the Senate, by granting Commissions which shall expire at the End of their next Session.

Section 3.

He shall from time to time give to the Congress Information of the State of the Union, and recommend to their Consideration such Measures as he shall judge necessary and expedient; he may, on extraordinary Occasions, convene both Houses, or either of them, and in Case of Disagreement between them, with Respect to the Time of Adjournment, he may adjourn them to such Time as he shall think proper; he shall receive Ambassadors and other public Ministers; he shall take Care that the Laws be faithfully executed, and shall Commission all the Officers of the United States.

Section 4.

The President, Vice President and all civil Officers of the United States, shall be removed from Office on Impeachment for, and Conviction of, Treason, Bribery, or other high Crimes and Misdemeanors.

Article III.

SECTION 1.

The judicial Power of the United States, shall be vested in one supreme Court, and in such inferior Courts as the Congress may from time to time ordain and establish. The Judges, both of the supreme and inferior Courts, shall hold their Offices during good Behaviour, and shall, at stated Times, receive for their Services, a Compensation, which shall not be diminished during their Continuance in Office.

SECTION 2.

The judicial Power shall extend to all Cases, in Law and Equity, arising under this Constitution, the Laws of the United States, and Treaties made, or which shall be made, under their Authority;—to all Cases affecting Ambassadors, other public Ministers and Consuls;—to all Cases of admiralty and maritime Jurisdiction;—to Controversies to which the United States shall be a Party;—to Controversies between two or more States;—between a State and Citizens of another State;—between Citizens of different States;—between Citizens of the same State claiming Lands under Grants of different States, and between a State, or the Citizens thereof, and foreign States, Citizens or Subjects.

In all Cases affecting Ambassadors, other public Ministers and Consuls, and those in which a State shall be Party, the supreme Court shall have original Jurisdiction. In all the other Cases before mentioned, the supreme Court shall have appellate Jurisdiction, both as to Law and Fact, with such

Exceptions, and under such Regulations as the Congress shall make.

The Trial of all Crimes, except in Cases of Impeachment, shall be by Jury; and such Trial shall be held in the State where the said Crimes shall have been committed; but when not committed within any State, the Trial shall be at such Place or Places as the Congress may by Law have directed.

Section 3.

Treason against the United States, shall consist only in levying War against them, or in adhering to their Enemies, giving them Aid and Comfort. No Person shall be convicted of Treason unless on the Testimony of two Witnesses to the same overt Act, or on Confession in open Court.

The Congress shall have Power to declare the Punishment of Treason, but no Attainder of Treason shall work Corruption of Blood, or Forfeiture except during the Life of the Person attainted.

Article IV.
Section 1.

Full Faith and Credit shall be given in each State to the public Acts, Records, and judicial Proceedings of every other State. And the Congress may by general Laws prescribe the Manner in which such Acts, Records and Proceedings shall be proved, and the Effect thereof.

Section 2.

The Citizens of each State shall be entitled to all Privileges and Immunities of Citizens in the several States.

A Person charged in any State with Treason, Felony, or other Crime, who shall flee from Justice, and be found in another State, shall on Demand of the executive Authority of the State from which he fled, be delivered up, to be removed to the State having Jurisdiction of the Crime.

No Person held to Service or Labour in one State, under the Laws thereof, escaping into another, shall, in Consequence of any Law or Regulation therein, be discharged from such Service or Labour, but shall be delivered up on Claim of the Party to whom such Service or Labour may be due.

SECTION 3.

New States may be admitted by the Congress into this Union; but no new State shall be formed or erected within the Jurisdiction of any other State; nor any State be formed by the Junction of two or more States, or Parts of States, without the Consent of the Legislatures of the States concerned as well as of the Congress.

The Congress shall have Power to dispose of and make all needful Rules and Regulations respecting the Territory or other Property belonging to the United States; and nothing in this Constitution shall be so construed as to Prejudice any Claims of the United States, or of any particular State.

SECTION 4.

The United States shall guarantee to every State in this Union a Republican Form of Government, and shall protect each of them against Invasion; and on Application of the Legislature, or of the Executive (when the Legislature cannot be convened) against domestic Violence.

Article V.

The Congress, whenever two thirds of both Houses shall deem it necessary, shall propose Amendments to this Constitution, or, on the Application of the Legislatures of two thirds of the several States, shall call a Convention for proposing Amendments, which, in either Case, shall be valid to all Intents and Purposes, as Part of this Constitution, when ratified by the Legislatures of three fourths of the several States, or by Conventions in three fourths thereof, as the one or the other Mode of Ratification may be proposed by the Congress; Provided that no Amendment which may be made prior to the Year One thousand eight hundred and eight shall in any Manner affect the first and fourth Clauses in the Ninth Section of the first Article; and that no State, without its Consent, shall be deprived of its equal Suffrage in the Senate.

Article VI.

All Debts contracted and Engagements entered into, before the Adoption of this Constitution, shall be as valid against the United States under this Constitution, as under the Confederation.

This Constitution, and the Laws of the United States which shall be made in Pursuance thereof; and all Treaties made, or which shall be made, under the Authority of the United States, shall be the supreme Law of the Land; and the Judges in every State shall be bound thereby, any Thing in the Constitution or Laws of any State to the Contrary notwithstanding.

The Senators and Representatives before mentioned, and the Members of the several State Legislatures, and all executive and judicial Officers, both of the United States and of the several States, shall be bound by Oath or Affirmation, to support this Constitution; but no religious Test shall ever be required as a Qualification to any Office or public Trust under the United States.

Article VII.
The Ratification of the Conventions of nine States, shall be sufficient for the Establishment of this Constitution between the States so ratifying the Same.

The Word, "the," being interlined between the seventh and eighth Lines of the first Page, The Word "Thirty" being partly written on an Erazure in the fifteenth Line of the first Page, The Words "is tried" being interlined between the thirty second and thirty third Lines of the first Page and the Word "the" being interlined between the forty third and forty fourth Lines of the second Page.

Attest William Jackson Secretary done in Convention by the Unanimous Consent of the States present the Seventeenth Day of September in the Year of our Lord one thousand seven hundred and Eighty seven and of the Independance of the United States of America the Twelfth In witness whereof We have hereunto subscribed our Names,

G°. Washington
Presidt and deputy from Virginia

DELAWARE
Geo: Read
Gunning Bedford jun
John Dickinson
Richard Bassett
Jaco: Broom

MARYLAND
James McHenry
Dan of St Thos. Jenifer
Danl. Carroll

VIRGINIA
John Blair
James Madison Jr.

NORTH CAROLINA
Wm. Blount
Richd. Dobbs Spaight
Hu Williamson

SOUTH CAROLINA
J. Rutledge
Charles Cotesworth Pinckney
Charles Pinckney
Pierce Butler
GEORGIA
William Few
Abr Baldwin

NEW HAMPSHIRE
John Langdon
Nicholas Gilman

MASSACHUSETTS
Nathaniel Gorham
Rufus King

CONNECTICUT
Wm. Saml. Johnson
Roger Sherman

NEW YORK
Alexander Hamilton

NEW JERSEY
Wil: Livingston
David Brearley
Wm. Paterson
Jona: Dayton
PENNSYLVANIA
B Franklin
Thomas Mifflin
Robt. Morris
Geo. Clymer
Thos. FitzSimons
Jared Ingersoll
James Wilson
Gouv Morris

UNITED STATES
BILL OF RIGHTS (1791)

A uthor's Note: A Constitutional Convention was held in New York City in 1789 to outline the rights that the founders believed important to specify. Twelve amendments were agreed upon, and they were sent to the states for approval. Articles 3–12 were ratified and became the Bill of Rights in 1791. The latest Constitutional Amendment, number 27, was adopted in 1992 and curiously was the first amendment in the original Bill of Rights, but it was not ratified for over two hundred years. It effectively prohibits senators and congresspeople from giving themselves salary increases while in session.

UNITED STATES BILL OF RIGHTS (UNABRIDGED)

The Preamble to The Bill of Rights

The Conventions of a number of the States, having at the time of their adopting the Constitution, expressed a desire, in order to prevent misconstruction or abuse of its powers, that further declaratory and restrictive clauses should be added: And as extending the ground of public confidence in the Government, will best ensure the beneficent ends of its institution.

RESOLVED by the Senate and House of Representatives of the United States of America, in Congress assembled, two thirds of both Houses concurring, that the following Articles be proposed to the Legislatures of the several States, as amendments to the Constitution of the United States, all, or any of which Articles, when ratified by three fourths of the said Legislatures, to be valid to all intents and purposes, as part of the said Constitution; viz.

ARTICLES in addition to, and Amendment of the Constitution of the United States of America, proposed by Congress, and ratified by the Legislatures of the several States, pursuant to the fifth Article of the original Constitution.

THE BILL OF RIGHTS (1791)

Amendment I
Congress shall make no law respecting an establishment of religion, or prohibiting the free exercise thereof; or abridging the freedom of speech, or of the press; or the right of the people peaceably to assemble, and to petition the Government for a redress of grievances.

Amendment II
A well regulated Militia, being necessary to the security of a free State, the right of the people to keep and bear Arms, shall not be infringed.

Amendment III
No Soldier shall, in time of peace be quartered in any house, without the consent of the Owner, nor in time of war, but in a manner to be prescribed by law.

Amendment IV
The right of the people to be secure in their persons, houses, papers, and effects, against unreasonable searches and seizures, shall not be violated, and no Warrants shall issue, but upon probable cause, supported by Oath or affirmation, and particularly describing the place to be searched, and the persons or things to be seized.

Amendment V
No person shall be held to answer for a capital, or otherwise infamous crime, unless on a presentment or indictment of a Grand Jury, except in cases arising in the land or naval forces, or in the Militia, when in actual service in time of War or public danger; nor shall any person be subject for the same offence to be twice put in jeopardy of life or limb; nor shall be compelled in any criminal case to be a witness against himself, nor be deprived of life, liberty, or property, without due process of law; nor shall private property be taken for public use, without just compensation.

Amendment VI
In all criminal prosecutions, the accused shall enjoy the right to a speedy and public trial, by an impartial jury of the State and district wherein the crime shall have been committed, which district shall have been

previously ascertained by law, and to be informed of the nature and cause of the accusation; to be confronted with the witnesses against him; to have compulsory process for obtaining witnesses in his favor, and to have the Assistance of Counsel for his defence.

Amendment VII
In Suits at common law, where the value in controversy shall exceed twenty dollars, the right of trial by jury shall be preserved, and no fact tried by a jury, shall be otherwise re-examined in any Court of the United States, than according to the rules of the common law.

Amendment VIII
Excessive bail shall not be required, nor excessive fines imposed, nor cruel and unusual punishments inflicted.

Amendment IX
The enumeration in the Constitution, of certain rights, shall not be construed to deny or disparage others retained by the people.

Amendment X
The powers not delegated to the United States by the Constitution, nor prohibited by it to the States, are reserved to the States respectively, or to the people.

AMENDMENTS TO THE UNITED STATES CONSTITUTION (1794–1992)

Author's Note: Amendments XI through XXVII represent changes to the Constitution that were adopted after the Bill of Rights. Particularly significant to the issue of human rights and social justice are Amendments XIII (1865) and XIV (1868), outlawing slavery and providing recognition of citizenship and full rights to anyone born in the United States. Amendment XIX (1920) gave women the right to vote. Also of note is Amendment XXVI (1971), which lowered the voting age from twenty-one to eighteen.

Amendment XI
Passed by Congress March 4, 1794. Ratified February 7, 1795.
Note: Article III, Section 2, of the Constitution was modified by Amendment 11.
The Judicial power of the United States shall not be construed to extend to any suit in law or equity,

commenced or prosecuted against one of the United States by Citizens of another State, or by Citizens or Subjects of any Foreign State.

Amendment XII
Passed by Congress December 9, 1803. Ratified June 15, 1804.
Note: A portion of Article II, Section 1, of the Constitution was superseded by the 12th Amendment.
The Electors shall meet in their respective states and vote by ballot for President and Vice-President, one of whom, at least, shall not be an inhabitant of the same state with themselves; they shall name in their ballots the person voted for as President, and in distinct ballots the person voted for as Vice-President, and they shall make distinct lists of all persons voted for as President, and of all persons voted for as Vice-President, and of the number of votes for each, which lists they shall sign and certify, and transmit sealed to the seat of the government of the United States, directed to the President of the Senate; -- the President of the Senate shall, in the presence of the Senate and House of Representatives, open all the certificates and the votes shall then be counted; -- The person having the greatest number of votes for President, shall be the President, if such number be a majority of the whole number of Electors appointed; and if no person have such majority, then from the persons having the highest numbers not exceeding three on the list of those voted for as President, the House of Representatives shall choose immediately, by ballot, the President. But in choosing the President, the votes shall be taken

by states, the representation from each state having one vote; a quorum for this purpose shall consist of a member or members from two-thirds of the states, and a majority of all the states shall be necessary to a choice. [And if the House of Representatives shall not choose a President whenever the right of choice shall devolve upon them, before the fourth day of March next following, then the Vice-President shall act as President, as in case of the death or other constitutional disability of the President. --]* The person having the greatest number of votes as Vice-President, shall be the Vice-President, if such number be a majority of the whole number of Electors appointed, and if no person have a majority, then from the two highest numbers on the list, the Senate shall choose the Vice-President; a quorum for the purpose shall consist of two-thirds of the whole number of Senators, and a majority of the whole number shall be necessary to a choice. But no person constitutionally ineligible to the office of President shall be eligible to that of Vice-President of the United States.

*Superseded by Section 3 of the 20th Amendment.

Amendment XIII
Passed by Congress January 31, 1865. Ratified December 6, 1865.
Note: A portion of Article IV, Section 2, of the Constitution was superseded by the 13th Amendment.

SECTION 1.
Neither slavery nor involuntary servitude, except as a punishment for crime whereof the party shall have

been duly convicted, shall exist within the United States, or any place subject to their jurisdiction.

Section 2.

Congress shall have power to enforce this article by appropriate legislation.

Amendment XIV

Passed by Congress June 13, 1866. Ratified July 9, 1868. Note: Article I, Section 2, of the Constitution was modified by Section 2 of the 14th Amendment.

Section 1.

All persons born or naturalized in the United States, and subject to the jurisdiction thereof, are citizens of the United States and of the State wherein they reside. No State shall make or enforce any law which shall abridge the privileges or immunities of citizens of the United States; nor shall any State deprive any person of life, liberty, or property, without due process of law; nor deny to any person within its jurisdiction the equal protection of the laws.

Section 2.

Representatives shall be apportioned among the several States according to their respective numbers, counting the whole number of persons in each State, excluding Indians not taxed. But when the right to vote at any election for the choice of electors for President and Vice-President of the United States, Representatives in Congress, the Executive and Judicial officers of a State, or the members of the Legislature thereof, is denied to any of the male inhabitants of such State, being twenty-one years of age,* and citizens of the United States, or in any way abridged, except for participation in rebellion, or other crime, the basis of representation therein shall be reduced in the proportion which the number of such male citizens shall bear to the whole number of male citizens twenty-one years of age in such State.

SECTION 3.

No person shall be a Senator or Representative in Congress, or elector of President and Vice-President, or hold any office, civil or military, under the United States, or under any State, who, having previously taken an oath, as a member of Congress, or as an officer of the United States, or as a member of any State legislature, or as an executive or judicial officer of any State, to support the Constitution of the United States, shall have engaged in insurrection or rebellion against the same, or given aid or comfort to the enemies thereof. But Congress may by a vote of two-thirds of each House, remove such disability.

SECTION 4.

The validity of the public debt of the United States, authorized by law, including debts incurred for payment of pensions and bounties for services in suppressing insurrection or rebellion, shall not be questioned. But neither the United States nor any State shall assume or pay any debt or obligation incurred in aid of insurrection or rebellion against the United States, or any claim for the loss or emancipation of any slave; but all such debts, obligations and claims shall be held illegal and void.

SECTION 5.
The Congress shall have the power to enforce, by appropriate legislation, the provisions of this article. *Changed by Section 1 of the 26th Amendment.*

Amendment XV
Passed by Congress February 26, 1869. Ratified February 3, 1870.

SECTION 1.
The right of citizens of the United States to vote shall not be denied or abridged by the United States or by any State on account of race, color, or previous condition of servitude--

SECTION 2.
The Congress shall have the power to enforce this article by appropriate legislation.

Amendment XVI
Passed by Congress July 2, 1909. Ratified February 3, 1913.
Note: Article I, Section 9, of the Constitution was modified by Amendment 16.
The Congress shall have power to lay and collect taxes on incomes, from whatever source derived, without apportionment among the several States, and without regard to any census or enumeration.

Amendment XVII

Passed by Congress May 13, 1912. Ratified April 8, 1913. Note: Article I, Section 3, of the Constitution was modified by the 17th Amendment.

The Senate of the United States shall be composed of two Senators from each State, elected by the people thereof, for six years; and each Senator shall have one vote. The electors in each State shall have the qualifications requisite for electors of the most numerous branch of the State legislatures.

When vacancies happen in the representation of any State in the Senate, the executive authority of such State shall issue writs of election to fill such vacancies: Provided, That the legislature of any State may empower the executive thereof to make temporary appointments until the people fill the vacancies by election as the legislature may direct.

This amendment shall not be so construed as to affect the election or term of any Senator chosen before it becomes valid as part of the Constitution.

Amendment XVIII

Passed by Congress December 18, 1917. Ratified January 16, 1919. Repealed by Amendment 21.

SECTION 1.

After one year from the ratification of this article the manufacture, sale, or transportation of intoxicating liquors within, the importation thereof into, or the exportation thereof from the United States and all territory subject to the jurisdiction thereof for beverage purposes is hereby prohibited.

SECTION 2.

The Congress and the several States shall have concurrent power to enforce this article by appropriate legislation.

SECTION 3.

This article shall be inoperative unless it shall have been ratified as an amendment to the Constitution by the legislatures of the several States, as provided in the Constitution, within seven years from the date of the submission hereof to the States by the Congress.

Amendment XIX

Passed by Congress June 4, 1919. Ratified August 18, 1920.

The right of citizens of the United States to vote shall not be denied or abridged by the United States or by any State on account of sex.

Congress shall have power to enforce this article by appropriate legislation.

Amendment XX

Passed by Congress March 2, 1932. Ratified January 23, 1933.

Note: Article I, Section 4, of the Constitution was modified by Section 2 of this amendment. In addition, a portion of the 12th Amendment was superseded by Section 3.

SECTION 1.

The terms of the President and the Vice President

shall end at noon on the 20th day of January, and the terms of Senators and Representatives at noon on the 3d day of January, of the years in which such terms would have ended if this article had not been ratified; and the terms of their successors shall then begin.

SECTION 2.

The Congress shall assemble at least once in every year, and such meeting shall begin at noon on the 3d day of January, unless they shall by law appoint a different day.

SECTION 3.

If, at the time fixed for the beginning of the term of the President, the President elect shall have died, the Vice President elect shall become President. If a President shall not have been chosen before the time fixed for the beginning of his term, or if the President elect shall have failed to qualify, then the Vice President elect shall act as President until a President shall have qualified; and the Congress may by law provide for the case wherein neither a President elect nor a Vice President elect shall have qualified, declaring who shall then act as President, or the manner in which one who is to act shall be selected, and such person shall act accordingly until a President or Vice President shall have qualified.

SECTION 4.

The Congress may by law provide for the case of the death of any of the persons from whom the House of Representatives may choose a President whenever the right of choice shall have devolved upon them, and for the case of the death of any of the persons from whom the Senate may choose a Vice President whenever the right of choice shall have devolved upon them.

SECTION 5.
Sections 1 and 2 shall take effect on the 15th day of October following the ratification of this article.

SECTION 6.
This article shall be inoperative unless it shall have been ratified as an amendment to the Constitution by the legislatures of three-fourths of the several States within seven years from the date of its submission.

Amendment XXI
Passed by Congress February 20, 1933. Ratified December 5, 1933.

SECTION 1.
The eighteenth article of amendment to the Constitution of the United States is hereby repealed.

SECTION 2.
The transportation or importation into any State, Territory, or possession of the United States for delivery or use therein of intoxicating liquors, in violation of the laws thereof, is hereby prohibited.

SECTION 3.
This article shall be inoperative unless it shall have been ratified as an amendment to the Constitution by conventions in the several States, as provided in

the Constitution, within seven years from the date of the submission hereof to the States by the Congress.

Amendment XXII
Passed by Congress March 21, 1947. Ratified February 27, 1951.

SECTION 1.

No person shall be elected to the office of the President more than twice, and no person who has held the office of President, or acted as President, for more than two years of a term to which some other person was elected President shall be elected to the office of the President more than once. But this Article shall not apply to any person holding the office of President when this Article was proposed by the Congress, and shall not prevent any person who may be holding the office of President, or acting as President, during the term within which this Article becomes operative from holding the office of President or acting as President during the remainder of such term.

SECTION 2.

This article shall be inoperative unless it shall have been ratified as an amendment to the Constitution by the legislatures of three-fourths of the several States within seven years from the date of its submission to the States by the Congress.

Amendment XXIII
Passed by Congress June 16, 1960. Ratified March 29, 1961.

SECTION 1.

The District constituting the seat of Government of the United States shall appoint in such manner as the Congress may direct:

A number of electors of President and Vice President equal to the whole number of Senators and Representatives in Congress to which the District would be entitled if it were a State, but in no event more than the least populous State; they shall be in addition to those appointed by the States, but they shall be considered, for the purposes of the election of President and Vice President, to be electors appointed by a State; and they shall meet in the District and perform such duties as provided by the twelfth article of amendment.

SECTION 2.

The Congress shall have power to enforce this article by appropriate legislation.

Amendment XXIV
Passed by Congress August 27, 1962. Ratified January 23, 1964.

SECTION 1.

The right of citizens of the United States to vote in any primary or other election for President or Vice President, for electors for President or Vice President, or for Senator or Representative in Congress, shall not be denied or abridged by the United States or any State by reason of failure to pay any poll tax or other tax.

SECTION 2.

The Congress shall have power to enforce this article by appropriate legislation.

Amendment XXV

Passed by Congress July 6, 1965. Ratified February 10, 1967.

Note: Article II, Section 1, of the Constitution was affected by the 25th Amendment.

SECTION 1.

In case of the removal of the President from office or of his death or resignation, the Vice President shall become President.

SECTION 2.

Whenever there is a vacancy in the office of the Vice President, the President shall nominate a Vice President who shall take office upon confirmation by a majority vote of both Houses of Congress.

SECTION 3.

Whenever the President transmits to the President pro tempore of the Senate and the Speaker of the House of Representatives his written declaration that he is unable to discharge the powers and duties of his office, and until he transmits to them a written declaration to the contrary, such powers and duties shall be discharged by the Vice President as Acting President.

SECTION 4.

Whenever the Vice President and a majority of either the principal officers of the executive departments or of such other body as Congress may by law provide, transmit to the President pro tempore of the Senate and the Speaker of the House of Representatives their written declaration that the President is unable to discharge the powers and duties of his office, the Vice President shall immediately assume the powers and duties of the office as Acting President.

Thereafter, when the President transmits to the President pro tempore of the Senate and the Speaker of the House of Representatives his written declaration that no inability exists, he shall resume the powers and duties of his office unless the Vice President and a majority of either the principal officers of the executive department or of such other body as Congress may by law provide, transmit within four days to the President pro tempore of the Senate and the Speaker of the House of Representatives their written declaration that the President is unable to discharge the powers and duties of his office. Thereupon Congress shall decide the issue, assembling within forty-eight hours for that purpose if not in session. If the Congress, within twenty-one days after receipt of the latter written declaration, or, if Congress is not in session, within twenty-one days after Congress is required to assemble, determines by two-thirds vote of both Houses that the President is unable to discharge the powers and duties of his office, the Vice President shall continue to discharge the same as Acting President; otherwise, the President shall resume the powers and duties of his office.

Amendment XXVI
Passed by Congress March 23, 1971. Ratified July 1, 1971.

Note: Amendment 14, Section 2, of the Constitution was modified by Section 1 of the 26th Amendment.

SECTION 1.
The right of citizens of the United States, who are eighteen years of age or older, to vote shall not be denied or abridged by the United States or by any State on account of age.

SECTION 2.
The Congress shall have power to enforce this article by appropriate legislation.

Amendment XXVII
Originally proposed Sept. 25, 1789. Ratified May 7, 1992.
No law, varying the compensation for the services of the Senators and Representatives, shall take effect, until an election of Representatives shall have intervened.

President Coolidge signs The Treaty for the Renunciation of War before a distinguished gathering in the east room of the White House, including Vice President Dawes, members of the Cabinet, and members of the Senate and House. In the front row, left to right: Vice President Dawes; President Coolidge; Secretary of State Frank B. Kellogg; Secretary of the Treasury Mellon; and Secretary of War Davis. In the back row, left to right: Senator William E. Borah; Senator Claude A. Swanson; Senator Thomas F. Walsh; Vice President-elect Charles Curtis; and Senator D.O. Hastings (1928). Image used courtesy of the Library of Congress.

TREATY FOR THE RENUNCIATION OF WAR (1928), AND PHOTOGRAPH (1928)

A uthor's Note: Following World War I, there were many international efforts focusing on peace and disarmament. Many women played a leading role following the successful bid to amend the Constitution to give them the right to vote. The Treaty for the Renunciation of War started as a pact between France and the United States. The idea of declaring war to be illegal was immensely popular in international public opinion after World War I.

On August 27, 1928, fifteen nations signed the pact in Paris. Signatories included France, the United States, the United Kingdom, Ireland, Canada, Australia, New Zealand, South Africa, India, Belgium, Poland, Czechoslovakia, Germany, Italy, and Japan. The US Senate ratified the agreement by a vote of eighty-five to one, though it did so only after making reservations to note that US participation did not limit its right to self-defense or require it to act against signatories breaking the agreement. President Calvin Coolidge signed the initial treaty in Paris in 1928. President Herbert Hoover signed the final agreement in 1929. Both were Republicans.

Eventually the treaty was expanded to include most of the established nations at the time: Afghanistan; Albania; Austria; Bulgaria; China; Cuba; Denmark; Dominican Republic; Egypt; Estonia; Ethiopia; Finland; Guatemala; Hungary; Iceland; Latvia; Liberia; Lithuania; Netherlands; Nicaragua; Norway; Panama; Peru; Portugal; Romania; Soviet Union; Kingdom of the Serbs, Croats, and Slovenes (later Kingdom of Yugoslavia); Siam; Spain; Sweden; Switzerland; Turkey; Persia; Greece; Honduras; Chile; Luxembourg; Danzig; Costa Rica; Venezuela; and finally Barbados in 1971, for a total of sixty-two countries. Although a common criticism is that the Treaty did not live up to all its aims, it was the base for the trial of Nazi leaders following World War II. Declared wars became very rare after 1945. The pact had no mechanism for enforcement, but it has served as the legal basis for the concept of crimes against peace.

TREATY FOR THE RENUNCIATION OF WAR
(UNABRIDGED)

Article I
The High Contracting Parties solemnly declare in the names of their respective peoples that they condemn recourse to war for the solution of international controversies, and renounce it, as an instrument of national policy in their relations with one another.

Article II
The High Contracting Parties agree that the settlement or solution of all disputes or conflicts of whatever nature or of whatever origin they may be, which may arise among them, shall never be sought except by pacific means.

Article III

The present Treaty shall be ratified by the High Contracting Parties named in the Preamble in accordance with their respective constitutional requirements, and shall take effect as between them as soon as all their several instruments of ratification shall have been deposited at Washington.

This Treaty shall, when it has come into effect as prescribed in the preceding paragraph, remain open as long as may be necessary for adherence by all the other Powers of the world. Every instrument evidencing the adherence of a Power shall be deposited at Washington and the Treaty shall immediately upon such deposit become effective as; between the Power thus adhering and the other Powers parties hereto.

It shall be the duty of the Government of the United States to furnish each Government named in the Preamble and every Government subsequently adhering to this Treaty with a certified copy of the Treaty and of every instrument of ratification or adherence. It shall also be the duty of the Government of the United States telegraphically to notify such Governments immediately upon the deposit with it of each instrument of ratification or adherence.

IN FAITH WHEREOF the respective Plenipotentiaries have signed this Treaty in the French and English languages both texts having equal force, and hereunto affix their seals.

DONE at Paris, the twenty seventh day of August in the year one thousand nine hundred and twenty-eight.

GUSTAV STRESEMANN
FRANK B KELLOGG
PAUL HYMANS
ARI BRIAND
CUSHENDUN
W. L. MACKENZIE KING
A J MCLACHLAN
C. J. PARR
J S. SMIT
LIAM T.MACCOSGAIR
CUSHENDUN
G. MANZONI
UCHIDA
AUGUST ZALESKI
DR EDWARD BENES

Certified to be a true copy of the signed original deposited with the Government of the United States of America.

FRANK B. KELLOGG
Secretary of State of the United States of America

AND WHEREAS it is stipulated in the said Treaty that it shall take effect as between the High Contracting Parties as soon as all the several instruments of ratification shall have been deposited at Washington;

AND WHEREAS the said Treaty has been duly ratified on the parts of all the High Contracting Parties and their several instruments of ratification have been deposited with the Government of the United States of America, the last on July 24, 1929;

NOW TIIEREFORE, be it known that I, Herbert Hoover, President of the United States of America, have caused the said Treaty to be made public, to the end that the same and every article and clause thereof may be observed and fulfilled with good faith by the United States and the citizens thereof.

IN TESTIMONY WHEREOF, I have hereunto set my hand and caused the seal of the United States to be affixed.

DONE at the city of Washington this twenty-fourth day of July in the year of our Lord one thousand nine hundred and twenty-nine, and of the Independence of the United States of America the one hundred and fifty-fourth

HERBERT HOOVER
By the President:

HENRY L STIMSON
Secretary of State

Eleanor Roosevelt holding the Universal Declaration of Human Rights (1948).
Image used courtesy of the United Nations.

UNITED NATIONS' UNIVERSAL DECLARATION OF HUMAN RIGHTS (1948), AND PHOTOGRAPHS (1948–1949)

Author's Note: The Universal Declaration of Human Rights is a milestone document in the history of the world. Drafted by representatives with different legal and cultural backgrounds from all regions of the world, the declaration was proclaimed by the United Nations General Assembly in Paris in 1948 as a common standard of achievements for all peoples and all nations. It set out, for the first time, fundamental human rights to be universally protected, and it has been translated into over five hundred languages. In the seventy-plus years since this document was signed, it has become the basis of international law and constitutions worldwide. First Lady Eleanor Roosevelt was instrumental in the conception and development of the Universal Declaration of Human Rights. She and other women leaders from around the world were instrumental in developing the language of gender inclusion used in the document. Though incomplete inclusive language to a modern reader, it was revolutionary in its time.

Eleanor Roosevelt leading educational discussion with world leaders on human rights (circa 1948). Image used courtesy of the United Nations.

UNIVERSAL DECLARATION OF HUMAN RIGHTS (UNABRIDGED)

Preamble

Whereas recognition of the inherent dignity and of the equal and inalienable rights of all members of the human family is the foundation of freedom, justice and peace in the world,

Whereas disregard and contempt for human rights have resulted in barbarous acts which have outraged the conscience of mankind, and the advent of a world in which human beings shall enjoy freedom of speech and belief and freedom from fear and want has been proclaimed as the highest aspiration of the common people,

Whereas it is essential, if man is not to be compelled to have recourse, as a last resort, to rebellion against tyranny and oppression, that human rights should be protected by the rule of law,

Whereas it is essential to promote the development of friendly relations between nations,

Whereas the peoples of the United Nations have in the Charter reaffirmed their faith in fundamental human rights, in the dignity and worth of the human person and in the equal rights of men and women and have determined to promote social progress and better standards of life in larger freedom,

Whereas Member States have pledged themselves to achieve, in co-operation with the United Nations, the promotion of universal respect for and observance of human rights and fundamental freedoms,

Press conference of the release of the United Nations Universal Declaration of Human Rights (1948). Note: Eleanor Roosevelt at the head of table in her role as leader of the United Nations committee that drafted the Universal Declaration of Human Rights. Image used courtesy of the United Nations.

Whereas a common understanding of these rights and freedoms is of the greatest importance for the full realization of this pledge,

Now, therefore,

The General Assembly,

Proclaims this Universal Declaration of Human Rights as a common standard of achievement for all peoples and all nations, to the end that every individual and every organ of society, keeping this Declaration constantly in mind, shall strive by teaching and education to promote respect for these rights and freedoms and by progressive measures, national and international, to secure their universal and effective recognition and observance, both among the peoples of Member States themselves and among the peoples of territories under their jurisdiction.

Article 1.

All human beings are born free and equal in dignity and rights. They are endowed with reason and conscience and should act towards one another in a spirit of brotherhood.

Article 2.

Everyone is entitled to all the rights and freedoms set forth in this Declaration, without distinction of any kind, such as race, colour, sex, language, religion, political or other opinion, national or social origin, property, birth or other status. Furthermore, no distinction shall be made on the basis of the political, jurisdictional or international status of the country or territory to which a person belongs, whether it be

Cornerstone laying ceremony for the United Nations headquarters in
New York. The ceremony was attended by United States President Harry
S. Truman, who was the principal speaker. Secretary General Trygve Lie
deposited copies of the United Nations Charter and the Universal Declaration
of Human Rights in the stone. The picture shows Secretary General Trygve
Lie and Wallace K. Harrison, Chief Architect, applying mortar to seal the
cornerstone (1949). Image used courtesy of the United Nations.

independent, trust, non-self-governing or under any other limitation of sovereignty.

Article 3.

Everyone has the right to life, liberty and security of person.

Article 4.

No one shall be held in slavery or servitude; slavery and the slave trade shall be prohibited in all their forms.

Article 5.

No one shall be subjected to torture or to cruel, inhuman or degrading treatment or punishment.

Article 6.

Everyone has the right to recognition everywhere as a person before the law.

Article 7.

All are equal before the law and are entitled without any discrimination to equal protection of the law. All are entitled to equal protection against any discrimination in violation of this Declaration and against any incitement to such discrimination.

Article 8.

Everyone has the right to an effective remedy by the competent national tribunals for acts violating the fundamental rights granted him by the constitution or by law.

Article 9.

No one shall be subjected to arbitrary arrest, deten-tion or exile.

Article 10.

Everyone is entitled in full equality to a fair and public hearing by an independent and impartial tribunal, in the determination of his rights and obligations and of any criminal charge against him.

Article 11.

1. Everyone charged with a penal offence has the right to be presumed innocent until proved guilty accord-ing to law in a public trial at which he has had all the guarantees necessary for his defence.
2. No one shall be held guilty of any penal offence on account of any act or omission which did not consti-tute a penal offence, under national or international law, at the time when it was committed. Nor shall a heavier penalty be imposed than the one that was applicable at the time the penal offence was committed.

Article 12.

No one shall be subjected to arbitrary interference with his privacy, family, home or correspondence, nor to attacks upon his honour and reputation. Everyone has the right to the protection of the law against such interference or attacks.

Article 13.

1. Everyone has the right to freedom of movement and residence within the borders of each state.

2. Everyone has the right to leave any country, including his own, and to return to his country.

Article 14.

1. Everyone has the right to seek and to enjoy in other countries asylum from persecution.

2. This right may not be invoked in the case of prosecutions genuinely arising from non-political crimes or from acts contrary to the purposes and principles of the United Nations.

Article 15.

1. Everyone has the right to a nationality.

2. No one shall be arbitrarily deprived of his nationality nor denied the right to change his nationality.

Article 16.

1. Men and women of full age, without any limitation due to race, nationality or religion, have the right to marry and to found a family. They are entitled to equal rights as to marriage, during marriage and at its dissolution.

2. Marriage shall be entered into only with the free and full consent of the intending spouses.

3. The family is the natural and fundamental group unit of society and is entitled to protection by society and the State.

Article 17.

1. Everyone has the right to own property alone as well as in association with others.

2. No one shall be arbitrarily deprived of his property.

Article 18.

Everyone has the right to freedom of thought, conscience and religion; this right includes freedom to change his religion or belief, and freedom, either alone or in community with others and in public or private, to manifest his religion or belief in teaching, practice, worship and observance.

Article 19.

Everyone has the right to freedom of opinion and expression; this right includes freedom to hold opinions without interference and to seek, receive and impart information and ideas through any media and regardless of frontiers.

Article 20.

1. Everyone has the right to freedom of peaceful assembly and association.

2. No one may be compelled to belong to an association.

Article 21.

1. Everyone has the right to take part in the government of his country, directly or through freely chosen representatives.

2. Everyone has the right of equal access to public service in his country.

3. The will of the people shall be the basis of the authority of government; this will shall be expressed in periodic and genuine elections which shall be by universal and equal suffrage and shall be held by secret vote or by equivalent free voting procedures.

Article 22.

Everyone, as a member of society, has the right to social security and is entitled to realization, through national effort and international co-operation and in accordance with the organization and resources of each State, of the economic, social and cultural rights indispensable for his dignity and the free development of his personality.

Article 23.

1. Everyone has the right to work, to free choice of employment, to just and favourable conditions of work and to protection against unemployment.
2. Everyone, without any discrimination, has the right to equal pay for equal work.
3. Everyone who works has the right to just and favourable remuneration ensuring for himself and his family an existence worthy of human dignity, and supplemented, if necessary, by other means of social protection.
4. Everyone has the right to form and to join trade unions for the protection of his interests.

Article 24.

Everyone has the right to rest and leisure, including reasonable limitation of working hours and periodic holidays with pay.

Article 25.

1. Everyone has the right to a standard of living adequate for the health and well-being of himself and of his family, including food, clothing, housing and

medical care and necessary social services, and the right to security in the event of unemployment, sickness, disability, widowhood, old age or other lack of livelihood in circumstances beyond his control.

2. Motherhood and childhood are entitled to special care and assistance. All children, whether born in or out of wedlock, shall enjoy the same social protection.

Article 26.

1. Everyone has the right to education. Education shall be free, at least in the elementary and fundamental stages. Elementary education shall be compulsory. Technical and professional education shall be made generally available and higher education shall be equally accessible to all on the basis of merit.

2. Education shall be directed to the full development of the human personality and to the strengthening of respect for human rights and fundamental freedoms. It shall promote understanding, tolerance and friendship among all nations, racial or religious groups, and shall further the activities of the United Nations for the maintenance of peace.

3. Parents have a prior right to choose the kind of education that shall be given to their children.

Article 27.

1. Everyone has the right freely to participate in the cultural life of the community, to enjoy the arts and to share in scientific advancement and its benefits.

2. Everyone has the right to the protection of the moral and material interests resulting from any scientific, literary or artistic production of which he is the author.

Article 28.

Everyone is entitled to a social and international order in which the rights and freedoms set forth in this Declaration can be fully realized.

Article 29.

1. Everyone has duties to the community in which alone the free and full development of his personality is possible.

2. In the exercise of his rights and freedoms, everyone shall be subject only to such limitations as are determined by law solely for the purpose of securing due recognition and respect for the rights and freedoms of others and of meeting the just requirements of morality, public order and the general welfare in a democratic society.

3. These rights and freedoms may in no case be exercised contrary to the purposes and principles of the United Nations.

Article 30.

Nothing in this Declaration may be interpreted as implying for any State, group or person any right to engage in any activity or to perform any act aimed at the destruction of any of the rights and freedoms set forth herein.

An Indian delegate, Swami Vivekananda, riveted the audience with his call for religious tolerance and an end to fanaticism (1893). Image used courtesy of the Art Institute of Chicago. Enhanced for clear visibility by John Dey.

PARLIAMENT OF THE WORLD'S RELIGIONS' FIFTH DIRECTIVE (2018), AND PHOTOGRAPHS (1893)

A uthor's Note: The Parliament of the World's Religions first met in Chicago in 1893. Religious leaders from all over the world gathered at a world's fair to share and learn about one another's beliefs, one of the most significant, if not the most significant, gathering of religious leaders in the history of the world at that time.

The Parliament of the World's Religions convened again in Chicago in 1993, on the centennial of the first meeting, and it has met six times since those first two initial meetings one hundred years apart. Meetings have taken place in South Africa (1999), Spain (2004), Australia (2009), the United States (2015), Canada (2018), and virtually in the fall of 2021. Attendance has ranged from seven thousand to twelve thousand people each time, including religious leaders and representatives from over eighty different religious traditions from around the world.

At the 1993 meeting in Chicago, it was decided to offer the world something it had never had—a declaration expressing the ethical commitments held in common by the

The first meeting of the Parliament of the World's Religions Chicago (1893).
Image used courtesy of the Art Institute of Chicago. Enhanced for clear
visibility by John Dey.

world's religious, spiritual, and cultural traditions. An Initial Declaration of Global Ethic was conceived. It expresses four ethical directives.

1. Commitment to a Culture of Nonviolence and Respect for Life
2. Commitment to a Culture of Solidarity and a Just Economic Order
3. Commitment to a Culture of Tolerance and a Life of Truthfulness
4. Commitment to a Culture of Equal Rights and Partnership between Men and Women

The complete document can be viewed online at https://parliamentofreligions.org, and a downloadable PDF can be found at https://www.global-ethic.org.

I was fortunate to get to attend the meeting of the Parliament of the World's Religions held in Toronto in 2018, at which the fifth directive was added. It calls for "Commitment to a Culture of Sustainability and Care for the Earth." I have included the complete text of the fifth directive here.

The Fifth Directive: Commitment to a Culture of Sustainability and Care for the Earth (Unabridged)

Numberless men and women of all regions and religions strive to lead lives in a spirit of mutual harmony, interdependence, and respect for the Earth, its living beings and ecosystems. Nevertheless, in most parts of the world, pollution contaminates the soil, air and water; deforestation and over-reliance on fossil fuels contribute to climate change; habitats are destroyed and species are fished or hunted to extinction. Over-exploitation and unjust use of natural resources increases conflict and poverty among people and harms other forms of life. Too often, the poorest populations, though they have the smallest impact, bear the brunt of the damage done to the planet's atmosphere, land and oceans.

a. In the religious, spiritual, and cultural traditions of humankind we find the directive: You shall not be greedy! Or in positive terms: Remember the good of all! Let us reflect anew on the consequences of this directive: We should help provide—to the best of our ability—for the needs and well-being of others, including of today's and tomorrow's children. The Earth, with its finite resources, is shared by our one human family. It sustains us and many forms of life, and calls for our respect and care. Many religious, spiritual, and cultural traditions place us within the interdependent web of life; at the same time, they accord us a distinctive role and affirm that our gifts of knowledge and of craft place upon us the obligation to use these gifts wisely to foster the common good.

b. All of us have the responsibility to minimize, as much as we can, our impact on the Earth, to refrain from treating living beings and the environment as mere things for personal use and enjoyment, and to consider the effects of our actions on future generations. Caring and prudent use of resources is based on fairness in consumption and takes into account limits on what ecosystems can bear. Wherever heedless domination by human beings over the Earth and other living beings is taught, wherever abuse of the environment is tolerated, and wherever development surpasses sustainable limits, we have the duty to speak up, to change our practices, and to moderate our lifestyles.

c. Young people should be encouraged to appreciate that a good life is not a life of outsized consumption or amassing material possessions. A good life strikes a balance between one's needs, the needs of others, and the health of the planet. Education about the environment and sustainable living should become part of the school curricula in every country of the world.

d. To be authentically human in the spirit of our religious, spiritual, and cultural traditions, means the following: Our relationship with each other and with the larger living world should be based on respect, care and gratitude. All traditions teach that the Earth is a source of wonder and wisdom. Its vitality, diversity, and beauty are held in trust for everyone including those who will come after us. The global environmental crisis is urgent and is deepening. The planet and its countless forms of life are in danger. Time is running out. We must act with love and compassion, and for justice and fairness—for the flourishing of the whole Earth community.

ACKNOWLEDGMENTS

A book is never the work of a single person. I have had the love and support of family, friends, and professionals throughout the years as this book moved from idea to printed page. First, I would like to thank my son Jordan Soltman for his input during the design of the book and for raising my awareness early on about the urgency of the climate crisis; this is one of the main things that motivated me to write this book. I would also like to acknowledge my son Matao Living Earth for his enthusiasm for this book, and his support of me as I wrote it.

I would like to thank my sister Beth Kellner for her careful reading of early drafts and her encouragement and ability to spot holes in the story I couldn't see—because I was standing in them. I would like to thank my sister Lynn Kellner for her unwavering support of me and for becoming the first of four Visionary Donors to support the book financially, alongside Oliver Max, Clay Philbrick, and my friend Phil Thompson, whose countless acts of help and kindness facilitated the completion of the first draft in 2019.

Thank you to my writing mentor and friend Kirk O'Donnell, and his four-legged sidekick Mousse, who always had a pen and paper handy in his breast pocket on our many walks and talks (Kirk, not Mousse—she was strictly a silent consultant at the end of her leash). I would like to recognize Sam Van Fleet for his lyrical phrasing and photographer's sense of style, which he lent to the book as an early reader. I would like to acknowledge my friend Forrest Kinney, who passed away before this book was published. His encouragement and wonderful sense of story was invaluable. I miss him every day.

Thank you to my cousins Dr. Brian Swanson, PhD, and Mary Laucks, MS, for lending me their scientific expertise and offering feedback as early readers. I'd like to acknowledge Matt Nelson for contributing his expert knowledge of sailing. I'd like to acknowledge Asha Azama, McKenna Niemer, and Bryttani Hatchel, for their invaluable help.

Thank you to all my friends and family who have offered encouragement and suggestions as the book developed, including Lauretta Hyde, Jill Heryford, Liz Lafferty, Kim Foley, Sara Van Fleet, David Kimura, Suzanne Northcott, Madelyn Koch, and Pam Weeks. I'd also like to acknowledge the ninety Kickstarter supporters who helped fund the book. Thank you to my publisher, Brooke Warner; my project manager, Shannon Green; my editors, Krissa Lagos and Barrett Briske; and all of the folks at SparkPress and BookSparks who have aided in its development.

Finally, thank you to Karen Gale—for her friendship of many years and for our conversations, which are always with me. And a special thank you to John Dey for his help with the photography in the book and to my dog, Pippi, for sticking by my side throughout it all.

INTERVIEW WITH
G.G. KELLNER

What inspired you to write this story?
In 2016, I began to feel the world needed a story of both hope and possibility out of the many calamities we faced. Seeing the state of the world and the sense of hopelessness in both my adult children and my students as they talked about the future of the planet, I decided to give notice at my teaching job and write this book. I broke into my tiny retirement account and moved to a remote cabin on an island just below Canada in the Pacific Northwest. With only an outhouse and a wood stove for distraction, I wrote *Hope, A History of the Future*.

What do you hope this book achieves?
My greatest aspiration for this book is to nudge the world toward a peaceful, just, verdant future by showing people it is possible and by taking a brave look at what we should be prepared for if we do nothing to correct the course we are on.

What parts are fiction, and what parts are fact?
"The Book of Changes" outlines the most extreme predictions of what climate change could lead to. Unfortunately,

so far, these more dire predictions of climate chaos seem to be unfolding.

On the positive side, the historical documents at the back of the book that could lead to the preservation of the planet and to a peaceful, just world are also very real. They give me hope that humankind can create a world I'd want to live in and one I can feel good about leaving to future generations.

Why did you bring religion into this book? It seems risky to touch on such a taboo topic.

My great-grandfather was a Methodist preacher, so I was brought up with some of the associated values. From an early age, I sought to understand spirituality and religion. As a young elementary-age child, I would attend the neighborhood Lutheran church alone, as my mother had given up on organized religion by then. We lived next to a Jehovah Witness Hall, and my curiosity about what went on inside was rivaled only by that of a cat's. Wherever I have traveled or lived, I have sought to understand the communities of faith that surround me. As an adult I've knelt in a Catholic mass in Mexico; witnessed voodoo ceremonies in Togo, West Africa; and taught schoolchildren in Hawaii about Pele. I've visited Celtic grave sites in Ireland, read inscriptions on gravestones on the island of Bermuda, and walked in monasteries in Europe. I've participated in Zen Buddhism ceremonies and attended Universal Unitarian services. I've sat in silence with Quakers, taken communion with Episcopalians, and visited Baptist churches in the southern United States. I watched the Pope perform a mass wedding at the Vatican and participated in Day of the Dead traditions in Guadalajara. I've attended Jewish gatherings and been served food by Sikh followers while listening to Muslims speak about peace. I'm curious and hopeful about the role religion can play in finding peace, creating social and economic justice, and preserving the environment. I think it is time we begin to talk to one another. We need to pull together—people of faith, agnostics, and atheists alike. We all must share in the love and care for our planet.

Will there be a sequel?
I have other stories and a book of poems I'd like to finish first, but then—*maybe*.

Do you have a cat?
I don't. I love cats, but I am actually allergic to them. I have a dog. She is a little mad she isn't the star character. Maybe next time, Pippi.

ABOUT THE AUTHOR

G ayle G. Kellner is a writer, an artist, a poet, and a former educator. She lives on an island in the Salish Sea in a home that has been in her family for five generations. When she isn't writing, reading, or working on her latest artistic interest (she created the block prints for the book), you can probably find her walking the beaches and forests of her island home with her dog. She is a regular guest and occasional host of a local radio show. Gayle is allergic to cats.

Follow the author on Instagram and Facebook or visit her website at www.gaylekellner.com for more of her story and to view her gallery of prints, paintings, and sculptures.

To request speaking engagements or educational workshops via Zoom or in person at your school, book club, library, church, or community gathering, you can contact her at ggkellner.info@gmail.com.

Author photo © John Dey

SELECTED TITLES FROM SPARKPRESS

SparkPress is an independent boutique publisher delivering high-quality, entertaining, and engaging content that enhances readers' lives, with a special focus on female-driven work. www.gosparkpress.com

Those the Future Left Behind: A Novel, Patrick Meisch, $16.95, 9781684630790. In a near future in which overpopulation, resource depletion, and environmental degradation have precipitated a radical population control program, people can volunteer to be culled at a young age in exchange for immediate wealth.

Gatekeeper: Book One in the Daemon Collecting Series, Alison Levy, $16.95, 978-1-68463-057-8. Rachel Wilde—sent from another dimension to bring defective daemons in for repair—needs to locate two people: a woman whose ancestors held a destructive daemon at bay and a criminal trying to break dimensional barriers. Helped by a homeless man with unusual powers, she uncovers a rising shadow organization that's changing her world forever.

Echoes of War: A Novel, Cheryl Campbell. $16.95, 978-1-68463-006-6. When Dani—one of many civilians living on the fringes to evade a war that's been raging between a faction of aliens and the remnants of Earth's military for decades—discovers that she's not human, her life is upended . . . and she's drawn into the very battle she's spent her whole life avoiding.

Deepest Blue: A Novel, Mindy Tarquini. $16.95, 978-1-943006-69-4. In Panduri, everyone's path is mapped, everyone's destiny determined, their lives charted at birth and steered by an unwavering star. Everything there has its place—until Matteo's older brother, Panduri's Heir, crosses out of their world without explanation, leaving Panduri's orbit in a spiral and Matteo's course on a skid. Forced to follow an unexpected path, Matteo is determined to rise, and he pursues the one future Panduri's star can never chart: a life of his own.

The Legacy of Us: A Novel, Kristin Contino. $17, 978-1-940716-17-6. Three generations of women are affected by love, loss, and a mysterious necklace that links them.

ABOUT SPARKPRESS

SparkPress is an independent, hybrid imprint focused on merging the best of the traditional publishing model with new and innovative strategies. We deliver high-quality, entertaining, and engaging content that enhances readers' lives. We are proud to bring to market a list of *New York Times* best-selling, award-winning, and debut authors who represent a wide array of genres, as well as our established, industry-wide reputation for creative, results-driven success in working with authors. SparkPress, a BookSparks imprint, is a division of SparkPoint Studio LLC.

Learn more at GoSparkPress.com